Xtina raised her l immediately and waited silently to hear what she had to say.

She turned to Mia. "May I put my hands on your head?"

Mia nodded and bowed her head a bit as Xtina approached and gently put both hands on Mia's head and closed her eyes. A warm wave flowed through Mia's body. She closed her eyes too but could still see the room in an even brighter light.

After a minute, Xtina spoke, her eyes still closed. "Mia, blessed are ye among women. I see that you have great strength of spirit and will, more than you know."

Xtina paused before speaking again. "And, Mia, I see you in the presence of a woman. There is great sorrow on her face. You will see great violence and evil. And you will wish to turn away."

Xtina's eyes opened, and she removed her hands from Mia's head. "Mia, you have a calling to fight against evil. And you have the power to do so. But even I cannot control your future. You will have to choose your own path."

Twice a Victim

by

Ralph Dellapiana

The Sisterhood, Book 1

Twice a Victim

Cover Art by *Kim Mendoza*

The Wild Rose Press, Inc.
PO Box 708
Adams Basin, NY 14410-0708
Visit us at www.thewildrosepress.com

Publishing History
First Edition, 2022
Trade Paperback ISBN 978-1-5092-4146-0
Digital ISBN 978-1-5092-4147-7

The Sisterhood, Book 1
Published in the United States of America

Dedication

For Nubia Pena. A dear friend and long-time victim advocate who breathed life into the character of Mia Montes and inspired The Sisterhood series of novels.

For Marc,
your heroic work
on the hardest cases
inspires many.
Thanks,
Ralph

Acknowledgments

A long list of people helped make this book better over the years it took me to write it, but I'm going to single out a few for special thanks who made the greatest impact. Melissa Jeglinski's diligent review of an early draft taught me a great deal about structure and style. Sherrie Clark provided numerous invaluable story and character tips. Ally Robertson and the production and artistic staff at The Wild Rose Press turned a stack of pages into a beautiful book. And last but not least, my wife Rocio's gift for understanding human nature added a layer of insightful emotion to my occasionally plodding action, and she patiently encouraged me to keep working until the novel became one that makes even me cry and cheer when I read it now.

Chapter One

It occurred to me, as I sat in my well-worn leather office chair staring forlornly at the new case file on my desk, that some things are always true. Two plus two equals four. Night never fails to follow day. That first pot of coffee in the morning takes too long to brew, every time. And jurors hate dead baby cases.

Dead baby cases are the worst. Jurors don't like to see pictures of dead babies. They can't look at them in their little pajamas and at their sad little faces without feeling a wrenching pain in the gut. Babies are so helpless, so dependent. Something inside of us, in the deepest essence of our humanity, instinctively moves us to protect them—most of us anyway. As a criminal defense lawyer, I would rather have practically any other kind of case.

I picked my reading glasses off the head of the Buddha on the credenza behind me, polished them on my shirt, and sat them on my ample Italian nose so that I could review the charging document of this new homicide case. I checked the name of the defendant— Kala Tausinga, the dead baby's mother. It went on to say that the cause of death was shaken baby syndrome.

Turning to the binder's tab labelled Medical Examiner for details, I found the autopsy photos and scanned through them. The first one was hard to view. I took a deep breath and held it as I cautiously flipped the page to the next photograph. It was worse than the first one. I let my breath out slowly and shook my head. The M.E. would want to use these photographs to illustrate his expert medical conclusion that the child had suffered a subdural hematoma. The jury won't care what the medical term is. They will be shocked. And angry. Angry at my client.

The district attorney will want to show these photos to the jury. I'll make a motion to exclude them. "Too gruesome," I'll argue. "The jury's passions will be too inflamed for them to be fair," I'll say. The judge will probably allow some of the photos anyway.

I closed the Tausinga file. During the course of my career, I had handled dozens of murder cases. Don't get me wrong. I don't mind trying murder cases. Give me a good old-fashioned drug deal gone bad any time. Jurors don't care much when two dopers try to kill each other. Sometimes it doesn't even make the news.

Same with gangbangers. Gangs claim territory. And other gangs challenge them for it. Violence always ensues—beatings, stabbings, drive-by shootings, and the inevitable retaliation in kind. Because gang members with guns are scary as a general proposition, you can usually argue self-defense.

Or give me a cheating-spouse murder. Jurors understand such a killing. You can argue that it wasn't premeditated; it was a crime a passion. Some jurors think such killings are justified. Historically such infidelity was a complete defense. At the least, many jurors agree that the shock of betrayal is a mitigating circumstance, perhaps reducing the appropriate verdict to manslaughter, not murder.

I leaned back into my chair and closed my eyes.

Working at The Defenders this long not only rewarded me with a corner office on the third floor big enough for a couch, but it also gave me the wisdom and experience to know that the law wasn't as black and white as people thought and that justice was often only aspirational.

I stroked my goatee, nervous about this new case. This one will be a difficult case, and it was one case too many at the moment. With murder cases, my clients face the possibility of spending the rest of their lives in prison. I hold their lives in my hands. It is a heavy burden to bear. Unlike private attorneys, because of our public defender contract, we can't turn away potential clients because we are too busy. Our contract with the county requires us to take all the cases the county sends us. Making matters worse, several experienced lawyers left our office in the last year, mostly because of the crushing case load, leaving the rest of us to try to pick up the slack.

Recently, as my work-life balance tilted farther and farther from the center, I pondered whether it was finally time for me to leave too. The office did hire some new lawyers, but they were fresh out of law school. Although they are enthusiastic and idealistic, you can't give them dead baby cases.

Taking a deep breath, I picked up my desk phone handset and punched a few numbers into the keypad to call my colleague Mary Swanson.

"Well, if it isn't Frank Bravo," she answered cheerfully. "Long time no see, my friend."

"Hi, Mary. It's good to hear your voice. Have you had a chance to review the copy of the Kala Tausinga case file I put on your chair this morning?" I asked hopefully.

"Yes. Let's talk." Her tone changed from light to serious. "Can you come to my office?"

"On my way," I answered, eager to get her take on the case.

At first glance, the hallways at The Defenders appeared to be like those in any office building. But if you were to examine them more closely, you would discover the colorful character of the motley assortment of attorneys who worked here. One colleague had "Get a Warrant" embroidered in large black letters into a small rug and placed it at his office's entrance. Gracing the wall of another was a life-size Wonder Woman poster with the caption from the movie "I will fight for those who can't fight for themselves." A pirate flag hung at the entryway of another, declaring her mutiny against the unjust exercise of power. No other law firm would tolerate such eccentricity. But the independent souls who chose to work at The Defenders would never conform to the demands of the usual Human Resources Department. They resisted authority. That was why they were so good at this job. It was why I loved this place and why I've stayed.

Upon arriving at Mary's office, I gave a quick knock on the open door. "Hello, my friend." I stepped in and made myself at home, flopping down into a soft gray chair on the other side of her desk.

"Let's catch up first," Mary said, easily turning her slim build around to the credenza behind her desk to grab the Keurig carafe sitting on its heating plate. "We haven't had a chance to chat for weeks."

"Great idea. Seriously, I could use a break right now."

"Careful, the coffee's hot." Mary handed me a cup.

I carefully took a sip, leaned back into the chair, and admired Mary's immaculate office and her bob cut that kept every brown hair in place. She wasn't only a colleague at The Defenders, but also a long-time friend since our days together in law school. We got well-acquainted in our second year after seeking each other out to work on a moot court appeal together for our Legal Research and Writing class. We spent many late nights with beer and pizza discussing research, editing our brief, and reviewing arguments.

After law school, I came straight to work at The Defenders, but Mary started out in medical malpractice. Prior to law school, she had worked with her father, a pathologist who performed autopsies. When she came to The Defenders, she spent two years in the Domestic Violence court before moving to the general felonies team.

It was largely because of Mary's medical background and experience with domestic violence cases that I asked for her help on the Kala Tausinga case. That was how we coped with the caseload at The Defenders—we helped each other. Whenever things got tough, we circled the wagons and defended our little family.

Mary asked, "So how are you doing? Did you finally get your divorce from that wench that was wrecking your life?"

"Yeah. The proceedings dragged on for ten months, as long as the marriage itself. But my divorce from Katrina was final about six weeks ago." I let out a grateful sigh.

"So, are you seeing anyone, or are you still in

mourning?"

"I'm done mourning, finally. But you remember what an emotional mess I was before I decided to file for divorce."

"Yes, I do," Mary said. "Very clearly. You were awful. You complained all the time and had a continual hangover. You quit shaving and were moping around here like Eeyore at a funeral." She mimicked me, swiping the back of her hand across her forehead. "I'm sooo sad. Life's a bitch. Then you die."

"Sorry about that," I said, grinning sheepishly. "I'm afraid I did have a continual hangover for a while, drowning my sorrows with booze. Good thing I found that Zen meditation group. They helped me let go of the emotional baggage that was pulling me down, which allowed me to swim back up to the surface."

Mary nodded. "Anyway—" She waited until she caught my eye. "—I'm sure glad to have the real you back."

"Thank you." I gestured toward the framed photo of Mary's husband sitting on the left side of her desk. "How is your husband, Philip? Is he still teaching philosophy at the university?"

"Yes. He loves life on campus." Mary grinned with pride. "I kid him that he's not in touch with the real world. But when I say things like that, he replies with something like 'Cogito, ergo sum' and smiles."

She took a sip of her coffee. "Hey, have you started dating again yet?"

I shrugged. "It took months, but I finally did open the door to seeking out a new partner. I've met a few women on Match."

"Any hot prospects?"

"Not so far. I had one date with a gal who warned me about how she had vowed to get even with the last guy who broke up with her. With disturbing glee, she described how she drove her car through the front window of his office."

Mary laughed. "With the emphasis on *one* date with her, I see."

I chuckled, enjoying sharing my dates-gone-bad stories with Mary. "Then there was Astriid, a Finnish woman. Never been married, no kids, but had two big dogs. The largest trophy I have ever seen dominated her living room. She won the Finnish National Judo Championships four years straight."

Mary's eyes opened wide. "Wow, how did that date go?"

"She took me down with one quick move. And let's just say that she had her way with me. Later, when I asked about her never having married, she said, 'I have had many partners, but dogs are much more loyal than men. And dogs love you unconditionally.'"

"Her logic is unassailable," Mary said.

"Hey! Thanks a lot," I replied, laughing.

"And there was the preacher's wife," I added.

"A preacher's *wife*?"

"Yep. She described in detail how sexually repressed she had been for the last fifteen years. Sermon after sermon about thinking righteous thoughts and rejecting carnal desires. She said she had decided to choose her own life, not to let others judge her according to their puritanical standards. She didn't tell me they were still married until after."

Mary asked, "After what?"

"Umm…"

"Oh. That! Sorry. This isn't sounding very promising, Frank."

I raised both hands in front of me and shrugged. "I know. I know. I'm about to give up. But I do have a golfing date set up soon. I haven't met her in person yet, but her picture's cute."

Mary quickly leaned forward in her chair and lifted a finger toward me. "Cute, huh? Your ex-wife was cute too. You can't go only by *cute*. Be careful."

"I won't jump into anything," I assured her. "I'm not dating merely to date. I'm hoping to find another partner, but she'll have to be someone special to persuade me to take the leap again. That was my second divorce, so I've got two strikes now."

Mary chuckled. "Speaking of your first marriage, Philip and I miss getting together with you and Janelle. I was sorry when you two broke up. But at least you have your daughter from that relationship. How is she taking all this?"

"Bella understandably has mixed feelings. She has always been supportive of her mother and takes her side when Janelle and I argue. But when Bella is with me, she says she only wants me to be happy."

Mary nodded. "What is she now, a junior in high school?"

"Yes. She just turned sixteen, and she is the junior class vice president. She's taking A.P. classes, plays cello in the orchestra, and is on the basketball team."

"Wow. You must be a proud papa."

"Very proud. That's probably the one thing I can say without hesitation that I have done well in my life. Raising Bella."

Mary let me sit with that good thought silently for

a while. I stared into my black coffee, thinking of better times, and took a big sip before grudgingly coming back to the present. To the case.

Finally, I raised my eyes to meet Mary's. "Meanwhile...did you get a chance to review the police reports I sent you from the Kala Tausinga case?"

Mary sat her coffee cup on the desk and reached for the file folder I had left her that morning. "Yes. But I don't think I got everything. The only police report I have is from December third, the day after the baby died. Do you have the other reports, or do we need to do a supplemental request for discovery?"

I replied, "Actually, I think those *are* the only police reports."

"You're kidding. A *one-day* investigation on a homicide?" Her jaw dropped, and she stared at me, apparently dumfounded.

"I'm not sure the police suspected foul play at the time," I offered as a possible explanation. "After all, they didn't arrest anyone until well after the medical examiner's report was finally released. Speaking of which, what do you make of the autopsy report?"

"There are a couple of noteworthy details," Mary said matter-of-factly as she picked up a page of handwritten notes. "No membrane had formed over the blood in the brain."

"Meaning?"

"If the injury were older, you would expect to see hemosiderin-laden macrophages or histiocytes. So, I would say that the injury that caused the bleeding occurred close in time of the child's death."

Nodding in understanding, I said, "Okay. Anything else?"

"Yes," Mary said. "The most notable detail in the medical examiner's report was his inability to determine the time of death. Rigor had already started to set in when the police arrived at midnight. And no one even tried to take the baby's temperature. And as you know, checking body temp is critical in time-of-death determinations. I can't believe that the paramedics on the scene didn't even try to check it. Anyway, because the M.E. didn't know time of death, he couldn't give the time of injury. So, the bottom line is that *when* the child was injured can't be determined medically."

I laid the notepad I had brought into Mary's office on the edge of her desk. "Can we brainstorm for a minute?"

"Go for it." She leaned back into her chair, interweaving her fingers on her lap.

"Since the time of injury can't be determined, can we tell the jury that it could have been Kala's husband who killed their sixteen-month-old son?"

"Maybe so." Mary shrugged. "I saw that the 911 call came at 11:55 p.m. Both Kala and her husband told the same story. They said that Kala found the baby in distress in his crib at about six p.m., before the husband got home from work. The funky thing is that they didn't call 911 until six hours later, and the baby had clearly been dead for a while by then. So, yes, medically speaking, the kid could have been injured *after* his father got home."

"Okay. That's good," I replied, relieved.

"But unfortunately, that's not what Kala told the police. She said she found her child injured *before* her husband got home from work."

"Oh yeah. There is that," I answered glumly, the relief leaving.

Without stopping her scan of the M.E.'s report, Mary asked, "Is there any history of domestic violence in the household?"

"I don't know." I tugged at my goatee while I considered what to do next. "I'll prepare a subpoena for all police calls to that apartment during the time they've been living there. And I'll get an investigator to interview the neighbors. People in apartment complexes usually know the dirt about their neighbors and like to gossip. Let's talk to Kala's friends and relatives also. Maybe someone has seen her fighting with her husband. Maybe we could argue that it was him after all."

"Frank, take a breath," Mary said calmly, peering over her readers. "I'm sorry to play the devil's advocate, but sometimes women *do* kill their children, like when Susan Smith ran her car into a lake with two toddlers in the back. Later, she said it was because her lover didn't want them around. And what about Andrea Yates? Satan told her to drown her five children to save them from eternal damnation, or something crazy like that. You never know what people are capable of doing."

God, I hate dead baby cases.

Chapter Two

Arriving at the visiting area of the recently constructed county jail the next morning, I slid my driver's license and Bar Association identification card out of my worn wallet and handed them to the deputy sitting behind the counter eating what appeared to be a blueberry muffin.

"Good morning. Sorry to interrupt. I work for The Defenders, and I've been assigned to represent Kala Tausinga. I'd like to see her."

The deputy flashed me a friendly smile despite that fact that I had arrived before normal visiting hours. "Please wait a moment." She laid the muffin on a small paper plate at her side and wiped her fingers with a napkin.

The deputy returned her attention to me. "Have you been here before? We have a new computer system, and we have to type in the name, profession, and contact information for all professional visitors."

"Yes. I've visited clients here several times already. I'm sure you'll find me in there somewhere."

She read my Bar Association I.D. and started typing on her computer. "Yep, here you are." Several keystrokes later she added, "Found Ms. Tausinga too. She's in B-Pod. Give me a few minutes to set up your visit," she said as she punched numbers on her desk phone.

I scanned the room behind me. The waiting room in the visiting area of the new county jail was large and well-lit with restrooms and a drinking fountain in the back. Lockers ran down the inside wall for visitors to lock up their phones, keys, and wallets. Dull, gray concrete slabs placed evenly throughout the room passed for seating for the friends and family waiting for the next thirty-minute time slot to visit inmates. Finding them all empty this early in the morning was welcomed, so I picked a seat and sat down and waited.

I thought back to the old metro jail. There, we didn't have to wait. The jail gave us public defenders a pass to go inside. Private lawyers didn't get to go in, though. They had to visit their clients through the glass. But we public defenders had the run of the place. At each heavy metal door we came to as we made our way to see our clients, we would wave our pass at the closed-circuit camera that was bolted to the metal wall by each door and wait until the guard let us through. But we went everywhere. We saw everything.

I remembered how in minimum security, due to overcrowding, inmates were herded into large rooms with rows and rows of cots. In maximum security, inmates with a history of violence were placed in small isolation cells. The women's shower area was open to the guards' view and had only waist-high walls, so it was easy to locate your female clients, albeit seeing them while they were showering could be somewhat disconcerting. In the suicide watch cell, mentally ill prisoners were detained naked to prevent them from using an item of clothing or a sheet to commit suicide. We saw it all.

Built like a medieval dungeon underneath the old

courthouse, the old metro jail had long, narrow hallways with rows of group cells that extended to more than a hundred feet away from the view of the nearest guard station. The guards called that part of the jail "Gladiator Row." Many of my clients housed in that section in the old jail showed up to court with black eyes and puffy lips. Some got it worse. I never knew even one who identified his attacker. No one talked, or worse would happen the next time. The old metro jail was dark and damp. There were bugs and the smell of urine. Muffled screams echoed off concrete walls...

"Yes. Got it," said the deputy behind me. Being the only one in the room, I justifiably assumed she was talking about me. I stood up and walked back over to the counter to see if I was correct and that she had finally been able to arrange my visit.

"Go to Pod B Section 6," she said. "There are signs in the hallway to show you how to get there."

"Yes, I know. I've been down there before. Thanks."

"Do you need a contact visit, or is the regular visiting area okay?"

"At this hour, no one else will be visiting in that pod, right?"

"That's right," said the deputy with a nod.

"The regular visiting area will be fine."

"Do you have anything you need to check into a locker?"

"Cell phone, wallet, and keys," I replied after patting down my pockets.

The deputy pushed with her feet and rolled her chair back to the wall behind her where she picked a key off a rack. "Okay, here's a key for the locker," she said, rolling her chair back toward me. "After you put your belongings in the locker, go through the metal detector."

"Yeah, I know the drill. Thank you."

After a slow walk down the long concrete tunnel to Pod B, I waited patiently by door number six. Then I remembered to push the button next to the door to announce that I had arrived.

The deputy quickly buzzed me through, and I opened the heavy door. I walked down one more short, narrow hallway to a row of large plexiglass windows with a single round metal stool mounted on a cement cylinder in front of each one.

On the other side of one of the windows sat a young woman with long and straight black hair who must have been Kala Tausinga. She sat hunched forward, her eyes and corners of her mouth downcast. As I approached her, she brushed her hair away from her face.

I settled onto the stool in front of the window and asked, "Are you Kala Tausinga?"

"Yes," she answered quietly, a small furrow wrinkling her forehead.

"My name's Frank Bravo. I was appointed by the court to be your attorney." I studied her, concerned about her demeanor. In a soft voice, I asked, "How are you?"

"Fine, I guess," she whispered with a slight accent I couldn't quite place. "I've been praying to my Heavenly Father a lot. That's helped." She finally raised her eyes as if talking about her faith gave her some courage. "And my bishop visited me yesterday."

"So, you're Mormon?" I asked, recognizing the

references to the principal religious organization in Utah.

"Yes," she answered, perking up on the topic. "My family is Mormon. Missionaries came to our town in Samoa and taught people about their church and beliefs. My parents liked the emphasis on the family and how the church helps its members. They joined when I was a young child. But my husband doesn't like to go to church, so we don't go very often."

Further questioning revealed that Kala was twenty-two years old and born in Samoa, but her husband Afa is Tongan. That explained her English; it was probably her second language.

"Your English is quite good. How long have you lived in the States?" I asked, glancing up from my note writing.

"Almost ten years now. I came to live with my aunt and uncle in Utah when my father died."

"When did you meet your husband?"

"I got pregnant while I was in high school and dropped out. My family urged me to marry the father. I did, and he's now my husband, and we have four children." Her soft voice got stronger when she mentioned her children.

As Kala told me all this, her manner remained meek the whole time. She sat with her hands folded in her lap. I tried to determine if this was her personality or if she were suffering from depression that might put her at risk for suicide or at least in need of counseling. We had licensed social workers on staff at The Defenders who provided counseling services to our clients.

Deciding that she was not in need of immediate

psychiatric care, I finally got to the point. "Kala, what happened to your son?"

Kala frowned and dropped her head. She wiped a tear from her cheek before speaking. "His name is Afa Tausinga, Junior, because we named him after my husband. My family and I call him Juna. The day Juna died, my husband Afa was at work, and I was home alone with Juna and my two daughters and was pregnant with my fourth child. I went to the manager's apartment to pay the rent and returned after about five minutes. When I got back to the apartment, I found my baby in his crib, and his arms were shaking. I picked him up and could tell he was having trouble breathing. I hit him on the back to see if he was choking on anything and tried to do CPR on him."

It was the same story she told the police on that fateful day of December second. And it was identical to the story her husband told police. I already had all the police and autopsy reports for this case because it had been two weeks since the baby died. The police arrested Kala only a few days ago, but they didn't arrest her husband.

I asked, "How do you know CPR?"

"Juna was born prematurely and almost died. The hospital staff wouldn't let me take him home until I learned CPR and showed them that I could do it." She wiped away another tear.

After scribbling some notes, I asked, "Do you have any idea how Juna was injured? Did he fall recently, or has he been in an accident?"

She shrugged. "I don't know. Maybe my two other children hurt him accidently. They can be rough with him."

"Your daughters, right? How old are they?"

"Three and four." Her eyes flooded with new tears.

This story that the kids could have hurt Afa didn't make sense when I read it in the police report, and it didn't make any more sense now. I told Kala about the medical examiner's report. "Your son apparently suffered a severe blow to the head—blunt force trauma more severe than could be inflicted by a child. It had to be an adult." I stared deeply into her eyes.

"I swear I didn't hurt my son," she said, returning my stare and speaking louder.

I was taken back a bit by the strength of Kala's denial. Almost all my clients denied their charges initially. I've learned the hard way that you can't draw any firm conclusions from their denials. For the moment, I decided not to challenge Kala's assertion but to seek other possible explanations.

"What about the baby's father? Could he have done it?"

"My husband isn't his father."

"But you named him Junior?"

"Yes. I named him after my husband hoping that Afa would come to love him, like he was his own son. But...I don't think he ever did."

"So, who is Afa Junior's father?"

She took in a deep breath and slowly exhaled. "A couple of years ago, I separated for a short time from Afa after he slept with my cousin. I also had an affair while we were separated and got pregnant with Juna. He's my third child."

"I understand now. Thank you for explaining."

I leaned back on the stool and tried to assess what Kala had told me. None of this was adding up for me.

Kala didn't seem like the kind of person who could kill her own son. But even good people can do bad things in a flash of anger or frustration. I've seen it my whole career. And Kala's own story proved that she was the only one at home with Juna when he died.

I gathered my notes together. "I'll do my best to help you. When you go to court in a few days, I'll be there with you."

"What will happen when we go to court?" Kala inched forward in her chair. "Can you *please* get me out of jail?" she asked, speaking more quickly now. "I want to be with my children. My baby needs me, and I want to be with oldest daughter on her birthday. It's less than two weeks from now."

I had to consider how to answer before I spoke. People charged with murder don't get out of jail, not unless they can afford a very high bail. Nevertheless, there was no direct evidence that Kala had killed her son. And, after all, the police didn't arrest her the night her son died. It was a stretch, but maybe I could make an argument for a lower bail on those grounds.

"Kala, do you or your relatives have any money or property that could be used for bail if I can get it reduced?"

"I don't have any money. But my aunt and uncle own a house. Maybe they could help. They're watching my children while I'm in jail. When I called them on the phone, they asked when I would be getting out. They're older and want me to take the kids as soon as I can. It's hard for them to take care of them, especially the baby."

"I understand. But it's not that easy."

She just stared at me with big, black, sad eyes.

Chapter Three

The next morning, I paced back and forth anxiously between the two brown synthetic leather couches and six gray fabric chairs in our office reception area. Mary, on the other hand, sat patiently, reading a magazine. Our white-haired investigator, Francis Benson, stood looking out the window toward the parking lot.

We were expecting Kala's aunt, Lovai Aleki, and her eighteen-year-old niece Lei to come to our office for interviews. Benson, as our investigator preferred to be called, told us that he had learned from the family that Lovai watched Kala's three children during the day, and Lei watched them in the evening after she came home from work.

According to Benson, Kala's daughters, Amanaki and Emeni, had been talking to Lovai and Lei. And what they said was shocking—*Daddy did it.*

My first instinct when I got Benson's report was to call the district attorney immediately to argue that he should dismiss the murder charge against Kala when we made our first appearance in front of the judge two days from now. After all, if we were to save these witnesses for trial, Kala would have to continue to wait in jail for a least a few more months.

Mary and I met with Benson to decide our best strategy for when to disclose our witnesses to the district attorney, evaluating the pros and cons. After much discussion, the three of us decided to get the witnesses on the record first. We would get recorded statements from the adults about what they had heard the children say, and, if possible, statements from the children as well. The children were very young. Although legally deemed competent to give testimony, often children don't have the intellect to tell a cogent story. But in our case, we hoped to have the corroboration of the adults who had been watching the children.

With recorded statements in hand, it would be harder for police detectives to try to strong-arm any members of the Aleki family into recanting or changing their story. A standard ploy in murder cases was for the police to threaten charges for Obstruction of Justice against family members who were going to testify for the defense. And in one of my earlier cases, police told one young mother that her children would be taken by the State if she testified for the defense. My take at the time was that the officers in that case wanted to make their arrest stick, and they believed that the ends justified the means. But that didn't make it right. In any case I wanted to take that option away from the cops in this case if I could.

The Alekis arrived fifteen minutes late, a fact not at all helpful to my nervous tension. As they approached the office, Benson opened the door for them, turned toward Mary and me, and said, "This is Lovai...and her husband Sione." Sione was a man with a big frown that didn't match the bold flower-print short-sleeve shirt he wore. He walked with a noticeable limp and settled heavily into a chair, filling it entirely. "And this is Lei," the investigator added as a young woman followed the others through the door, holding the hands of two very young children who had to be Kala's daughters.

Before we could even get started, there was already a problem.

"Why did you want us to come here?" Sione asked. His voice was quiet and sort of high-pitched, belying the strength of his bulky frame.

The answer to Sione's question was at once simple and at the same time by far the most consequential thing in my life at this moment. I forced my answer to sound calm. "We need you to tell us what the children are saying about who hurt Juna. It will help us win Kala's case."

Sione's reply made plain that he had other priorities. "We don't want to get involved. We're trying not to talk about this in the house. The children cry. It's not good for them."

"I understand your concern, Mr. Aleki," Mary interjected, perhaps seeing the bewilderment on my face. "I assure you that we will be as brief as possible. Frankly, we are hoping that by providing this information to the prosecutor, we may be able to avoid a trial altogether, and no one would have to testify in court."

Mary glanced at me for support. I knew that what she had just said about avoiding a trial was wishful thinking, but it was *theoretically* possible, so I nodded enthusiastically at her side.

"Okay," Sione said. He didn't sound convinced, but for now, at least he wouldn't impede our efforts to interview Lovai and Lei.

Mary and I led the women one at a time into the

nearby conference room while the rest of the family waited in the lobby. Standard procedure was to interview witnesses separately. That way, there was less chance that one would influence the other's memory of an event, a circumstance that a prosecutor would use on cross-examination at trial to call into question the truthfulness or accuracy of their testimony.

We started with Kala's aunt Lovai. Benson was present with his tape recorder. The four of us huddled around one end of a large, long, polished wood table which could seat up to sixteen. Hopeful to get some helpful evidence for Kala's case, I began the interview.

"Lovai, what is your relationship to Kala Tausinga?"

"She is my sister's daughter."

"By the way, where *is* Kala's mother?"

"She lives in Tonga."

"And who are Amanaki and Emeni?" I asked, certain I had massacred the pronunciation.

"They are Kala's girls."

"Okay. So, Lovai, do you spend any time with Amanaki and Emeni?"

"Yes. I watch them and Kala's baby during the day until my daughter Lei gets home from work."

"I see. Do they ever talk about what happened to their little brother?" Having asked the key question, I held my breath for the answer.

"Not very much. We don't talk about it in the house. But once Amanaki said something about it."

My anxiety turned into excitement. I leaned forward. "What did she say?"

"Well, she doesn't talk very well. It's gibberish. She hasn't learned English well because she hears a combination of English, Tongan, and Samoan at home. But she said, 'Ditty hit Juna head door,' I think."

"I'm not sure I understand," I said cautiously.

Lovai said, "What I think she said is that her daddy hit Juna's head on the door. That's how she talks."

"Tell me more about that," I said, feeling my body relax a bit. "What was going on when she said that?"

"It was in the evening a few days ago. Her father had not visited her or his other kids since they came to stay with us, but he called earlier that day to say he was coming. Around seven in the evening, I told Amanaki that her daddy was coming. That's when she said something like, '*No. Daddy stupid. Hit Juna head door.*' "

"So, you hadn't even *asked* her what happened to Juna?"

Lovai replied, "No, like I told you before, we don't talk about it."

"Had Kala or the police given you any information about the case at that point?"

"No," said Lovai. "We didn't know anything about what happened. We only knew that they had arrested Kala."

"What did you do then?" I fully expected some dramatic revelation.

"Nothing. Like I said, we try not to talk to the children about their brother. It upsets them."

"How about Emeni?" I asked, hiding my disappointment. "Has she said anything?"

"Yes, Emeni says the same thing— 'Daddy hit Juna.'"

This was good information. If both children say that it was their father who hurt Juna, we should be in good shape at trial.

"But Emeni repeats everything her older sister says," Lovai said. "So, I don't know if maybe she's just copying her sister."

I decided I didn't want to pursue the "just-copying" issue any further and turned to Mary to see if she had any other questions. She shook her head, so we thanked Lovai and took her back to the reception area and brought Lei into the conference room.

"Lei," I asked once we had all settled in, "what is your relationship to Kala Tausinga?"

"She's my cousin."

"Do you spend any time with Amanaki and Emeni?"

"Yes. I watch them and Kala's baby boy from around five or six when I get home from work until they go to bed at about nine."

"I see. Do the girls ever talk about what happened to their little brother?"

"Not very much. But once while I was watching Amanaki, she said something about it. She said that her daddy hit Juna's head on the door, or on the wall, or something like that."

This was exactly the answer we needed, so I eagerly followed up with Lei to get some more details. "What was going on when Amanaki said that Daddy hit Juna's head on the door?"

"We were looking at the photos of Kala and her family we had put up on the wall. I took one of them down and pointed at the people in the photo. I asked Amanaki who each one was to teach her the names of the family. When I asked her about Juna, she said, 'Daddy hit Juna head. Juna in Heaven now.'"

"Then what happened?" I asked.

Without any hesitation, Lei said, "I was surprised. What she said didn't make sense. It was Kala who was arrested, *not* her husband, so I asked Amanaki, 'Don't you mean Mommy?'"

"What did she say?"

"She was *very* upset at me. She said, 'No, not Mommy. Mommy not stupid. Mommy not hurt Juna.'"

"What did you do when you she said that?"

"We didn't talk about it again until the man from your office called us. And we told him."

Lei leaned back in her chair and folded her arms, apparently done with her story. Mary and I thanked her and asked her to wait for us in the conference room.

"This is great for Kala's defense," Mary said. "Amanaki said that it was Daddy, not Mommy."

"And the statement was spontaneous, not an answer to a question, which makes it reliable," I added, feeling so much more confident than I did before the interviews.

"But," Mary added, "the statement of a relative of the defendant is usually viewed suspiciously."

"True enough," I agreed, wishing Mary would have let me relish in my confidence a little longer. "But I seem to recall seeing a photograph of the crime scene where there was an indentation in a door or wall. So, the statement would match that fact. And in this case, we do have *two* relatives willing to testify, not only one."

"Whether they're actually *willing* to testify is an open question," Mary said. "You heard what Sione said. The family does not want to get involved at all. And besides, what Lovai and Lei said about Amanaki's statement is inadmissible hearsay. The adult members of the family can't repeat it in court." She tilted her head to the side in the direction of the children. "So, let's interview the four-year-old, Amanaki."

Mary went out to ask Lovai to bring Amanaki into the conference room. Amanaki had been clinging to Lovai since they arrived at our office. I asked Lovai to please stay in the room and to let Amanaki sit on her lap, thinking that having Lovai right there would make Amanaki feel comfortable enough to talk to us.

I was wrong. As I tried to engage Amanaki in casual conversation about her favorite toys, she slid off Lovai's lap and squatted under the table. With one hand, she squeezed Lovai's leg. The thumb of her other hand was jammed deep in her mouth. And she stayed there until we finally gave up and left the room, extremely disappointed. If the children couldn't testify in court, we couldn't use their statements in Kala's defense. Or putting it another way, we didn't have a defense.

After seeing the Aleki family out and thanking them for coming, Mary and I waited for the elevator to go back to our offices.

"Mary?"

"Yes, Frank," she said with concern on her face. "What is it?"

"Do you ever feel like saying *fuck it*?"

"What do you mean, Frank?"

I scanned the room to make sure no other lawyers could hear what I was going to say next. "Maybe we could both go open our own private practice. We would have fewer cases. Maybe only misdemeanors and drug cases or the occasional forgery. No damn dead baby cases. I'm beat down right now. I don't know how many more fucks I have left to give."

Mary didn't answer right away. The elevator opened, and we walked into it, and the doors closed behind us.

Mary pushed the stop button on the wall and grabbed me firmly by the shoulders.

"I know you, Frank Bravo. I've known you for more than twenty years. There is a reason you have the Don Quixote statue on your desk. That is *you*. Full of idealism. Fighting for the powerless." Mary's stare was penetrating. "You'd fade away and slowly die if you left this office. I for one think you still have more fucks to give," she said, smiling at the end.

I nodded and took a deep breath.

"And sure," said Mary, pushing the start button. "If you ever decide to go, let me know. I feel your pain. Maybe I would go with you after all... But not yet. Not now. Kala needs us."

Chapter Four

Mia Montes flexed her knees, braced herself, and exploded forward, kicking Carlos between his legs as hard as she could, screaming in primal rage. Balling her right fist, she punched him in the face, imagining she could push his nose up into his brain and then jammed her hand into his throat as hard as she could, her lethal intention obvious to any observer.

In fact, this Carlos would be dead for sure by now if he were not a dummy. A man-size training partner made of wood and rubber under foam padding. Mia named the dummy after her ex-husband, a violent and abusive man who had tried and almost succeeded in killing her ten years earlier. The dummy Carlos stood a bit crookedly now after Mia kicked through his knee, breaking the board beneath it a year ago. An extra slat of wood and a roll of duct tape kept him upright now.

Mia herself stood only five feet two inches tall. Her six-days-a-week training schedule, which her girlfriends thought insane, resulted in a slim but muscular body. Motivated by her promise to herself to never be bullied or abused again, she committed to achieving top physical conditioning and to mastering martial arts. On Tuesdays and Thursdays, she started with three sets of ten pull-ups to warm up followed by thirty minutes on the stationary bike, the Mount Kilimanjaro sim, max level, and a full range of upper body free weight routines.

Every Monday, Wednesday, and Friday, Mia rotated through several martial arts studios where she maintained memberships. Aikido, jiujitsu, and judo were her favorites because she learned how to fight against larger opponents and how to use their size and momentum against them. But it wasn't until she met Tito, an MMA trainer, that she learned the street fighting techniques she practiced on Carlos in her basement.

As she did her workout, Mia reviewed in her mind what Tito had taught her. "Use your feet. Your legs are stronger than their hands. Go for their knees to cut them down to size. A hard enough punch to the throat can take down anyone. Get a rear naked choke hold and don't let go, no matter what."

Saturdays Mia ran, as far and as fast as she could. She raced as often as possible and regularly won her age group. "Pace is my trick," she told her friends. But in her heart Mia knew that she just wanted it more than the other competitors and was willing to suffer more for the victory.

After completing this day's workout, Mia hurried to get ready to go to court. She peeled off her sweat-soaked tank top and tight spandex shorts and turned on the shower. Stepping in lightly, she grabbed the shampoo, squeezed a generous dollop over her head, and began to wash her thick and luxurious, straight black hair that would fall gracefully to her shoulders if she didn't keep it in a ponytail or hidden under a baseball cap.

After showering, she put thick makeup on her forehead. Though she had been told she was naturally beautiful and didn't need to wear cosmetics, Mia was merely trying to cover the long scar crossing the left front of her forehead from the machete her ex-husband Carlos plunged into her forehead the night she died. That's what the paramedics told her later. She had lost too much blood and was not breathing when they arrived. It was the dark night Mia finally decided to leave Carlos.

Mia walked out onto the balcony of her apartment on the hill overlooking the downtown area to check the weather. She recognized that the rent for the apartment was probably too expensive to pay by herself, but the view was awesome and the neighborhood safe, so it was well worth it. Besides, her car was paid off, so that helped.

Mia had chosen to live alone these last ten years. It was peaceful. No noise. No crises. She got to choose what she did and when she did it. She had accepted an occasional date request but had never found a man she liked enough, or trusted enough, to make a commitment to.

It was chilly, so Mia put on a wool pants suit, slipped her feet into some sensible black heels, and picked up a file folder off the glass-top desk in her home office. She reviewed the summary of her assigned case for that morning's court hearing as she walked toward the elevator to go down to the parking area. It was a murder case. A dead baby.

Anger stirred inside her as she read the probable cause statement. The case was State of Utah v. Kala Tausinga. *That's odd. It was the mother this time.* In Mia's experience, it was most often a drug-addled boyfriend who physically abused his girlfriend or hurt her children, or both.

On arriving at her space in the parking garage, she slid into the driver's seat of her red Honda Civic and moved her gym bag from the front passenger's seat onto the floor in the back seat so that she could set her file down. But first she double-checked the names of her new clients—Afa, Kala Tausinga's husband, and the couple's three surviving children.

When Mia arrived at the courthouse, she saw a Polynesian family in the hallway in front of the courtroom of Judge Russo. Since the defendant Kala Tausinga would be appearing before him, she guessed they might be there for that case.

Mia approached the family. "Hello. My name is Mia Montes. I'm a victim advocate from the District Attorney's Office. Are you the Tausinga family?"

The woman, who was holding a squirming newborn, answered. "We're the Aleki family. My name is Lovai, and that is my husband, Sione," she said, pointing to a large man also sitting on the bench. "Kala Tausinga is our niece." She tilted her head toward the baby in her arms and the two little girls sitting between her and the man. "And these are her children."

Mia replied, "It's very nice to meet you all. By the way, is Kala's husband, Afa, here with you?"

"No," Lovai said, "he's not here. I don't know where he is, or even if he is coming."

Lovai and Sione both averted their eyes and gazed down the hallway behind her. Mia turned and saw a man and woman walking toward them. She recognized them as two lawyers from the public defender's office approaching the Aleki family.

The man, tall and thin with a balding head, reached

out his hand to Mia. "Pardon me," he said. "I'm Frank Bravo."

Mia glanced down at his hand and back into his face without shaking his hand. "I know who you are." She frowned. She knew Frank Bravo's reputation. He would sometimes have the defendant's family testify for the defense and get the guilty defendants released. But in this case, those family members were the victims and her clients, so Mia moved directly between Bravo and the Aleki family and planted her heels firmly on the ground.

Mr. Bravo hesitated a moment before speaking. "My colleague Mary here and I represent Kala Tausinga." Then he smiled and asked, "Are you with the family?"

Mia didn't return his smile. She didn't trust defense attorneys. Sometimes they used trickery to get their clients off. She had been instructed that it was the policy of the District Attorney's Office that the defense attorneys should be discouraged from interviewing the victims in a case.

"Yes, I'm with the family. My name's Mia Montes. I'm the victim advocate in this case."

Mr. Bravo nodded at Mia and started to walk around her toward the family. But Mia moved with him, blocking his approach. She put her chin up and crossed her arms.

Apparently deciding not to challenge Mia further, Mr. Bravo cleared his throat. From where he stood, he directed his eyes to the Aleki family. "My plan is to ask the judge for a bond reduction. I'm going to inform the judge that because almost all of Kala's family live in Salt Lake City, she's not a flight risk. She doesn't have a criminal record of any sort, and she's not a danger to the community. And, due to the lack of evidence of intentional harm to the deceased child, the police didn't even arrest her at the time. I hope the judge will reduce the bail enough so that if you can use your house to post a bond, we can get her released."

Sione turned away and said nothing in response to the question about using the house to post bail for Kala. After a moment, Lovai quietly responded. "Recently, Sione was hurt and has not been able to work. Our house has gone into foreclosure."

"I'm very sorry to hear that," said Mr. Bravo, shrugging his shoulders and taking a deep breath. "I guess we'll see you inside," he added as he turned to go. He frowned at Mia as he walked away. And she frowned right back at him.

As the lawyers entered the courtroom, someone else approached the Aleki family. It was a big guy with an unkempt Afro wearing a collared shirt with the name of a company on it. Mia figured he was coming from work.

"Ms. Montes?"

Mia turned toward Mrs. Aleki. "You asked about Afa Tausinga. That is him."

Chapter Five

Disappointed that the Aleki family was not going to be able to post bond to get Kala released, Mary and I tracked down the prosecutor in Kala's case, Randy Johnson, to see if we could discuss Kala's case prior to the scheduling conference set to begin soon.

The three of us crowded around a little round table in a small conference room next to the courtroom. Mary and I planned to reveal to Johnson the details of the children's shocking Daddy-did-it revelation. I was hoping that dismissal was at hand, but Mary urged me to wait and see. At a minimum, we wanted to arrange Kala's release until trial in consideration of the new information. A sense of anticipation filled the tiny area.

After briefly laying out the basics for Johnson, I reviewed in some detail how the children said that it was Daddy, not Mommy who had killed the child. I explained how this information changed everything. I asked Johnson if he would agree to Kala's release and waited for his answer.

"They probably just made that up," Johnson said quickly.

What the.... I glanced at Mary with my mouth agape. She frowned at me and shook her head at my apparent soon-to-be explosion. I took a deep breath.

"Now look, Randy," I began, intentionally using Johnson's first name to attempt to create a more amicable discussion. "The circumstances surrounding the children's statements show that they weren't made up. After all, Amanaki's statements to the Alekis were spontaneous. The Aleki family didn't ever talk about what happened to Juna because they didn't want the children to relive the trauma. The statement that Daddy did it only came out when Mrs. Aleki told the children that their daddy was coming to visit. Only *then* did Amanaki say that it was Daddy who hit Juna's head. Moreover, when Lei heard what Amanaki said, Lei *challenged* her, saying, 'Don't you mean Mommy?' And Amanaki adamantly insisted that '*No. Mommy not stupid.*' "

Johnson faced me and met my eyes as I spoke to him, so I continued. "Plus, the Alekis didn't know *anything* about the case. They didn't have any police reports. So, the Alekis *couldn't* have suggested that answer to Amanaki. And, to top it off, Amanaki's little sister Emeni said the same thing as Amanaki!"

I sat back in my chair, certain I had cleared it all up for Johnson.

"But this is the first time the kids are saying this," said Johnson. "They would have said it before now if it were true."

Johnson didn't hesitate. He defended his position. It's like he was saying, "My mind is made up. Don't confuse me with facts." Unfortunately, to some extent, this is an unfortunate characteristic among lawyers in general. We were trained to take sides and to fight over details. This was a useful skill for court hearings, but not so good for personal relationships. But I digress.

"Actually, Randy," I said, forcing myself to be as polite as I could, "the police reports show that the night

Juna died, Emeni refused to go to an interview room with the officer. And Amanaki *did* answer questions from the officer. But he couldn't understand her. He didn't even try to get an interpreter or family member to help. If the cops had done more than a *one-day* investigation, they would have figured it out."

"There is other evidence as well that implicates Kala," Johnson asserted defensively. "The house was *very* messy, and the children were *very* dirty when they were checked by the nurse. Plus, the children don't speak well or know their colors. They are well below age level. And Juna was well below the normal weight for his age."

Johnson said all this with a straight face, as if it were sufficient justification for a murder charge. I had hoped the statements of Kala's children gave us all we needed to resolve this difficult case, but now a wave of anger built inside me. Mary was squirming in her seat and leaning forward as if she wanted to intervene, but I raised my hand in her direction. I was too upset to be quiet. Fortunately, Mary jumped in anyway.

"Come on, Randy," Mary said in a chiding tone, "the house was messy because Kala was nine months pregnant. Have *you* ever been nine months pregnant?"

That at least got a grin from Johnson and significantly reduced the tension that had built up between him and me. Thank God for Mary.

"Besides," Mary said, "why do people assume that taking care of children is the job of only the mother? We're not in the 1950s. Kala's husband, Afa, works at a *soap* factory. He's a big, strong guy. Surely, he could bring some of that soap home and spread it around the house a little."

Mary's disarming style elicited a chuckle from both Johnson and me. Johnson nodded as Mary laid things out in her pleasant and common-sense way.

"I too saw the nurse's report about the how dirty the children were," Mary said. "But that was two days after the incident. The police reported that they gave the girls to Afa's father the night of the incident. *He's* the one who didn't bathe them. And Juna was small because he was only sixteen months old and was born prematurely. We can get you those records to review. So you see, *none* of those things prove murder at all. Under the circumstances, it's no wonder the police didn't arrest anyone. In fact, we frankly can't even see why Kala was even charged."

Johnson hesitated, finally. He put his hand to his forehead and tapped it with his fingers, seemingly considering Mary's thoughtful explanations of the circumstances. Maybe he was going to come around after all.

"Well, I'll offer her manslaughter," Johnson offered after several moments of contemplation.

"Jesus, Randy," I blurted. "Manslaughter is still up to fifteen years in prison. We're saying that we think there is evidence that she is *innocent*. Manslaughter isn't going to do it." I stood up and walked out of the conference room without my file. I was thinking I needed to get out before I said something I regretted.

I took some deep breaths as I marched to the end of the long hallway. Closing my eyes, I visualized myself in front of my Zen master, sitting on my pillow with my legs crossed, hands resting lightly on my knees with palms facing upward and open to let all things go.

Not until my mind was at peace did I start to walk

back toward Judge Russo's courtroom. Mary was waiting for me in the hallway with concern on her face. She checked me over apparently to see if I was okay, and then nodded toward the courtroom door.

Inside the courtroom, Mary and I waited our turn to call Kala's case. Since the Aleki family could not afford to post any bail, all we could do now was to use today's court appearance to schedule another hearing.

When it was our turn, I stood to walk to the lectern in front of the judge's high bench, sighing audibly. "If it please the court," I said firmly, summoning my courtroom voice, "could we call the matter of Kala Tausinga?"

"Yes, of course, Mr. Bravo," replied Judge Russo. "Bailiff, please bring out Mr. Tausinga."

The bailiff started shuffling nervously through the loose pages of his transport list. I could see that he was confused, and I knew why. The judge had never seen our client and had assumed he was a man. Now the bailiff was reading through the list of men he had transported for court today. I let him struggle for a minute before intervening.

"Actually, Your Honor, it *should* be *Mr.* Tausinga who is coming out," I asserted, staring down Johnson. "Unfortunately, however, the State has *instead* charged *Mrs.* Tausinga in this case."

The judge smiled. I imagined he thought I was joking or merely saying one of those things that defense lawyers are supposed say. Johnson had a smirk on his face but said nothing.

I turned to give the Aleki family an I'm-so-sorry look. Afa Tausinga glared at me from the back row. *Shit.* I recognized him immediately from the photos taken by police the night that Juna died. Afa leaned forward on the bench and placed his hands on the bench as if he were about to push himself up to his feet. But he was trapped at the end of the bench against the wall.

When Afa moved, he bumped Mia Montes, who was seated next to him. She quickly scooted a few inches to the side and leaned away from him. She stared first at me and then at Johnson and shook her head slowly.

The bailiff disappeared. A moment later, he brought Kala out of the holding cell and led her over to the lectern next to me.

"Keep your eyes on the judge," he told her.

"Very well, Mr. Bravo," said Judge Russo. "How would you like to proceed?"

"Judge, we need to ask for a continuance. There's some additional investigation that we'd like to do in this case before we schedule a firm trial date."

Judge Russo agreed to my request without objection. Delays are common in homicide cases. There's so much at stake that there is usually no complaint from the court about delays.

Kala's brow furrowed. She shook her head. I could see that she for one did have a complaint.

Judge Russo turned to his clerk. "Give us a date about thirty days out."

Kala spoke, loud enough for Judge Russo to hear. "Does this mean I'll have to stay in jail? I don't want to wait."

"Yes, I'm sorry," I said, turning toward Kala while glancing sideways at the judge. "The prosecutor wants to go forward with the case against you. We need more time to prepare."

"Mr. Bravo," said Judge Russo, apparently having overheard my conversation with Kala, "is your client willing to waive her constitutional right to a speedy trial?"

Kala shrugged. Over the years I have seen this puzzled expression on the faces of many if not most of my clients at some point when they struggled to interpret the legalese we lawyers spoke in the courtroom. Realizing I was caught between a rock and a hard place, I explained her rights. "Kala, you have a right to have a jury trial and to have it sooner rather than later. I suggest that you allow us to delay the case to have more time to prepare."

"Sooner," she said simply.

I stared at her for a minute, knowing she couldn't possibly imagine all that was required to prepare for a murder trial.

"No, Your Honor, Ms. Tausinga does *not* waive her right to a speedy trial."

Smiling almost imperceptibly, Judge Russo again directed his gaze and voice at his clerk. "Give us a date for trial, the soonest available."

The clerk busily tapped keys on her computer. "April eighteenth."

"How many days will we need, Mr. Bravo?" asked the judge.

I turned to Johnson. "Five?"

"That should be fine, Your Honor," Johnson said.

I nodded at Kala as the bailiff took her away. I picked up my file and signaled to Mary to come with me into the holding area to speak further with Kala about everything that had just happened.

Mary took me by the elbow after we stepped past

the big metal door leading to the holding area that the bailiff was keeping open for us. "While you were at the lectern, Johnson passed me an offer sheet. He already had it written up. It's what he told us before—manslaughter."

I had recovered my composure a bit since I stormed out of the conference room. I decided to at least consider the offer.

"Well, manslaughter's not a mandatory prison charge. Will Johnson agree to probation?" I asked Mary.

"No. He's asking for the maximum prison commitment—fifteen years."

"Well, that's a piece of shit offer," I pointed out needlessly.

"It's worse," Mary added. "He said we would have to stipulate to the prison commitment."

"Well, no fucking way that's going to happen."

"What does all that mean?" Kala asked after quietly watching us decide her future without consulting her.

I glanced at Mary who turned toward Kala. "It's an offer to reduce the murder charge to something less serious. The prosecutor offered to let you plead guilty to manslaughter instead of murder."

"I'm sorry. Does that mean I would be admitting that I killed my baby?"

"Yes," Mary said. "The only difference is that the charge is less serious, so you would not be incarcerated for as long."

"But I can't say that I killed my baby," Kala blurted, crying. "I didn't do it."

Over the years, almost all my clients have

professed innocence at first, no matter the quantity or quality of evidence against them. So, Kala's emotional outburst was not unexpected. According to the evidence, she was home alone with Juna when he was fatally injured. I know the State's shaken baby syndrome experts. All will claim that, according to all the scientific studies, there was no "lucid interval" between a child's injury and the onset of symptoms of lethargy, difficulty breathing, unconsciousness, and eventually death. Therefore, according to the theory, the last adult with the child was logically the killer.

"Don't worry, Kala," I said with as much emotional support as I could muster. "We're not telling you to accept this offer. We're just obligated to tell you about it. At this point, we're still planning on going to trial for you and fighting this case."

Kala stared at me with those big, sad black eyes, tears still running down her cheeks. It was killing me because so far, I hadn't been able to help her.

Kala turned away from me and stared at Mary. Mary found a Kleenex in the pocket of her jacket and handed it to Kala while nodding in agreement with me. Mary told Kala that we would continue to try to find evidence and witnesses for her defense.

Soon, a transportation officer came to take Kala back to the jail. We waited with her while he checked her leg chain and handcuffs. By the time Kala left, she was no longer crying. But she peeked over her shoulder at me as the officer led her away with that same despondent expression on her face.

Kala seemed sincere when she insisted that she didn't kill Juna. But what she told police left her as the only logical suspect.

Chapter Six

While driving my Jeep Cherokee toward the Glendale Golf Course a couple of days later, I tried to forget about the pile of cases stacked on my office deck and reflected on the unsettled state of my personal life. Before my divorce was final, it had been hard to date. "Hi. I'm still married, but I'm lonely" isn't that great of a pick-up line, I guess. Even now that I had started to date, I wasn't sure I was ready for a new commitment yet. I wanted to find a new partner, but something inside of me was damaged. The trust gland maybe. Or the unconditional love organ. Maybe I just needed more time to heal. But I was hoping that at least this date would get my mind off dead babies for a while.

When I arrived at the golf course, I found Dora already waiting for me in front of the clubhouse. I had been attracted to her photo on Match and was intrigued by the self-description in her profile, "Adventurer Seeks Companion." But Dora was even more beautiful in person than in her profile. I admired her athletic figure. Her long brown hair was highlighted with blonde streaks, and her big, dark-brown eyes sparkled from within.

We signed in, got a cart, and drove to the first tee. While we waited for the group ahead of us to get to their balls, I discovered that Dora was the chief financial officer for a regional chain of jewelry stores.

She had two children, both adults. She was forty-five years old and divorced.

Dora moved up onto the tee box when the prior group was almost far enough down the fairway for us to hit. She started taking practice swings with a driver. She paused during each backswing as she focused intently on the angle of her takeaway. It was Dora who had suggested that we play golf for our first date. On one hand, golfing eighteen holes took at least four hours. That would suck if we didn't get along. On the other hand, it was an unusually warm spring day. I liked golf. And Dora was a hottie.

"We can hit now," Dora said as she walked to the front of the tee box and planted a tee. She moved behind the ball to line up the shot. She got in her stance and wiggled her firm little butt back and forth as she found a comfortable position. Lowering her chin, she slowly drew her club away from the ball into a high position over her head. With a quick but controlled turn of her torso, she powerfully spun and drove her arms and the club head through the ball. *Ping!* The ball flew long and straight.

"I like your form," I said admiringly.

"Thanks," she replied simply.

"And you play golf well too!"

She turned and grinned at me this time. Bright white teeth gleamed between glossy red lips.

We talked about the layout of the course and the various joys and challenges of golf as we played the first eight holes. "I love these carts that have built-in GPS—you get the exact yardage to the pin"; "The greens are certainly in good repair today"; "The light breeze is perfect—it cools without affecting the ball flight too much"; "And the water hazards make the course more interesting, don't you think?"

We complimented each other's good shots and gave encouragement after a bad one. She didn't make many bad shots. It was a pleasant conversation for a first date. We were hitting it off.

After the ninth hole, we stopped to grab a couple of hot dogs and drinks. I liked that Dora wasn't snooty about eating golf course grub. After lunch, we went back to the golf course, but there was a little bit of a backup on the tenth hole. So, we sat in our cart and chatted.

I said, "Your profile said you have two kids. Do they see their father much?"

"No. My kids have different fathers. My daughter Jewel is twenty-six. Her father and I were high school sweethearts. The problem was that he never left high school. He didn't have any goals. He was *so* immature. He only wanted to shoot pool with his friends all the time. We broke up but stayed friends. He has been somewhat involved in Jewel's life but never helped me financially."

"Sounds like he's a bum."

"No, not really. My son Max is twenty. It's *his* father that's the real bum. He kept a job, but he was a bad alcoholic. Before I met him, it was hard for me to raise my little girl as a single mom. The jobs I could get with my high school education didn't pay well. Then I met him, and it helped financially. And he was nice to me, at first anyway."

"I don't mean to pry, but what do you mean *at first*?"

"It's okay," Dora said with a little smile. "It was a

long time ago. When he got drunk, he was abusive. It was mostly verbal. If I said anything about his drinking, he'd call me names and tell me that I was good for nothing and that I couldn't get along without him."

Dora paused, apparently deep in some old memory. "Then one day, he hit me right in the face," she said, not smiling now. "After he finished his bottle and passed out, I took my kids and our clothes and went to a girlfriend's house. Later, he tried to get me to go back. But I didn't trust him. And I didn't want to live in fear. I didn't want that for my kids."

Dora fell silent again, staring into the distance.

After a moment, I said, "So... what did you do?"

"I took charge of my life." That sparkle in her eyes returned. "I got a job and registered for college. I raised my kids by myself. It took me six years, but I graduated with an accounting degree."

"How are your kids doing now?"

"My daughter is married to a great guy. He loves her and takes good care of her. She's eight months pregnant. So, I'm about to be a grandmother."

"That's exciting. What about your son?"

"He's twenty now and a good kid, but he inherited a bad gene from his dad. At eighteen, he got hooked on heroin. I got him into a treatment program. And I moved him in with me so I could keep an eye on him. He's okay now. He's got a job and an apartment and seems to be doing well."

"That's great. You're a good mother."

"Thanks, Frank. But you should know this about me. My kids come first, no matter what. Some guys can't deal with that."

Dora stared directly into my eyes. I imagined that I

could see the question in her mind that she didn't ask. She was wondering if I was one of those guys.

The sound of a cart's motor as it drove away provided an opportunity to break the awkward silence. "Your kids *should* come first," I agreed, drawing a nod of agreement from Dora. "And any man who truly cares about you should care about your children also." I started up our cart. "And by the way, I have a daughter too."

In between shots over the next few holes, I told Dora about my teenaged daughter Bella and what a joy it was to have her in my life.

The thirteenth hole was a short par three. The carts were backed up again. I found a tree and parked underneath it to wait.

"So, Frank," Dora said, turning sideways in the cart to talk to me. "What kind of law do you practice?"

"I'm a criminal defense lawyer. Or, more specifically, I'm a public defender."

"You work for the State?"

"Actually, that's a common belief. In some states, the public defenders do work for the State. But here in Salt Lake County, it's different. I work for a private firm. We have contracts with the city and the county to defend people who can't afford to pay for a lawyer."

"What's that like?"

"It's great. Defending people's constitutional rights is a good reason to get up every morning. I love the people I work with. Everyone helps each other. And it's a gas to be in court all the time. There's nothing quite like doing a closing argument to a jury in a murder case to get your adrenaline pumping." I glanced at Dora. Her eyes popped open.

"You do *murder* cases?" she asked.

Dora appeared to be quite impressed. Maybe she was only being polite, but I was eating it up.

"I handle all kinds of felony cases," I answered, a little embarrassed. "But, yes, it seems like I always have at *least* one homicide open. Right now, I have one with a woman who they *say* killed one of her kids. But I'm not sure she did it. I think it might have been her husband."

Dora said nothing this time. And she was no longer smiling. Her grim gaze was one I got a lot lately when I told people about the new case. No one was very sympathetic to my client. She was either a mother who killed her own child, or she was a mother who didn't protect her child from lethal injury. It was like I somehow had gained psychic powers. I could see these very thoughts quite clearly in Dora's eyes. *Shit. I hate dead baby cases*.

"Well, never mind work!" I said, perhaps a little too enthusiastically. "It certainly is a beautiful day to golf," I added, desperate to change the subject.

Gratefully, we did change the subject, and we finished a pleasant round of golf. I drove the golf cart to Dora's car in the parking lot. She grabbed her golf bag off the cart and swung it effortlessly into her trunk. We agreed to stay in touch and get together again sometime soon.

I waved at her as she drove away and cranked the handle on the little golf cart to search for my red Jeep on the other side of the parking lot.

Dammit! As soon as I approached, I could see that my tires were flat. I screeched the cart to a stop and hopped out. A deep meandering scratch was etched into the driver's side door.

Another golfer was closing his trunk two spaces away from the passenger side of my car.

"Hey, man. Can I ask you a question?"

"Yeah, sure. What?" He walked a little closer to me.

"Did you happen to see anyone hanging around my Jeep just now? My door was keyed, and my tires are flat."

"No. Sorry," he said. "I just got here myself. But it looks like it was done with a knife."

"A knife. How do you know?"

He pointed to the back tire on the passenger's side. "It's sticking out of your tire over here."

I hurried around to the other side of my Jeep. Yep. It was a knife.

"Can I give you a hand?" he asked.

"No. Thanks, though. I'll call a tow truck."

He nodded, got in his car, and drove away.

Who? Why? Could it have been Afa? Daggers flew from his eyes when I accused him of murder in open court. But without a witness, I couldn't file a police report against him. I scanned the parking lot. No one else was around. *Shit!*

Chapter Seven

The holding cell next to the courtroom was empty today, except for one small figure sitting silently in the corner. It was Kala. She sat with her hands over her face, her elbows on her knees.

Almost a week had passed since our first court appearance. Kala had called my office yesterday and told my secretary she wanted to see me and Mary as soon as possible because she had a hearing today in family law court.

Dreary and stark, this holding cell was identical to the holding cells for the criminal courts. A cement slab about eighteen inches high extended all the way around the cell. It seated maybe fifteen. A toilet was installed at the back of the cell, concealed only partially by a three-foot-high wall. A drinking fountain jutted incongruously out of the top of the toilet's tank.

The bailiff opened the holding cell for Mary and me so that we could go in and speak with Kala. "You won't have much time because court's starting soon," he informed us in a monotone voice before closing the door behind us to give us privacy. Still, he remained right outside the holding cell.

Kala started to talk as soon as we entered, but she was sobbing and speaking so rapidly that I couldn't understand anything she was saying.

Mary put her hand on Kala's shoulder. "Slow

down. Take a deep breath. Tell us what's wrong."

Mary's compassionate touch helped. Kala nodded and relaxed a bit. She stopped trying to talk and took a deep breath. After a moment, her crying subsided, so Mary and I sat down on the cement bench across the cell from her.

"They said they are going to take my kids!" Kala said finally, brushing her long hair from her wet eyes. Her dark brown eyebrows were bunched together around deep furrows in her forehead.

I asked, "Who said that?"

"Two ladies from the Department of Family Services."

"That is a fairly standard procedure in this sort of situation," Mary explained. "When abuse is suspected, the juvenile court has hearings to determine custody, especially if there's a death."

"Isn't there anything we can do?" Kala asked, whimpering.

"No, probably not," Mary said. "Because you're in jail, you won't be able to complete the requirements of the court's reunification plan. You have to have a job, a stable residence for the children, and must complete parenting and anger management classes, among other things."

I could see that this explanation, while completely accurate, did nothing at all to placate Kala. In fact, tears began streaming down her cheeks again.

"But my kids are my life! They are all I have. If I can't have them, nothing else matters."

Kala's nose was running now too. She raised an arm and wiped the snot on the back of her wrist. I check my jacket pocket but didn't have a tissue.

"When I go into my cell to go to bed at night, I wish I would just go to sleep and not wake up," she said. "If I can't be with Amanaki, Emeni, and Malohi, then I might as well die so I can be with Juna. At least I could be with my baby." Kala's head was down now, and she was quiet.

I sat in stunned silence. The profound intensity of Kala's emotion staggered me. She would rather *die*. Until this very moment, I had not even begun to grasp the depth of her hopelessness. I was merely working a case. I had heard Kala's words but had not comprehended them. I needed to swallow but couldn't do it. My throat was too tight with emotion.

The young bailiff came to the door of the cell and tapped on it. I don't know if he heard our conversation through the glass or if he had only been able to observe Kala's body language.

I couldn't quite hear him, but I could read his lips as he pointed at Kala. "Is she okay?"

I shook my head no. *She is pretty damn far from okay.* I waved him away.

Mary stared at me like I should do something. I shrugged helplessly.

"Kala," Mary said after a minute, "you will *always* be your children's mother. The State can't change that. And the children are with your aunt Lovai. She and her husband will probably get custody. Kinship placements are preferred by the courts. So, the court will probably give custody to them. And you should be able to still see your children and still be a part of their lives."

Finally, Kala raised her head, a tiny glimmer of hope in her eyes. Mary had come to the rescue again.

"But yesterday when I called Uncle Sione to talk to

my kids, he told me not to call the house anymore," Kala blurted. Whatever spark of hope I thought I saw faded away.

"Kala, I don't understand," Mary interjected. "Did your uncle say why you shouldn't call?"

"He said the kids cry when I call, and they ask when I will be home. But my uncle said that he and my aunt have custody of my kids now and want to adopt them. They say I will be a bad influence on my kids when I get out. *How* can they *say* that?"

Kala had just popped Mary's happy balloon. I had imagined that things couldn't get any worse for Kala than being charged with murder. But now this. They were trying to take away her other children.

"My kids are all I have. If I lose them, I don't care what happens to me," she repeated.

I sensed that Kala was on the verge of giving up all hope. I reached deep inside myself, searching for an answer for her, anything that might help.

Glancing at Mary and back at Kala, I said, "Um, we still care about what happens to you, Kala." I usually make a point not to get emotionally involved in my client's lives, but what was happening to Kala had gotten to me.

"Don't worry about your children, Kala," I continued. "Like Mary said, at least they're with family right now and not with strangers. After this case is over, maybe we can get counseling arranged for you, the kids, and the Alekis. The counselor can explain to your aunt and uncle why it's okay for you to still be involved in your children's lives. It'll work out."

"Promise?" she asked, her eyebrows raised in hope.

Now what was I supposed to say? I was definitely

not sure things would work out. Kala was facing life in prison. I didn't know how I could *possibly* promise her anything. But she was in such desperate despair. Finally, I said the only thing I could bring myself to say. "Yes, I promise."

The bailiff opened the cell door and told us that we had to leave because the judge would be taking the bench momentarily. Mary and I went into the courtroom and checked the court calendar that the clerk had placed on each of the two attorney tables. We learned that the court had assigned Kala a lawyer who specialized in family law, and a separate lawyer had also been assigned for Kala's husband, Afa. Today was a parental rights termination hearing for both Kala and Afa.

Mary and I sat in the gallery simply for moral support for Kala. But to tell the truth, I was also desperate to see Afa. Although Kala's aunt and uncle had temporary custody of Kala's children, Afa, as the children's father, was the presumptive choice to take custody. Yet I didn't see him.

So far, my investigator had been unable to contact Afa. He had been living with his father but had reportedly moved, and his phone had been disconnected. I wanted to see if he got custody of the kids. Plus, after what happened to my Jeep, I had some questions I wanted to ask Afa for personal fucking reasons.

The plaque on the judge's bench had the name Judge Angeline Kronig. While we waited for the judge to take the bench, I was surprised to see Mia Montes, the victim advocate, come into the courtroom with Kala's aunt Lovai and Kala's children. They sat on the back row. It was odd to see Mia here because the victim advocates in the District Attorney's Office normally only attended the criminal case hearings. Mia had apparently taken a particular interest in Kala's case.

When Judge Kronig entered the courtroom, she first called Afa's case. Afa still had not appeared. His court-appointed attorney explained that she had been unable to contact him and that his phone number was disconnected. She made a formal motion to withdraw as his counsel, which the court granted.

The attorney representing the State of Utah asked the judge to take judicial notice of the legal file of the Department of Family Services regarding Afa Tausinga, and the court's prior orders, and rested its case. There was, of course, no rebuttal. No one was there to dispute the State's case.

Judge Kronig made the following findings: The court had jurisdiction. The children were residents of the State of Utah, and Afa Tausinga was their father.

The judge said, "For the record, I ordered the Department of Family Services to design a reunification plan for the father. The plan requires him to complete parenting classes, a mental health assessment, and maintain stable housing and employment. All this information was served upon Mr. Tausinga before he moved from his last known address. Mr. Afa Tausinga has substantially neglected or willfully refused to comply with the service plan ordered by the court. Consequently, I'm concluding that Afa Tausinga Sr. is an unfit or incompetent parent, and that therefore, it is appropriate that his parental rights be permanently terminated."

I quickly started wondering if I could somehow get

the court ruling that Afa was an unfit parent admitted into evidence in Kala's murder trial.

The judge called a ten-minute recess before calling Kala's case. Mary stayed with Kala while I went to look for Kala's attorney, Tori Nakamura, whom I had met at an earlier attorney event. I found her out in the hallway speaking on her phone.

I waited impatiently until she slid the phone into the pocket of her jacket and approached her. "Hi, Tori. I'm Frank Bravo. I represent Kala in her criminal case."

"Hi, Frank. Yes, I remember meeting you at the annual bar meeting—"

"I'm sorry for interrupting. But this is urgent." I waved toward the courtroom and asked, "Isn't there some way to stop this?"

Tori shook her head. "Kala hasn't completed the court's reunification plan. She's going to do a VR."

Mia Montes walked up and stood beside us. Not able to think of a decent reason to shoo her away, I continued speaking to Tori Nakamura.

"A VR?" I asked, my tone incredulous. "She's agreeing to a voluntary relinquishment of her rights to her children? How can it be *voluntary*? She's locked up. They won't let her *out* to comply with the service plan. Kala doesn't *want* to give up her children. They're all she has."

"But she's in jail for murder," Tori replied with a shrug.

"What if she's innocent?" I protested. "Our own investigation suggests that it may have been Kala's husband who killed the baby."

"Well, it's not that simple," Tori said. "The juvenile court has specific rules. If a parent does not comply with the service plan, there are only two options. Either the court finds the parent unfit and terminates his or her rights, or the parent does a voluntary relinquishment, and the court terminates his or her rights."

"Well, the juvenile court has some *stupid* rules," I complained helplessly. "Termination is the result either way? If it's the same result either way, wouldn't it be better if Kala didn't go on the record to say she *volunteered* to *give up* her rights? Shouldn't she *fight* the termination so that her children would know she didn't *abandon* them?"

"Actually, it is better to do the VR," Tori explained patiently. "If Kala fights and the court declares her to be an unfit parent, the State will automatically take away any children she might have in the future. Plus, a finding of unfitness would make it harder for her to have any contact with her children when she gets out of jail. Umm, that is, if she gets out before they become adults."

Tori spoke these harsh words to me without emotion. She appeared to have become hardened, or at least accustomed to the human drama of the government tearing children out of their parents' arms.

"But with the VR there's no finding of unfitness, and so they couldn't take any future children from her. Plus, she can explain right on the record how she's giving them up *not* because she doesn't want them, but because she *loves* them and feels it would be in the children's best interest for her to relinquish her rights."

"But how can it be in the children's best interest to be separated from their own mother? She is the one person in the world that loves them more than anyone else could possibly love them. It's *because* she loves them that it's not in the children's *best interest* to be taken from her."

"I'm sorry," Tori said. "But there's really no better option."

"What about a motion to continue?" I urged desperately. "If the hearing could be put off until after her trial, maybe she could start working to complete the reunification requirements, and—"

"That won't work," Tori said more loudly now as she cut me off, her patience with me obviously wearing thin. "The statute limits the time. And Kala is in jail and charged with murder. The legislature has concluded that it's in the child's best interest to have closure."

"Closure? How about due process? Can't the statute be challenged on constitutional grounds? The statute should be declared unconstitutional!"

Tori said, "We already tried that, years ago. The state supreme court rejected the challenge. I'm sorry. I have already explained all of this to Kala. She knows what she has to do."

The bailiff came into the hallway and said that the judge was back on the bench. Tori returned to the courtroom and sat down at the table with Kala. Judge Kronig took her chair, banged her gavel, and called Kala's case.

Judge Kronig's clerk asked Kala to stand and raise her hand. The chain that was wrapped around Kala stopped her hand a little above her waist. Kala swore to tell the truth.

Tori announced for the record, "Kala will now give her statement in support of voluntary relinquishment."

Turning to Kala, Tori asked, "Are you the natural

mother of Amanaki Tausinga, Emeni Tausinga, and Malohi Tausinga?"

"Yes, I am." Kala almost whispered, her head down.

"Have you read and do you understand the written statement in support of your voluntary relinquishment?"

She nodded before lifting her head back toward her attorney. "Yes."

"Has anyone coerced you into doing this?"

Kala's eyes furrowed. "What does that mean?"

"That is, has anyone forced you into doing this?"

"No."

"Are you doing this because you love your children and wish the best for them?"

"Yes."

"Do you understand that your rights and responsibilities regarding your children will all be terminated, and you will have no say in the adoption or selection of a guardian?"

Kala lowered her eyes and nodded.

"I'm sorry, we have to make a record," interjected Judge Kronig sternly. "You need to answer out loud."

"Yes," Kala responded, her voice barely above a whisper.

"Do you understand that this is an irrevocable act?" Tori asked.

"I'm sorry," replied Kala, "what does that mean?"

"It means that you can't change it later," Tori explained.

"Oh… Yes." She hung her head again.

The judge then asked the other parties to the hearing if they had any questions to ask Ms. Tausinga. Present were the guardian ad litem, the assistant attorney general, and a DFS caseworker. They were all women. Each responded, stating, "No, Your Honor, I do not have any questions."

"Ms. Tausinga," said the judge, "do *you* have any questions?"

Kala spoke up, in a surprisingly and uncharacteristically loud voice. "I want to say that I understand that the reason I have to give them up is because I can't take care of them because I am in jail."

The judge frowned. This was not part of the normal script. But Judge Kronig must have heard this sort of thing before. They all must have heard it before. It clearly didn't matter to any of them. Everyone must be able to see that there is nothing *voluntary* about this voluntary relinquishment. But everyone moved forward anyway as if it were.

I wondered if these women had any children of their own. Did they have any empathy or compassion? If they did, none of them were showing it at this moment. They all appeared to have resigned themselves to fulfill their little roles in the big system.

Judge Kronig put pen to paper and signed her name. She declared, quite matter-of-factly, "Kala Tausinga's parental rights are hereby terminated."

Kala craned her neck toward the back of the courtroom where her two young daughters, Amanaki and Emeni, sat with Kala's aunt Lovai. Kala's daughters could not have grasped any part of what had just happened. They both smiled and waved at their mother. Kala mouthed "I love you" to them as the bailiff took her by the arm.

Kala didn't immediately follow the bailiff back to the holding cell, so he pulled her by the arm, a bit roughly, and she stumbled off behind him, her leg chains limiting the length of her step. After she was taken away, I got up and walked slowly to the back of courtroom, shaking my head.

I pushed open the courtroom door. Mia Montes rushed to me with deep concern etched in the furrow between her dark eyebrows.

"It's Frank, right?" Mia's tone and demeanor had changed dramatically from the day she confronted me in the hallway at Kala's first court appearance.

"Yes," I said cautiously, wondering why she was waiting for me.

"Can we talk for a minute?" Mia's body language was more open than before, and she even offered a small smile, easing my doubts.

"Sure, I guess so."

"I'd like to see Kala," Mia said, getting right to the point. "I need to talk to her."

I was dumbfounded. The victim advocates all work for the prosecution. No good thing could come from this.

I got right to the point also. "For what purpose? You work for the State. Wouldn't you report back to Randy Johnson?"

Mia glanced around and waited a minute as a couple of lawyers walked past us down the hallway. She motioned me over to a spot against the wall.

"No," she said quietly. "If Johnson found out I'm even talking to you about this, I would probably be in a lot of trouble. So please don't tell anyone I asked."

"Then why are you doing this?"

With a conspiratorial grin and a sparkle in her eye, Mia leaned into me and whispered, "I think Johnson has this case all wrong. After hearing you talk about Kala's case and seeing how scary Afa really is when he sat next to me the other day in court, I've come to believe that Kala might be the actual victim here. But I need to be sure before I do anything or say anything to Johnson. I need to talk to Kala. I need to hear her tell me her story. Then I'll know. I'm sure I'll know."

I liked this new Mia. "Mia, I'm truly very happy to hear that you feel the same way that I do about Kala and her case. Mary and I think that Kala isn't telling us the truth about what happened that night. Even after we told her she's likely to be convicted of murder if she doesn't testify, she won't talk about it. She's afraid of her husband. I'm not sure she'll even talk to you."

"Let me try at least." She cocked her head to the side and raised an eyebrow. "From what I've seen so far, it looks like you have nothing to lose."

Chapter Eight

Kala's name, written in large blue capital letters, dominated the month of April on the wet-erase calendar hanging on the wall next to my office desk. A week had already passed since we set the case for trial, and I was getting nervous about whether we would be ready.

"Mary?" I asked loudly into the desk phone in my office when she picked up my interoffice call. "Do you happen to have a little time to review our discovery and investigation on Kala's case?"

"Sure. In fact, I've been preparing a timeline for the day of the murder. Do we have Afa's timecards yet from the soap company? I'd like to know what time he left work."

"No. I'll have our investigator follow up with the company. But we did receive the results back from our subpoena to the police department requesting all police calls to Kala's apartment."

"That's great," Mary said. "What did we get?"

I picked up the pile of police reports and started rescanning it. "Four calls in the last two years. All domestic violence calls."

"Wow. Who called the police? Kala?"

"No. The neighbors called. And almost every time, the neighbors reported that the reason they called police was because it sounded physical."

"So did they arrest Kala's husband?" Mary asked.

"No. I don't think there were any arrests."

"What? Are you sure?"

"Yes, I read all the reports. Each time the police showed up, Kala and her husband *both* told police that there was no physical violence. They said they were only arguing."

Mary said, "But Utah is one of the states that has a statute *requiring* police to arrest someone in those situations, even if it's only to spend one night in booking. You know, keep them apart until tempers have cooled down to try to make sure that no one gets hurt."

"Well, they didn't do it here. Not even once." I tossed the reports down on my desk. "And I'm not very surprised. Kala claimed that every time, she hadn't been injured. So maybe that justified the police's failure to arrest her husband."

"You know, I shouldn't be surprised," Mary said. "I spent almost two years in DV court. It seems that even when a woman *did* report domestic violence, by the time court came around, she would either not show up, or she would show up and recant, say that nothing actually happened. And then she would make some excuse, like she was mad at her husband or boyfriend at the time or something like that. It's the classic battered woman syndrome behavior cycle. First, he hurts her. If it's worse than usual, she might complain to friends or even call the police. Then, he says he loves her and promises to be better. She gets the charges dropped. She goes back to him. And, soon after that, the cycle starts over."

I said, "Well, there was obviously *something* going on in Kala's relationship. The neighbors said it sounded physical. And to have *four* different calls? Where there's smoke... And never mind the little detail of the dead baby."

"I have an idea," Mary said. "Let's call the YWCA. They have programs for battered women. Let's see if there's something they can do. Maybe they can send a caseworker or counselor to the jail to talk to Kala. Maybe she'll open up to someone trained in crisis intervention. I made some contacts with domestic violence counselors that helped the women staying at the YWCA when I was working in DV court. Let's call and see if we can get someone to go see Kala."

"That's a good idea. I'm not sure what went on between Kala and her husband, but I'm sure we don't have the whole story yet. So far, she's only told us that she didn't kill her baby. But she seems afraid to say anything else. Why don't you come to my office? We'll make a call."

"Be right there."

A few moments later, Mary came into my office and plopped down onto the blue microfiber couch that didn't match any of my other furniture. She adjusted a pillow at her side.

"First let me apologize," I said.

"Why? For what?" Mary's eyebrows knitted together.

"I had no idea how much work this case was going to be. And the judge gave us such a short date. I know you have lots of other pending cases to work on. I know I do. Anyway, I'm sorry for getting you into this."

Mary pursed her lips. "We can do this. We're not just lawyers. We're *public defenders*."

"Well, I am grateful for your help. Very much."

"But you owe me one," Mary said, laughing.

I glanced at the phone number on the YWCA website and punched it into my desk phone.

Mary and I had the YWCA on speakerphone. The receptionist transferred us to a young female caseworker, and we described the circumstances of Kala's history with her husband and the police calls.

Then Mary asked, "Is there a counselor who could see her at the jail?"

"We don't provide services to offenders," said the caseworker.

"But just because they arrested her doesn't mean she's guilty," I explained matter-of-factly. I've learned over the years that most people don't grasp the constitutional right to be presumed innocent. They believe that if you were arrested, you must be guilty.

The caseworker paused a moment. "Well, has her husband been arrested or convicted in the past?"

"Well, um, no, but…"

"Then I'm sorry. There's nothing we can do. It's our policy only to help the *victims* of abuse."

We went back and forth with the caseworker but didn't get anywhere. She didn't budge even an inch. Mary shook her head. I hung up.

"That was disappointing," Mary said.

"That's an understatement. There's nothing like mindless bureaucratic protocol to prevent good things from getting done."

Mary leaned forward in her chair. "Don't be too hard on them. The local YWCA has done a lot of good work for battered women here in Utah over the years. We just haven't convinced anyone that Kala is the victim in this case."

I said, "Yeah. You're right, as usual. But if we

can't convince anyone Kala is the victim here. She'll be going to prison with a life sentence."

Chapter Nine

Mia was already in the visitor's room at the jail when the deputy brought Kala in. Mia stood and offered her hand to Kala.

"Hi, Kala. I'm Mia. Do you remember me from court?"

"Yes. I saw you. You were sitting with my family at the back of the courtroom during my first court date. And you were with them again a few days ago when they took my children from me."

"I was very sorry to see that happen."

The two women stared for a couple of moments as if sizing each other up. Mia moved the plastic chair opposite Kala around to the side of the small white table and sat down. She wanted to close the distance between them in the hopes of creating more intimacy.

"I'm here today because Frank and Mary said I could come visit you," Mia said. "I'm a victim advocate. I'm trained to help women who've been abused."

Kala didn't reply.

"Most of the women who are in abusive relationships are afraid to tell anyone else everything that's happened to them because they fear their abuser." Mia paused, her eyes searching Kala's face. "They're afraid that somehow he'll get back at them for going forward with their case against him. So, the women change their story, or they don't show up to court. But the problem is that they often go back to the abusive relationship. And the abuse continues. There's only one way out for these women. They must speak up. Say what happened. Make sure their abusers are held responsible. Or it never ends. And it usually only gets worse."

Mia waited a minute, letting all she had said sink in.

Kala sat quietly, staring at the tabletop.

"So, it's not only you who are afraid, Kala. You have lots of company."

Kala still didn't respond, so Mia tried something else to get Kala to open up. "Would you tell me about your son, Juna?"

Kala lifted her head, and her face brightened. "My husband Afa had cheated on me with my cousin. I told him to get out, and he left. Later, I met Vai. He treated me with such kindness and respect." Kala's gaze returned to the table. "Eventually, we had sex. The first time, I only did it to get back at Afa for having sex with my cousin. But I liked Vai. And we got together several times." Kala shrugged her shoulders and paused. She took a deep breath and added, "I got pregnant with Juna."

Mia asked, "If you liked Vai, why did you go back to Afa?"

"For a while, I thought I might be able to make a life with Vai. He treated me so much better than Afa did." Kala's gaze strayed as she apparently reminisced. "But my family made me go back to Afa, and the bishop told me that I should go back too. Besides, Afa would be so angry. He said he would kill me if I ever left him. And Afa told me that if I left him, the court would give the kids to him. So, I knew I couldn't be with Vai."

"I understand," Mia said, nodding. "But what did Afa say about you being pregnant?"

"I tried to tell him that it was his baby. But he found out how many months along I was and figured out that it wasn't his baby." She searched Mia's face as if seeking validation. "But I wouldn't admit it. And I couldn't tell him about Vai. The Polynesian community is big, but everyone knows each other. Afa would know who Vai is. And he would have hurt him. In fact, later it got out that Vai got me pregnant. People were talking. I told Vai he should leave town, and he said he would go to Alaska, to work on a fishing boat."

Kala fell silent again. Mia directed her back to the reason she was there.

"Kala, Frank and Mary believe that you've been abused by your husband and that it was probably him that killed your son. But they told me you wouldn't open up to them about what happened."

"But I did tell them what happened," Kala said while still staring at the tabletop. "I told them the same thing that I told the police."

"But did you tell them everything?"

"Well, maybe not everything," said Kala, her eyes on her hands.

"I know what you're going through. I was once in your shoes. I was in an abusive relationship. Do you want to hear my story?"

Kala nodded.

Mia gave some background about how she and her boyfriend Carlos met, how they liked each other and

71

eventually moved in together and how they even spoke of marriage. "We were so happy, well, most of the time at least," she said. "Over time, Carlos became more and more abusive. I found out that violence ran in his family and that they had connections to a drug cartel in Mexico. His father and brothers beat their wives and girlfriends too."

Now it was Mia's turn to stare at the tabletop. The volume of her voice lowered as she went back in time in her mind. "Carlos promised he'd quit hitting me. But he never did. So, one night, when Carlos was drunk and hit me again, I decided to leave."

Mia looked up. Kala's attention was completely focused on her, so she continued. "When Carlos turned his back, I ran out the front door of our apartment. But I didn't get fifty feet away before he tackled me and dragged me back inside the apartment by my hair. I screamed for help, hoping a neighbor would come or would call the police. But that made Carlos even angrier, and he pinned me down on the kitchen floor and squeezed my throat so that I couldn't yell. He kept squeezing until I couldn't breathe. He laughed at me, and I remember clearly what he said to me: 'You can't leave me, you stupid whore!' I scratched and hit him until he let go, but then he grabbed a steak knife off the table and started slashing the knife across my chest while he sat on me, shouting, 'I'll kill you, you fucking bitch!' "

Mia stopped, overwhelmed by the terror of the memory.

Although Kala had her hands chained together, she reached out and touched Mia's arm gently. Mia kept her eyes down; she didn't want Kala to see her tears. Then she took a deep breath and resumed her story with a trembling voice. "I was desperate. He was going to kill me. I remember shouting, 'Don't hurt me. I love you.' That stopped him for a moment. When he put the knife on the counter, I managed to get to my feet and scrambled back to the front door. But he kicked the door shut, smashing my hand between the door and the door frame. He picked me up like a rag doll and carried me into the bedroom and threw me onto the bed. He punched me in the face until I passed out."

Tears rolled down Mia's cheeks. She allowed herself a few seconds to summon up enough strength to finish telling her story. "When I came to my senses, I saw that he had pulled off my pants and was about to rape me. He was trying to stick it in me when I started to kick at him as hard as I could. Somehow, I rolled off the bed, but I was dazed and too weak to move. The last thing I remember after that was seeing the machete Carlos kept up on the closet shelf swinging down at me. Later, at the hospital, the doctor told me that my heart had stopped, that I had died I guess, but the paramedics resuscitated me."

Both Mia and Kala were crying now.

Mia was determined to tell the rest of it. "The police arrested Carlos for attacking me, but the judge had to let him go when I didn't show up to testify against him. A victim advocate tried to reach me several times to get me to go to court. But I moved, and I was afraid Carlos would find me in my new apartment and kill me for sure the next time. So, I hid from the constable who tried to serve me the subpoena to appear at trial, and I made sure I was out of town when the trial date came."

Kala asked, "What about your family? Couldn't they help you?"

Mia shrugged. "I don't have any family. They died in a car accident when I was about twelve years old, and I grew up in a place for orphaned kids and abused women called The Refuge. I didn't think the people I knew on Carlos's side of the family would help me. I had some distant relatives, I guess, but I didn't think to call them. I was in a dark place and started using heroin myself. I lost my job. My life was over."

Mia sat quietly for a long time. "One day, someone from The Refuge came looking for me. Later, they told me that they had found me unconscious in my apartment and took me back to The Refuge. Physically, I recovered over time. They helped me with counseling and job training. I feel like I'm a different person now. I even changed my last name to make it harder for Carlos to find me."

Mia took Kala's hands into hers now.

"But I remember everything," Mia said, her voice stronger now. "That's why I do what I do now. That's why I help women who've been abused. That's why I want to help you." Mia paused for a moment. "Will you let me help you?"

Kala nodded slightly.

"Good. Now tell me, is what you told the police the *whole* story of what happened the night that Juna died?"

"No. It wasn't the whole story."

"And is the reason you didn't tell the whole story because Afa threatened you?"

"Yes, it is," Kala said, more firmly now. "Afa threatened to kill me and my kids unless I said what he told me to say."

"Was it Afa who killed Juna?"

"Yes," Kala blurted, sobbing into her hands.

Mia leaned toward Kala and put her arms around her, holding her as best as she could from her chair. Mia remembered vividly her own feelings of helplessness and fear when she was with Carlos. She hoped her caring touch would ease Kala's distress now.

Mia didn't see the guard approaching. He pounded on the door to the visitor's room and shook his head.

"No touching," he shouted through the glass, frowning.

Please. Not right now. Mia was upset at the timing of the interruption by the guard but let go of Kala and scooted her chair back. Mia didn't reply vocally to the guard, but she did tap her watch and pointed toward the door to signal to the guard that she intended to leave before he came in to pull her out for violating the jail rules. The guard nodded but was still frowning.

Mia pushed her chair back and stood up slowly. "Thank you for sharing that with me, Kala. But you also need to tell Frank and Mary, okay?"

Kala nodded. "Okay, I'll tell them."

Kala stood by the door, waiting for the guard to let her out. "Will I be able to see you again?"

Mia smiled. "Yes. I'll come visit again for sure."

Chapter Ten

The following Monday, Mary and I sat in the waiting room of the Granger Medical Clinic, flipping through various issues of *Pregnancy* and *American Baby* magazines. Unlike the sterile space in most doctors' offices, colorful photos of animals covered the walls, and children's toys lay scattered around on the floor.

With Kala's trial fast approaching, Mary and I were trying to finish interviewing all the possible witnesses that we had found so far. We had sent out several subpoenas and releases to get medical records for Kala and her children. Today we hoped to interview Patricia Poulson and Melinda Ramirez, two nurse-midwives whom we learned provided prenatal care for Kala with two of her children.

"Mr. Bravo, the nurses are ready to see you now," the receptionist said, motioning toward an open door. "Walk through here"—she pointed—"and go into the second room on the left."

Mary led the way as we entered a small exam room.

"Hmmm," I mused when I saw the cramped space. "There aren't enough chairs in this exam room for all four of us, Mary, so why don't you get up here on the exam chair? You can put your feet in these stirrups."

"Sure. I'll do that if you put on a gown during this

interview and leave the back open," Mary said before laughing.

Soon the nurses came in, fortunately toting an extra chair with them. A tall, slim brunette introduced herself as Patricia, and a petite blonde introduced herself as Melinda. We introduced ourselves and inquired about Kala's prenatal care.

Patricia answered, "We assisted Kala with her fourth child, Malohi. From what I understand, he was born a few days after Juna's death."

Mary glanced up from her notes. "Did Kala report any problems with her husband?"

Both women nodded affirmatively.

Melinda said, "Kala had mentioned her intent to seek a divorce, but she lacked the resources to get one. Plus, she told me that the bishop of her church urged her to try to work things out with her husband instead of leaving."

I asked, "Did you happen to notice any bruises on Kala? Do you know whether she had reported any domestic abuse?"

Patricia said, "I don't remember any bruises."

Melinda interjected. "I do. I saw bruises. When I asked Kala about them, she explained them away. She didn't claim any abuse. In retrospect, I guess Kala's reluctance to admit the reasons for the bruises may have been because her husband brought her to all of her appointments and stayed right out in the waiting room until she was done."

I quickly searched our list of prepared questions, and found that I had asked them all. "If Kala denied she was abused when you asked her that specific question, then we probably won't ask you to testify," I said, putting my pen in my pocket and standing up to go. "But I want to thank you for meeting with us."

"You're welcome, of course," Melinda said. "We were wondering when you would come. We've been waiting for you for weeks."

Mary abruptly stopped putting files in her folder. "Waiting for us? We just found the records with your names on them. How could you possibly know we were coming?"

"We called and asked who Kala's defense lawyers were," Patricia said, matter-of-factly.

I sat back down. "No one told us you had called."

"Well, so how did you know to come talk to us?" asked Patricia.

"We're just trying to do a thorough investigation," I said. "But why was it that you were trying to reach us?"

"We saw on TV that Kala had been arrested," Melinda said. "We were shocked. We were sure there must have been some sort of mistake. We called the police. I asked if they could tell us how to contact Kala's defense attorney."

Mary and I stared at each other with jaws dropped. I took my pen back out of my pocket.

I asked, "Melinda, do you remember who you talked to at the police department?"

"No. I called three times. I left voice messages."

"Did you call 911?" Mary interjected. "They record all those calls."

"No," Melinda said. "We found the number for the West Valley City Police Department. I think they transferred me to the detective's division, or something like that."

"Hmmm. I'm guessing that if you told the police that you were looking for a *defense* attorney, they may not have been too interested in helping you." My tone held a hint of sarcasm.

"But, Melinda," Mary asked, "why did you call in the first place?"

She hesitated. I couldn't tell if she was trying to recall something or if she was wondering whether she should answer.

"Tell them, Patricia." Melinda lightly tapped Patricia's arm with her elbow.

"Well," Patricia started slowly, "I assisted Kala with the birth of her youngest on about December 8th. Kala's husband came with her, and he wouldn't leave the delivery room, even when I asked him to. He stayed there all night. She delivered without complications around midnight. In the morning, I went in to feed her and see how she was doing. Her husband was asleep, and Kala started whispering to me. She said that she had been having a hard time with him. She asked me if I had heard what happened to her son, that her son had died about a week earlier. She glanced over at her husband and asked me if I thought she was the type of person who would kill her own child. But there was a sound. Her husband had woken up. He sat forward in his chair glaring at her and making a fist. He didn't say anything, but Kala recoiled from him and turned away from me. She didn't say another word the whole time she was there. If I even asked her how she was feeling, it was her husband who answered for her. She was under his thumb."

Mary glanced at me with eyes wide. "We didn't see any notes about that in the medical records."

Patricia shrugged. "Well, he didn't *do* anything. It was more his controlling and aggressive demeanor. But I do remember being frightened of him at the time."

Scribbling notes furiously, I asked, "Do you have training in diagnosing battered women's syndrome?"

"I'm not a psychologist," Patricia said, "but we are concerned about both the physical and mental health of our clients. The subject does come up in our training."

"Did you share your concerns about Kala's arrest with anyone else?"

"Yes. When we didn't get any answer from the police, we called the Department of Child and Family Services."

"And the District Attorney's Office," Melinda added.

"Do you remember who you talked to?" I put pen to paper to write down the name.

"No. We had to leave messages. But we called so many people. We thought we had done what we could do."

The four of us sat silently. I didn't know exactly what the others were thinking, but I was stunned. What was wrong with the system? How could everyone ignore these calls? What dumb luck that Mary and I had stumbled upon these women. I shook my head in wonder as I wrote additional notes for follow up.

"I have one more question for you, Patricia," Mary said after a moment. "It's about the question Kala asked you the morning after she gave birth. *Do you* think that she is the sort of person who would hurt her own child?"

"No," Patricia said. "You never can know for sure, but I don't think she could do such a thing. No way."

Chapter Eleven

After a long day at work, I left a pile of files on my desk and walked the block between my office and the one-bedroom apartment I rented when I split with my ex-wife. The apartment was in a '70s-era three-story complex surrounded by even older, rundown apartment buildings. But it was close to work. That's what I cared most about at the time. I signed a six-month lease because the move was supposed to be temporary.

However, recently I had renewed the lease for another six months. It wasn't so bad. The apartment must have been remodeled somewhere along the line because now it had a walk-in closet and a six-foot bathroom vanity. I added a couch, a bed, a 75-inch 4K OLED TV, a microwave, a small set of dishes, and most important, a framed photograph of my daughter, Bella. Recently, I bought two wine glasses, just in case I decided to bring someone home with me.

My cell phone rang halfway to the apartment. Bella's name and picture appeared on the screen.

"Hi, Daddy."

"Hi, sweetheart. What's up?"

"I wanted to see how you are. It's been a while since we talked. How is work?"

"Work's good. Busy. I'm getting ready for a murder trial." A lady passed by pushing a stroller. I gave a quick nod, but she put her head down and pushed faster when I spoke the word murder.

"Hey, can I come watch? I haven't been to court with you since I was ten."

"I remember that day well." A grin spread across my face as that day flashed back in my mind. "I still tell my friends and colleagues about it. Your school was doing mock trials, and you had volunteered to be a defense attorney and wanted to see how to do it, so I brought you to a preliminary hearing. You sat behind me while I cross-examined a cop about his investigation of a drug distribution case, and you kept saying, 'Daddy, Daddy,' until I apologized to the judge and asked for a moment to see what you needed. You said, I'll never forget, 'Daddy, can *I* ask some questions?'"

We both laughed at the memory. "In fact, until you were about fourteen, when people asked what you wanted to be, you'd say, 'I want to be a lawyer like my daddy.'"

"Yes, I did. But lately, I'm leaning toward being a doctor."

"Oh? Why is that?"

"We're studying anatomy in my A.P. Biology class. It's fascinating. They let us cut a cadaver last week to see the musculature and ligaments under the skin."

"Woah." I visualized that scene. "If that didn't freak you out, you probably would make a good doctor."

"But I still want to see you in action in court."

Happy she still wanted to see me in my element, I came up with an idea. "How about this. The trial starts in a couple of weeks. I'll invite you to come to court the day the medical examiner is scheduled to testify."

"That would be perfect," she said.

"But can you get off of school?"

"Don't worry, Daddy. Not only will I get out of school, but I'll find a way to get extra credit."

I chuckled. "That's my girl."

"K, Daddy, I gotta go now. Someone's calling."

"Who? A boy?"

"Bye, Daddy," Bella replied, answering my question by refusing to answer it.

As I entered my apartment, I kicked off my shoes by the door and laid my phone on the counter. The small apartment included a kitchenette that combined with the living room and had just enough space for a two-person table. The other half of the apartment contained the single bedroom and the bathroom. Yet the apartment was big enough for me because I didn't take much with me when I left my ex.

As I closed the door behind me, I remembered the emptiness of the apartment when I first moved in. Except for my clothes I had left behind everything when I moved out of the house I owned with my ex-wife. To avoid a protracted divorce, fighting over assets, and being pulled into the blame game, I had simply walked away and left her the house.

I left the burdens of a dysfunctional relationship behind as well. I didn't feel sad about leaving with nothing. Not carrying any things and not carrying that emotional baggage made me feel light. Made me feel free.

I sat on the couch, leaned back, closed my eyes, and remembered how quiet it was in the new apartment. When I first moved in, I used to sit on this couch alone for hours at a time. Grateful for the peace. Grateful for the quiet.

My phone rang again, stirring me from my reverie.

"Hi, Frank. It's Dora. Can I come over, or do you have plans?"

My heart jumped. "Yes. Please come. I was just about to settle in and watch an NBA game."

"I can dig that."

Dora and I had texted a bit since we played golf. I was happy to hear from her. I liked her and was hoping that the relationship would continue, and maybe grow into something regular, something serious.

Plus, Dora had been on my mind a lot lately. As I learned more about the abuse that Kala had endured for years, I thought about how Dora had left her husband the first time he hit her and considered the multitude of circumstances that made one woman stay in an abusive relationship and another leave.

I put my coffee cup from breakfast in the dishwasher and carried my shoes to the closet. The apartment was simple. When I had started to date again, I worried that some women might write me off because I lived in a dumpy apartment complex. But I decided that I wanted to find a woman who wanted to be with me for me and not because of where I lived.

Dora arrived shortly, kicked off her own shoes, and plopped onto the couch like it was her own place. No complaints at all about the apartment. A good sign.

"Is this your daughter?" Dora pointed at the only thing hanging on any of my walls.

"Yes, that's Bella." My heart swelled with pride.

"Oh, my God, she's beautiful. I love her olive-toned skin and green eyes. And are those ringlets in her hair natural?"

I couldn't help but grin. "Yes, they are."

"You said she's a junior in high school?"

"That's right. But she's acting more like a senior. She's already talking about college."

"Is she going to go to the University of Utah?"

I frowned. "No. Her grades are good enough that she could get a free ride here at the U. But she told me that she's going to apply only out of state. And when I said, 'But, honey, Daddy lives here,' she said, 'Sorry, Daddy, but I need to go somewhere that is, well, more diverse.'"

I turned to Dora. "By the way, welcome to my humble abode."

Dora smiled and said simply, "I'm happy to be here."

We settled in and watched basketball. My ex-wife never sat down to watch basketball with me. But Dora was into the game. I nuked some popcorn, ordered some pizza, and grabbed a six-pack of beers. We drank. We laughed. We shouted at the TV when there was a bad call or a good play. It was nice to have a friend. It was a good evening, a very good evening.

Once the game was over, Dora announced, "It's getting late. Maybe I should go." She laid her hand on my thigh.

"Baby, you've been drinking. I don't think you should drive." After a moment I added, "You can stay if you like."

"I have a bag in my car," she responded quickly. "I'll be right back."

While Dora went to her car, I cleaned up and dressed down.

"Give me a minute to freshen up," she said when she returned. She went into the bathroom with her bag. I turned down the covers and sat on the edge of the bed.

Wow. Dora came out of the bathroom in a frilly sexy top with a garter belt and G-string. She walked slowly toward me, keeping her eyes on mine.

I took her by the hand and guided her down onto the pillow. Pulling her gently toward me, I kissed her. Her lips were moist and soft. I slid my hand under her top onto her left breast. She squeezed my hand and pressed it hard against her, moaning softly. I slid back the right side of her top and put my mouth on her breast and circled my tongue around her nipple. She pulled my head tight against her chest.

I reached and touched gently between her legs. She was wet, so wet. She pushed back against my touch. I lightly circled her wet spot with my fingers. She started to moan more loudly. I dipped my middle finger gently inside her. She grabbed my hand and pulled it against her. I pushed two fingers inside her. She moaned louder and pulled my hand hard, inside her. "Deeper, reach deeper!" she begged. She was pushing and moaning. "*Omigod, Omigod, Omigod!*" she cried out, pulling my hand into her in a frenzied passion as she pushed against me. "*Oh, Oh, Oh, OH, OH, OH, Oohh, Oohh, Oohh...*" After a minute, she quit pushing against me and let go of my hand. She lay back onto the pillow, eyes closed, mouth open, breathing heavily, but more slowly now. I lay down by her, touching her very softly, amazed.

"Are you okay?"

She nodded. "It's been a long time for me." She breathed. "And I was horny when I got here three hours ago."

"Glad I could help."

Dora rolled over and spooned up against me. I reached across her to turn off the lamp by the bed and snuggled her as close to me as I could.

In the morning, I got up to go shower. I kissed Dora and left her in the bed. She opened her eyes and smiled. I think I could get used to seeing that smile in the morning.

"I'll make coffee while you shower," she said, swinging her legs over the edge of the bed. "Your coffeemaker is exactly like mine."

When I got out of the shower, Dora was up, dressed, and standing in front of me, holding her cell phone. Her face wore a profoundly disconcerting frown.

"My mother just called. My son has relapsed. It's the heroin. And he's cut his wrists again! They're taking him to the hospital."

"Oh, no! Can I give you a ride?"

"No, that's okay. I'm meeting my mother there. I don't know how long I'll be there. But thanks for the offer."

"Okay. Well, after you see him, would you please give me a call and let me know how he is?"

"Of course. Look, I've got to go now, but there's something else I need to tell you."

"What is it?"

"I'm afraid that I'm going to have to get my son into treatment and have him move in with me. I'll have to stay close to home, to keep an eye on him while he's recovering. I don't know how long it might take. It could be months."

She walked to my front door, and I followed behind her. She opened it and stepped into the hallway.

Before she closed the door behind her, she turned back toward me. "I can't let a relationship come between me and my son."

"But I…"

And then she was gone.

Chapter Twelve

A few days after seeing Kala at the jail, Mia went to the District Attorney's Office to visit Kala's prosecutor, Randy Johnson. She had her mind made up about what she would tell him before she entered his office—Kala didn't do it.

Seeing that the door to Randy's office was open, she tapped lightly on its frame. He looked up from the something he was reading on his desk and smiled when he saw her. "Hello, Mia. Good to see you. Please have a seat." He motioned to the black chair in front of his desk with his hand. "My secretary said you wanted to see me. What's this about?"

"The Kala Tausinga case," Mia said.

"Yes, the child homicide case. Very sad," Randy said. "How are the victims doing?"

Mia took a breath. She understood very clearly that Randy was not thinking of Kala when he asked about the victims in the case. She hesitated.

"Well," Mia said, summoning her courage, "Kala's other children seem to be thriving with her aunt and uncle."

"Okay," said Randy, stretching out his pronunciation of the word and raising the tone at the end as if it were a question. "Tell me why you wanted to see me."

"I'm not sure that Kala killed her child," started

Mia, hesitantly. Randy didn't speak, his eyes boring into her as he waited for her to finish. After a moment, she continued. "I think she's innocent. In fact, I'm sure she's innocent."

Randy raised an eyebrow but didn't answer right away. The victim advocates who worked for his office didn't give such opinions. She worried that he might be angry.

"Okay, tell me why you think so," Johnson said.

Mia dove right in. "I talked to Kala. She told me that it was her husband Afa who killed her child. I believe her."

"What do you mean you talked to her?" Randy asked. "She's the defendant. And she's represented by counsel."

"I asked her lawyer first. Mr. Bravo said it was okay for me to talk to her," Mia replied defensively. "I only want to help her."

"It's not your job to help her," Randy said, raising his voice now. "*Your* job is to help the victims."

"But I think that she *is* the victim," Mia said, raising her voice too. "You should be prosecuting Afa, not her."

Randy paused for a moment before continuing. "We are prosecuting Kala, not Afa. And frankly, it would be difficult to prosecute Afa now, after the police arrested Kala, especially now that we've charged her, not him. A good defense attorney would have a field day with that type of indecisiveness, arguing that we didn't even know who committed the crime. That would be 'reasonable doubt' right there."

Mia set her chin, unpersuaded by Randy's reasoning.

"My job is to prosecute the accused. Your job is to help me do it. *That's* the job. If you can't do it, you should find another job. Do you understand me?"

Mia sat back, shaken by Randy's blunt threat. "Yes," she responded after a moment. "I understand." Mia wasn't ready to walk away from a job she loved. A job she was good at. She chose her words carefully. "Thanks for hearing me out at least."

Johnson nodded and stood up. He reached out his hand, and Mia accepted the handshake and walked out.

Somehow, I've to help Kala anyway.

She strode through the long hallway toward the elevators, her mind racing. *But how?*

Mia finally reached her car in the six-story parking structure next to the District Attorney's Office and turned on her engine. She sat there for a minute, thinking. *Xtina! Maybe she would help.*

Mia opened the contact list on her phone and found Xtina's number. She tapped out a text message: "Hi, Xtina. It's Mia Montes. Sorry it's been so long since I've called. I grew up in your orphanage, and later you took me into The Refuge after my boyfriend tried to kill me. You said I could contact you if I ever needed you, right? Well, I need your help now. Please!"

Chapter Thirteen

"Frank, a Bishop Kimball is in the lobby asking for you," said The Defenders' receptionist on the other end of my desk phone, "and he has an attorney with him."

Bishop Kimball was the equivalent of a priest or a pastor in the Mormon Church, according to our investigator Francis Benson. Francis had been talking to Kala about people she had spoken to about her marital problems, trying to identify potential witnesses. I called Mary and asked her to meet me and Francis in the third-floor conference room. I was glad to get this interview scheduled as quickly as we did because we only had about two weeks left until trial.

When we were all present, we introduced ourselves to each other. It was a very friendly exchange. As we sat down, I was feeling optimistic about the meeting.

"So, Bishop Kimball," I asked, "you are Kala's bishop?"

"Yes, I am."

"I understand that she came to you to talk about the problems in her marriage?"

"Excuse me, please," the lawyer interjected, "I'm afraid I can't let my client answer that question."

Carefully folding up my optimism, I put it back into my pocket. "Why not?" I queried cautiously.

"The communication is privileged."

"Are you referring to the clergy communication

privilege?"

"Yes," the lawyer said. "It's Rule 503."

"I know the rule. But my investigator told me he found Mr. Kimball at an *accounting firm*," I pointed out, cleverly quashing the lawyer's legal assertion. "So, he must not be a clergyman."

"Yes, he is," the lawyer said. "I have a case in which an appellate court ruled that a Mormon minister is a member of the clergy within the meaning of the clergy-penitent privilege."

"Where, in Utah?"

"No, Oregon."

Mary must have sensed I was getting on edge because she intervened, probably to salvage the interview.

"But we're not in court, *examining* him as a witness," explained Mary in her usual, professional tone. "We're only *talking*. And we're not asking about any *confession* Kala may have made. We're asking if she came to the bishop for marital advice."

"Nevertheless," the lawyer answered, "based on my research I believe that the rule covers all communications between the bishop and the members who speak with him in his role as bishop."

I put my hand on my forehead and closed my eyes, trying to remember the details of the rule. "I believe that a person talking to a clergyman can *consent* to discussing the details of any communication. And I'm confident that Kala *will* consent to have us speak with the bishop."

Smiling snidely, the lawyer asked, "Do you have a notarized waiver and consent form?"

"No, but I'm positive we can get one."

"Well," the lawyer said smugly, "even a signed waiver may not be enough in any case because Mrs. Tausinga cannot consent for her husband, and questions about the marriage may affect *his* privilege."

"But we're not asking about her husband or anything *he* said." I was growing frustrated by the lawyer's obstinance and by my own need to speak more loudly than I should. I thought of my Zen meditation class and took a breath. "Look, we only want to know if she came for marital advice. You can leave the husband out of it."

"Well," said the lawyer, appearing to become annoyed by my continued assertiveness, "I can't let him answer your questions. All I can say is that he tried to save the marriage."

Bingo! That's exactly what I needed to know. That's enough to argue to the jury that Kala at least *asked* for help, that she tried to do *something* to protect her son. I quickly made a note on my legal pad.

"But why save a marriage where the wife says she wants a divorce?" Mary asked.

"Women have a duty to obey their husbands," the lawyer replied. "And, besides, a woman has to be *married* to enter into the celestial kingdom."

I could see that it was Mary now who was about to totally lose her normally cool professional demeanor and pounce all over the duty-to-obey statement, but I had already lost mine and beat her to the punch.

"Pardon me. Can you explain to me the celestial kingdom thing? And what's this about a woman having to be married to go there?"

The bishop glanced toward the lawyer and took this question himself. Not a legal matter, it fit squarely within his wheelhouse as a man of the cloth—not law of man but law of God.

"The celestial kingdom is the highest of the three degrees or kingdoms of glory in Heaven," he began to explain, a little too self-righteously for my taste. "Those in this kingdom dwell forever in the presence of God the Father and his son Jesus Christ. And a woman can only attain this glory through temple marriage to a worthy man."

"I'm not a priest or anything," I said quickly. "But I have read the Bible, and I'm pretty sure there's nothing in it that says anything like that."

The bishop frowned. "It's clearly stated in a Mormon scripture, the Doctrine and Covenants, Chapter 131, verses 1-4."

"Okay. I get it now. So...a woman must be married to go to Heaven, to be with God, no matter how righteous or good a person she is? Is *that* what you told Kala? That she *had* to go back to her husband, or she wouldn't go to Heaven?"

I wasn't asking questions anymore. I was shouting in righteous indignation. The bishop shrank back into his chair.

"It's no wonder she went back to her husband. But, sir, *you* put her back in danger right when she had finally worked up the courage to get out!"

The lawyer raised his hand like an officer at an accident scene in a busy intersection to stop the onslaught. "I'm sorry," he declared. "This is the end of the interview."

Chapter Fourteen

Mia pressed her foot harder onto the accelerator as she raced down Interstate 80 along the dead-straight road between Salt Lake City and Wendover, Nevada. The Refuge was about halfway along that road.

Xtina had returned Mia's call promptly and invited her to come see her at The Refuge. It was short notice, but Mia was desperate.

The ground by the highway was so dry that almost nothing grew. Only sturdy weeds survived in the salty alkali dirt. Mia had heard that in ages past, the whole region had been covered by Lake Bonneville, an ice age lake the size of Utah. *Must have been a very long time ago*, *because now this area is bone dry*.

Finally arriving at the turnoff, Mia followed the road south until she arrived at the large building that housed The Refuge. She knew the place well having stayed there for several years as a child and then returning to stay for another two months after she fled from Carlos. She found a parking spot and saw Xtina on the porch waiting for her. She didn't look a day older than when Mia last saw her ten years earlier. Flowing black hair that fell halfway down her back and her smooth dark skin tone reflected her Middle Eastern heritage. As Mia climbed the stairs to the porch, she saw and remembered Xtina's radiant eyes that sparkled like pure emeralds in front of a fire, and seemed to change hues depending on the light.

Xtina approached Mia and embraced her warmly. "I'm happy to see you, Mia."

"Me too, Xtina. It's been too long."

Xtina nodded in agreement. "I hear you've been well."

Mia cocked her head. "What do you mean? Heard from whom?"

"We follow the lives of the women who've come here for refuge from abuse, to make sure they're okay, and to make sure their abusers can't hurt them again. Besides, you've been very special to me ever since you first came here after your parents died. You were only twelve years old and scared. You ended up staying with us for quite some time. You became like a daughter to me."

Mia felt her skin tingle with warmth upon hearing Xtina's kind words, and she put her hand on Xtina's arm. After a moment she gestured with her other hand. "I hardly recognize the place. There are so many buildings. It's like a little city here now."

"Yes, we have The Garden where we now house and raise orphaned and refugee children, and we have expanded The Refuge to house many more abused women. We still have the full-service gym there on your left where Sensei Gozen gave you your first martial arts training. She said no one so young had ever mastered the naginata as well as you did."

Mia fondly recalled her days with Xtina as a teenager, the sparring sessions with Sensei Gozen, the professors who came to The Garden to teach the girls there, and the happy hours she spent tending plants in the greenhouse.

Xtina spoke again, waking Mia up her from her daydream. "And in this new building over here on your right, we now teach college courses and provide technical training to help our guests start their new lives."

"That's great. When I was here ten years ago, there was only one greenhouse. Are all of those huge buildings out there greenhouses now?"

"Yes. We feed ourselves and export our all-organic food to several surrounding states. If you like, I can take you on a tour later. But come with me now," Xtina said as she opened the door, "and tell me what you need. I've invited someone to join us."

Xtina led Mia through a door to an office area at the front of the building. In Xtina's office a beautiful blonde woman stood to meet them.

Xtina pointed her hand toward the woman. "Do you remember Victoria? She was a rape victim who we rescued and brought to The Refuge. Later, we hired her to work here. She was your caseworker when you were here at The Refuge. Now, she's the Executive Director of the Western Division of The Sisterhood."

"Yes, I thought I recognized you," Mia said. "It's good to see you again."

"You too, Mia," Victoria said warmly.

"But what is The Sisterhood?"

"Aha," Xtina said. "You have asked a very important question. This is a topic we did not discuss with you when you were young. What I will tell you for now is that The Sisterhood is an organization of women who help other women who have suffered abuse. A woman alone may be weak, but women together can be strong. The Sisterhood intervenes to get justice when the legal system fails. We balance the scales of justice."

Xtina sat down behind her desk. "As you already know, we operate The Refuge here for victims of abuse. And as you may have surmised when Carlos stopped harassing you, we do other things to make sure that abusers can no longer victimize anyone."

At the time of Carlos's disappearance, Mia had speculated about where he was. Was he hiding from the law? Did he finally understand that she was not going to be with him and decided to leave her alone? She had bumped into Carlos's older brother Enrique a year later and found out that not even his own family had seen him. What *other things* was Xtina talking about?

Victoria raised both her eyebrows and glanced at Xtina. "Should we be talking like this in front of Mia?"

Xtina sighed. "I understand your concern. But I believe that Mia may be joining us in The Sisterhood if she chooses to follow the path that will surely open before her."

Victoria turned and gazed intensely into Mia's eyes as if trying to see deep inside her. Her scrutiny made Mia uncomfortable enough that she had to turn away.

Victoria turned back to Xtina. "You are The Sisterhood's very own oracle. If you've seen that future for Mia, that's good enough for me. I still clearly remember the day you told me of the future you saw for me when I met you here at The Refuge. You said you saw me being a leader in this organization. Back then I had only worked as, shall we say, an exotic dancer, and I doubted you."

Xtina nodded. "I saw Mia's future the first time I put my hands on her head."

Mia remembered all that Victoria and Xtina had done for her at The Refuge. When Mia first arrived, she was at life's lowest point, convinced she had no future at all. She said, "Xtina, I don't think I ever properly thanked you for helping me start a new life. I want you to know that I am very grateful."

Victoria said, "Funny you would put it that way—a new life. When you arrived here sometime after leaving Carlos, you had OD'd. I think you were dead."

Mia quickly turned toward Xtina with her mouth agape. "Is that true?"

Xtina nodded. "Yes, dear. When our sister Zena found you, she called me and said you weren't breathing. I told her to bring you to me straightaway. I learned I had the gift when I was young, in the old country."

"But how is it possible?" Mia asked. "I don't understand."

Xtina's penetrating gaze filled Mia with light and peace. "I do not speak of this, and you should not repeat it. People don't understand."

Xtina and Victoria quietly stared at Mia, waiting for a response of some kind from her. As Mia struggled to grasp the full significance of the words Xtina had spoken, Xtina finally broke the silence. "Mia, come with us. Let us show you an example of what The Sisterhood does. Victoria was about to review a new potential case with me."

Victoria went to a table in the office and turned on a projector attached to a laptop. She clicked her remote, and the first image of a PowerPoint presentation appeared on a screen on the wall. "This is the Utah attorney general. One of his campaign promises was to investigate and end human sex trafficking, particularly of underage girls, and he created a large and expensive task force to that end. The Sisterhood actually made a substantial contribution to his campaign."

Victoria clicked to a blowup of a news article. "But after almost two years without any type of success or apparent progress, and after a critical news report by an investigative journalist, the attorney general became desperate for results. He demanded action and personally joined a police raid on a massage studio. Police arrested two customers who were inside at the time, both of whom admitted to being pleasured sexually during their massages."

The next photo showed police congregating in the parking lot. "Here is the attorney general gloating outside of the massage shop. He turned this police fiasco into a political photo op. But here's the bigger problem. Not only was nothing at all done to help the two undocumented Chinese girls found working at this massage shop, but the police arrested the girls for sex solicitation. My question is, should The Sisterhood aid these young women?"

Xtina asked, "Victoria, what sort of assistance do you propose? This seems different than the types of cases we usually take. It sounds more like a legal issue."

"I know a couple of lawyers," interjected Mia. "I've seen them work. They're smart and dedicated to helping people. Their names are Frank Bravo and Mary Swanson."

"Frank, you say?" said Victoria. "A man?" She glanced at Xtina. "Aren't we committed to using only women in our work?"

Xtina replied, "The Sisterhood is indeed dedicated to empowering women to help themselves and other women. But there is nothing in our bylaws requiring us to exclude men from the work. When it comes to who may stand with us, I say by their fruits shall ye know them."

Victoria smiled at Xtina. "Why do you always speak in parables?"

"Like Jesus, I was born in Bethlehem," Xtina said. "Although unlike Jesus I'm not a turn-the-other-cheek enthusiast. I saw that didn't work out so well for him. I am more of a Law of Moses fan, you know, an eye for an eye."

Xtina turned back to Mia. "Sorry for the digression. You can tell your story in a minute. But first let's wrap up our discussion of the young women who were arrested. Referring that matter of the arrest to a lawyer seems appropriate because this particular circumstance is not clearly within the ambit of our mission."

"Perhaps not," Victoria said, "unless the girls were coerced into working at the massage parlor. If so, it could be human trafficking, the type of case we would take on."

"Yes, you're right," Xtina said. "Assign someone to investigate the trafficking issue. Also, have someone check out this Frank Bravo fellow. Meanwhile, I have an immediate solution for these young women. I will post their bail and invite them into The Refuge until we decide if intervention by The Sisterhood is appropriate."

Xtina turned to Mia. "Now, tell us briefly why you called."

"Well, here's the short version. I guess you know that I'm a victim advocate. I have a case where a baby was killed. The police arrested the mother. Her name is Kala Tausinga. The more I learn about the case, the more certain I am that Kala is innocent and that it was her husband who killed the child. But her husband is abusive and has threatened her, so she's unwilling to tell anyone what really happened. Right now, if nothing changes, I'm afraid that she will be convicted of murder, and her husband will go free."

"Yep, that's clearly the type of case we could help with," Victoria said.

"Mia, The Sisterhood is having a board meeting next week," Xtina said. "I suggest that you come. You could meet the board members and tell them your story. They will decide whether we'll take the case."

"Yes, okay," Mia replied.

Xtina added, "I should tell you that this is not the normal procedure. Usually, Victoria would present the possible new cases to the board. But I think that you are a good candidate to join The Sisterhood. The board would need to approve that as well. What do you say?"

"Umm, I don't know. I will come to the board meeting and tell them about Kala." Mia paused and shook her head. "But I don't know about joining The Sisterhood. I don't understand what that would entail. I would have to know more."

"Victoria will give you the time and directions to the board meeting. But as you seem unsure about joining The Sisterhood, there is one thought I would like to leave you with." Xtina signaled to Victoria to turn off the computer and turned her full attention to Mia. "In life, you cannot choose what happens to you, but you can choose what you do about it. Most people go through their lives like a rowboat without oars, being tossed to and fro by each storm on the sea. But others have the power to pick a port, put up a sail, and choose their destination. Choose their life."

Mia nodded. "I think I understand."

Xtina opened her hand and extended it toward Mia. "You, Mia, have that power. But only if you resolve to use it. I will tell you now, there will soon come a time when you will have to make that choice."

Chapter Fifteen

I waved at Mary as I walked toward her down the courthouse hallway. We were meeting for lunch after a long morning of case hearings. But Randy Johnson, Kala's prosecutor, reached me first and stopped me.

"I have something for you." Johnson handed me a court document just as Mary arrived.

I glanced down at the paper. "Notice of Expert? It's too late to be giving notice of an expert in a murder trial. We're less than two weeks from trial. You're supposed to give at least thirty days' notice. What did you do, sandbag this to get an advantage, so we wouldn't have time to prepare to respond?"

"Well," said Johnson, "your remedy is to file a motion to continue the trial if you need more time. I won't object."

"Our client would probably object to a continuance," interjected Mary, as she took the paper from me to see the name of the expert. "And what is this Alicia Simpson going to testify about anyway?"

"Alicia is the director of the Children's Justice Center. She is an expert in protocols for interviewing children. As you know, children can be easily manipulated by adults into saying things that aren't true."

"Look at this." Mary pointed at the description of Alicia Simpson's testimony. "She's supposedly going to testify that in her opinion, the two Tausinga girls appear to have been *coached*."

"Oh, come on, Randy," I said, raising my voice. "That's as good as saying that they've been told to lie. You can't have an expert say that."

"I understand your position," replied Johnson dismissively. "There's one other thing. I have a new investigative report of a recent interview our investigator conducted with Afa."

"Where?" I asked. "Do you have an address? My investigator couldn't find him at his old address."

"Actually, he's now living in the basement at his father's house. Here's a copy of our investigator's report."

I took the report and scanned it quickly. I saw that it was written by a Detective Peterson, who I know works exclusively for the DA's office, not the police department. Peterson wrote that Afa admitted hiding from the DA's investigator because he had warrants outstanding for his arrest. Peterson also noted that he checked the warrants database and did locate warrants for criminal mischief and terroristic threats.

When I finished reviewing the report, I lifted my head. "This is great stuff. Thanks, Johnson, I told you that Afa was a bad guy. Here's proof. *Terroristic threats*! What were the circumstances of those charges? Who did he threaten?"

"I don't know." Johnson shrugged. "Detective Peterson neglected to include the details of those cases in his report to me."

Mary remained calm, as usual, as she spoke. "So, is Afa in jail now? Terroristic threats is a serious charge."

"Well, um, no." Johnson stated in a matter-of-fact

tone. "We didn't arrest him."

"Why the hell not?" I asked.

"We need him to cooperate in the case. We made a deal with him. If he cooperates and doesn't get in any more trouble, he doesn't go to jail."

I shook my head. This was not the first time a bad guy got a walk, in exchange for cooperating with the prosecution. The damned thing was that what I called a miscarriage of justice, the courts have upheld as within the discretion of the prosecutor.

"Well, in any case," I asserted, "the fact that he was hiding shows he's guilty."

"I don't necessarily agree," Johnson said. "He may have been hiding because he didn't want to assist us in the prosecution of his wife. Or maybe it was just what he said, because he had warrants."

Someone needed to talk sense into Johnson, and at this moment in time, that person was me. "But these warrants, along with those other domestic violence calls, are more evidence that he's a violent son of a bitch."

Johnson voice remained calm, and the only parts on his body that moved were his lips to speak and his eyes to appraise Mary and me. "Detective Peterson said that Afa is quite soft spoken and not at all intimidating," Johnson retorted, obviously unpersuaded by my rant. "I've asked Detective Peterson to talk to Afa's side of the family and see if we can find some evidence that Kala is actually the abusive one in the relationship."

Although frustrated, I could understand that Johnson was a professional doing his job, trying to gather evidence against the accused. "Well, try to keep an open mind, okay?" I urged.

Johnson simply shrugged in response.

Mary nodded toward the exit. We walked the short distance from the courthouse to a local deli and ordered two gourmet sandwiches before sitting down at a small wooden table. While waiting for our order, we discussed ways we could investigate Afa's recent terroristic threats case, thinking that if Johnson tried to paint Afa as the hapless victim in the relationship with Kala, then we might be able to present rebuttal witnesses to show his history of violence.

I pondered the possibilities. Mary broke into my thoughts. "Frank, let's take a break from Johnson, at least during lunch, and talk about something else."

I nodded, grateful for the idea.

Mary asked, "How's your personal life going?"

After I recounted a G-rated version of my very happy, then very sad evening a week or so earlier with Dora, Mary said, "I'm sorry to hear that. Have you met anyone else you liked?"

I shook my head. "Don't get me wrong. Dora did sort of make it sound like she didn't think she could continue with our relationship. But I haven't given up on her. We hit it off and have a lot in common. It may be a while, but I'm hoping it'll work out for us somehow down the road. Other than that, I'm not sure dating is worth the hassle."

"I totally get it." Mary nodded. "To borrow a phrase, dating is like a box of chocolates; you never know what you're going to get."

"Yeah, and I would add that if you try too many chocolates, you get an upset stomach," I replied, shaking my head. "Besides, right now we're swamped with work, so there's not much time to fool around."

"Yes, I totally agree," said Mary, chuckling.

"Having said that, though, there is a woman who contacted *me*. Her name's Julie. Her online profile was very impressive. We chatted on the phone. She asked a lot of questions about me, then I got my turn. This woman has got it together. She owns the penthouse in the condo tower on the hill. She's president and CEO of an industrial bank here in town and manages about twelve billion in assets. Her story is amazing. She started as a bank teller in a small town in Idaho. Her family sent her away to business school, and she worked her way up the ladder from there."

"So, she sounds promising." Mary folded her arms and leaned forward on the table.

"Yes. Julie is special. Man, Kala is so different, so emotionally insecure. If she were more like Julie, or even Dora, maybe she could have—"

"She's *not* them," Mary interrupted with an intensity that drew stares from two nearby tables. "She got pregnant and didn't finish high school. She didn't have a family to send her away to school. Her father's dead, and her mother's in another country. She's been abused and repressed by a bully for several years. You *can't* compare her to *them*! And you *can't* blame the victim."

My face flushed with shame. I knew she was right, of course. I shut up and waited silently for my sandwich.

Chapter Sixteen

Mia turned off the freeway at the exit to The Refuge, but the directions to the board meeting sent her down a small side road. She ended up at an outwardly plain building that seemed like nothing more than a storage building for equipment and maybe some support staff. She parked and went in to see if she could find out if she was at the right place or not.

Inside, Mia found the building to be modern and well-appointed. An attractive brunette receptionist in a white blouse and tan skirt walked up to meet her. "You must be Mia," she said in a pleasant and disarming manner that somewhat lessened Mia's stress level. "I'm Jenny." She offered her hand toward Mia.

Jenny's handshake was brief yet firm. "Please follow me."

Mia followed her to a locked door labeled "Private." Jenny unlocked the door and pointed to a chair inside the room. "Please sit down. Someone will be here shortly to assist you." Jenny locked the door behind her as she left, revving Mia's nervousness back into the red zone.

Before Mia had time to sit, a large woman wearing a security uniform and her hair tightly pulled back approached. "Come with me." She did an about-face and led Mia to a door with no handles or visible controls of any kind.

The security guard lifted her wrist to her face and spoke into what appeared to be a bracelet. "She's here." The door opened immediately, revealing an elevator. They entered, and again Mia saw no visible controls. Yet when the door closed, down they went several levels.

The elevator door eventually opened to Xtina standing there beaming warmly. Seeing her face eased Mia's nervousness. Xtina tilted her head in the direction of a closed door. "They are waiting for you in there."

Mia took in a big breath and walked behind Xtina into a large boardroom. Six women sat around an ancient oak table with shiny black stone insets in the table in front of each seat. Mia also noticed what looked like ancient swords, helmets, breastplates and other artifacts on the walls and on shelves around the perimeter of the room.

Xtina scanned the room. "Mia, welcome to this quarterly meeting of the board of The Sisterhood. We have added you to the agenda."

She ushered Mia to a seat close to the door.

"You already know me and Victoria." Both Victoria's mouth and eyes smiled at her. Using her right hand to wave from one side of the table to the other, Xtina added, "Let me also introduce you to the other six directors of our North American organization and tell you a little bit about each of them.

"This is Zena." As Zena stood, her large frame caused Mia to involuntarily jerk back in her chair. Zena was a muscular woman standing over six feet tall and must have been wearing heels as well. She dominated the room. "Zena owns and operates several gyms and gives self-defense classes, which she offers free to teenaged girls."

Zena nodded at Mia and sat down.

"The Sisterhood also calls on Zena's exceptional physical capabilities from time to time for other purposes."

Zena raised an eyebrow but said nothing.

"Next is Sariah." Sariah had long curly gray hair with a slight peppering of the chestnut brown it used to be. "Sariah earned her stripes fighting for women's rights since the '60s." Sariah did not stand but gave Mia a small nod.

"This is Alowana," Xtina said. "She is a Sioux Indian from South Dakota who earned an eagle feather from her tribe for her efforts to investigate and stop the epidemic of vanished or murdered indigenous women and girls. The Sisterhood has helped her bring some of those responsible to justice."

Alowana sat silently as she watched Mia.

Xtina pointed to the women on the other side of the table.

"Next is Laushana." Xtina pointed her chin at a heavy-set black woman with gray peeking through her dark short hair. "Laushana became a leader in the #blacklivesmatter movement by organizing protests, press conferences and instigating legal action. She eagerly agreed to join the board needing to find hope in a system of justice outside the one that consistently fails her and her community.

"Now, this is Sally, if that is her real name." Xtina winked at Sally, who returned a wry grin. Sally had straight light-brown hair pulled back into a tight ponytail. "Sally worked overseas with the CIA for two decades and has a particular set of skills that come in handy in the cases she handles for The Sisterhood.

"Finally, up there is Julie," said Xtina, pointing at a forty-eight-inch flat screen on the wall at a woman wearing her brown hair coiled in a tight sleek bun. "Julie is the president of an industrial bank here in Utah and today is joining us via WebEx from New York where she sits on the board of an investment firm. She chairs our organization's board."

Julie waved.

"Before we get started," Xtina said, "I would ask that Alowana ground us in our work with the sacred Red Sand Ritual to remind us what we do and who we do it for."

Alowana stood and revealed a beaded bag decorated with indigenous markings from inside her jacket. She centered herself at the head of the large oak table and began to take small and intentional steps, swaying slightly as she circled the room, singing quietly in her native tongue. Mia couldn't understand the words, but the emotion was easy to translate. It was raw, full of reverence, and something that spoke to the significance of the work imagined and carried out in this room.

Alowana's song ended, but she continued to walk around the room. She undid the purse string and began to pour what appeared to be red sand onto the floor around the table

Alowana's voice disrupted the reverent silence. "We join this table as sisters in search of complete justice for the harmed and the voiceless, the shamed and the silenced, those lost to us at the hands of careless cruelty, and those taken before their time. As each grain of sand returns to the earth to come full circle where it began, we too do this work to return balance, closing the circle of harm to claim full unabridged justice."

With that final statement, Alowana walked back to her seat and resumed her place at the large table. Mia focused on the face of each woman. The group was silent. They each showed immense respect, love, and, it appeared, admiration for what had transpired.

"Thank you, dear sister," Xtina said, bowing toward Alowana. "May we never forget the reason we exist—to serve, protect, and restore balance to the scales."

Once Alowana was seated, Xtina spoke again. "Now, you will see on your agendas that the purpose of this meeting is to discuss two new cases that we might take on. But first let me introduce Mia Montes, the victim advocate I told you about. I am recommending her to be considered as one of our frontline advocates in The Sisterhood network. I know Mia well. She lived on-site in The Garden for about six years as a child and later returned when she escaped an abusive marriage and stayed in The Refuge for a while. Given Mia's life history, training, and substantial experience serving survivors, together with her firm commitment to help other women, I propose that we consider inviting her to join our organization. Are there any questions or comments regarding my proposal before we vote?"

A hand raised at the other end of the table. "Yes, Zena?"

"Mia, you work in the courts," Zena said, staring harshly at Mia. "The courts follow the law." Zena paused, before adding, "Sometimes, well, very often, the work deemed necessary by The Sisterhood is...beyond the law. What would you do if asked to do something you knew fell outside the bounds of what was considered...legal?" Zena stood up now, startling Mia. "Would you report us to your boss at the District Attorney's Office?"

Mia's chest tightened. She had not anticipated this sort of accusatory questioning. Xtina made it seem like she would be welcomed into this group because of her work as a victim advocate and her commitment to survivors. Now she wondered if she should even be here, and exactly what "outside the bounds" actions could be expected of her.

Mia cleared her throat. "Let me say this. I've seen firsthand how the law doesn't always protect victims. Society doesn't always protect victims. Xtina told me that The Sisterhood steps in and succeeds where the law fails. I want to help."

"You haven't answered the question." Sally spoke with the air of one accustomed to performing interrogations. "Will you continue to bind yourself with the constraints of our legal system, or are you willing to help us seek justice when our legal system fails?"

Without waiting for Mia to answer, Laushana interjected. "It is not *our* system. The system doesn't respond to all of us or represent all of us the same way. But I also want to know if you will, with us, be willing to step out of bounds where required. We don't do this work without sacrifice or take these cases lightly, and we need to know we can trust you."

Mia hesitated, not sure what to say or how to answer the barrage of questions. She glanced at Xtina in the hopes that she would intervene and save her, but Xtina also waited for her response.

Finally, Xtina spoke. "Mia, let me assure you that

The Sisterhood is not a gang of mindless vigilantes. We act according to a strict moral code. We do no more than is necessary but no less than is deserved. Each action is approved only after due consideration by the board."

Mia took a deep breath, grateful for Xtina's explanation.

"We are women," Xtina continued. "We can be beautiful and gentle like the petals of the rose. But, if necessary, like the thorns on the stem of the rose, we can draw blood."

Xtina's eyes searched Mia's face. "Consider this, Mia"—her voice gentle— "if a bad man committed an evil act against an innocent victim, do you think it would be just to do to him what he did to that person?"

Mia still hesitated. She could sense that all the women staring at her were pressing for an answer. When she finally spoke, her words came out in a stutter. "I, I, um, I don't know. I think it would depend on the circumstances."

Some of the women stared at Xtina, concern evident on their faces.

Xtina raised her hand. Everyone stopped speaking immediately and waited silently to hear what she had to say.

She turned to Mia. "May I put my hands on your head?"

Mia nodded and bowed her head a bit as Xtina approached and gently put both hands on Mia's head and closed her eyes. A warm wave flowed through Mia's body. She closed her eyes too but could still see the room in an even brighter light.

After a minute, Xtina spoke, her eyes still closed.

"Mia, blessed are ye among women. I see that you have great strength of spirit and will, more than you know."

Xtina paused before speaking again. "And, Mia, I see you in the presence of a woman. There is great sorrow on her face. You will see great violence and evil. And you will wish to turn away."

Xtina's eyes opened, and she removed her hands from Mia's head. "Mia, you have a calling to fight against evil. And you have the power to do so. But even I cannot control your future. You will have to choose your own path."

After a long moment, Julie's voice broke the silence. "I suggest that we take the question of Mia's membership under advisement. We normally don't accept new members until and unless they have proven their allegiance to the organization in some way and their commitment to our mission."

Mia sighed. She was disappointed but grateful for a welcome reprieve from the overwhelming tension that had built up in the room.

"Very well," Victoria said. "The next item on the agenda is the question of whether The Sisterhood will take action on a new case. Mia will describe a case in which she has become personally involved."

Relieved by the change of topic, Mia's confidence began to return. "It's a long story…"

Chapter Seventeen

"I am so sorry I didn't tell you guys everything before," Kala told Mary and me after we all got seated around the white plastic table in the jail's small contact visit room. "I was afraid. But Mia told me what she went through with her ex-boyfriend and why she became a victim advocate. She told me she has helped a lot of women in my exact same situation and that several women have testified against their husbands or boyfriends who were abusing them. She said that Afa should be held responsible for what he did."

Mary raised her eyebrows. We were only a few days from trial, and we were concerned because we believed that Kala hadn't told us the truth about what had happened to her.

"Mia convinced me that I should tell you what I have been going through." She lifted her head, her eyes landing on Mary. "Thank you for sending her. She was nice to me. She said you are here to help me and that I should try to be strong."

"That's right," Mary said. "We are here to help you. But for us to help you, we need to know what happened, everything you can tell us. For starters, we obtained some records from the police department that show how they received several domestic violence calls regarding your apartment over the past couple of years. But the police never arrested anyone. Tell us about that.

We brought the police reports with us today."

Mary scanned through the papers in her hand. "Here's one from about two years ago. When the police came, you were on the floor under a blanket. It says here that Afa answered the door, sweating profusely. The police said they questioned both of you and that you both said you were only arguing. What was going on there?"

"Afa was raping me," Kala said matter-of-factly as she brushed hair from her face with her hand. "That was shortly after our separation. After Vai made me pregnant. Afa was angry almost all the time after that."

Kala's calm tone in describing a violent assault stunned me, but I didn't know how to respond. I said nothing.

"The day before the police came, Afa had choked me until I passed out," Kala continued. "If I didn't want to have sex when he did, he would just take me. If I fought him, he would hurt me."

I grabbed the pen from the inside pocket of my sport coat to make some notes.

Mary asked, "Didn't the police examine you to see if you had bruises or other injuries?"

"I had on a turtleneck that covered the bruises on my neck, and I guess they didn't have a female cop to check me."

"Wouldn't the police think it odd that you were wearing a turtleneck in the summer?" Mary asked.

"I got up off the floor and wrapped the blanket around my waist when the cops came through the front door. I think they must have guessed that I was half naked. They didn't even try to check me."

Mary flipped through more pages. "What about the

time toward the end of last August. Do you remember what happened that time?"

"August? Oh, yes. That was one of the times I tried to leave Afa. I told him I can't do this anymore. He accused me of leaving to be with Juna's father. I told him no, but he wouldn't listen. He was so mad. He punched a hole in the wall right next to me. He said, 'If you leave me, I'll kill you!' And he said he'd kill himself because he wouldn't want to live his life without me."

"So, you stayed?" Mary asked.

"Yes. Afa said that if I left, the children would be without their father. And my father died when I was two, so I grew up without a father. I didn't want that for my kids. He also told me that since I didn't have a job, and he did, the courts would take my kids from me and give them to him. I *couldn't* lose my kids." She stared down at her fidgeting hands. "He promised he would be better. He said he loved me."

I said, "I'm so sorry. That must have been hard."

Kala shrugged. "He didn't hurt me that time."

He didn't hurt her? He threatened to *kill* her. He threatened to take her children from her, and she played it off like it was nothing. I threw my hands up. Mary shrugged.

"Kala," Mary asked, "what about last October? The police reported that the neighbors said the argument sounded physical. But again, you both said it was only a verbal argument. Do you remember that one?"

Kala squeezed her eyes closed. "Yes, I remember," she said. "I was about six months pregnant with my last son Malohi at the time. I was talking on the phone with my cousin when Afa came home. I hung up when he came in. He didn't like me talking on the phone. He was so mad. I didn't know why. He kicked me in the stomach, and I fell. When I asked him why, he said I must have been talking to my baby's father. I told him it was my cousin, but he wouldn't listen. He yelled. He threatened to kill me. He was always saying things like that. When the police came, they asked me if I was hurt. I guess I must have been bending over or holding my stomach or something."

"Did you seek medical attention?" asked Mary.

"Yes, they took me to the hospital. But I didn't tell them what happened. They said the baby would be all right as far as they could tell. But he did come early, and he wasn't as strong as my other kids."

Mary and I sat silent, waiting to see if she was going to add more. When she didn't, Mary spoke. "Thank you, for sharing all of that. It couldn't have been easy."

"By the way, we do have some good news to tell you," I said. "We went to talk to the two nurses who had been doing your prenatal care. They said they were waiting for us to come. One of them, Patricia, told us about the night you went in to give birth and how you tried to talk to her about what had happened to Juna, but Afa heard you and threatened you. We believe she'll be a good witness for us at trial."

"I like them. They were nice to me."

"There's one more thing," I added. "It's about the night Juna died. What you told the police didn't make sense. You and Afa both said that maybe the other kids hurt Juna. But the medical evidence shows that he was hurt too severely for a child to have caused the injury. Can you tell us what really happened?"

121

Kala nodded. "Well, it was Saturday. Afa had just got home from work, and he was angry again. He said he heard from someone at the soap factory that Juna's father had come back to town. I tried to calm him down. I told him I wanted to be with him, not Juna's father, hoping that would calm him down, but he kept yelling at me and threatening me.

"The next day was Afa's birthday, and I told him I wanted to make him a nice cake. We had just bought a car, so I said I would go buy some eggs and frosting so that I could make him a cake. He was mad, but he let me go."

I asked, "How long were you gone?"

"I don't know. Maybe between a half hour to an hour."

"Okay, so what happened when you got home?"

"When I got back, Afa was sitting on a chair in the front room. I remember it perfectly. He was holding the girls, one on each leg, and was pulling them close to his chest. The girls were crying, and he was crying too. I stared at him. I didn't know what to think. I'd never seen him cry before. He said, 'I'm so sorry, I'm so sorry.' But he wouldn't tell me what happened. I glanced around the room but didn't see Juna, so I went to find him. Something was wrong."

Kala sat up straighter and started speaking faster and louder. "I found Juna in his crib. His face was bruised, and he was having trouble breathing and was turning blue. His body was stiff, and his little arms were shaking. I yelled for Afa. I asked him what happened. He wouldn't say. I went to pick up the phone to call 911, but Afa grabbed my arm and took the phone away from me. I didn't know what to do. I turned Juna over and hit him on the back in case he was choking on something. I tried CPR."

Kala was openly crying now without constraint. She had her arms wrapped around herself and was rocking back and forth, moaning in between sobs but saying nothing.

Mary urged Kala to continue, asking, "Okay, what happened after that?"

"Juna died in my arms... Afa wouldn't let me call! He said he would kill me and the other kids if I did. But I should have called anyway. It's my fault my baby is dead!" She shook uncontrollably, and her sobs got louder.

"I should have left Afa. When my son was born, I named him after Afa so that Afa would love him. But he never did. He told me he never would. I should have left him." Kala was quiet and appeared to be trying to calm herself. Finally, after a long silence, she asked, "What's going to happen to me now?"

"I don't know," I answered with the same honesty that Kala finally used with us. "But we're going to fight your case. We're going to help you every way we can. We can explain to the jury how abusive Afa was. We can explain how Afa was angry when he got home from work that day. We can tell them how you were gone when Juna was hurt and how Afa threatened you to keep you from calling 911."

Mary nodded supportively.

Hope glimmered in Kala's eyes for the first time in a long time.

"Kala," I said, "did you tell *anyone* about how Afa abused you? Did you ask anyone for help?"

"I was too ashamed to say anything to my family. I

prayed to the Heavenly Father to help me and to protect my children. I did go to my bishop, though. I had a strong feeling he would help me. I told him I wanted to leave Afa, that I wanted a divorce."

"Did you tell him that Afa hit you, Kala?" asked Mary.

"Yes. But I didn't tell him everything."

"What did the bishop do?" asked Mary.

"He told me I should not get a divorce. He told me to do marriage counseling. He gave me a referral for counseling and said the church would pay for it. I believed that God had inspired me to go the bishop, and the bishop in his wisdom had showed me the way God wanted me to go. I prayed to the Heavenly Father and thanked him."

"So, did you and Afa go to counseling?" Mary asked.

"No. Afa tore up the paper with the address. He said that counseling was for white people, and he slapped me in the face over and over until I apologized to him. He made me promise I would never leave him." Kala put a hand over her eyes.

Mary's eyes met mine. There would be no more talking today. There had been enough crying for one day. Mary put her hand on Kala's arm, and we all sat quietly.

"I'm okay," Kala said after a while. "So, what do you think? Am I going to be okay at trial?"

"We think things are shaping up pretty well for us at trial," I said, noncommittally. "There is one thing we should bring up first, though. Our investigator couldn't find Afa to question him, but the prosecutor said they found him. They apparently are going to call him to testify against you."

Kala eyes opened wide, and she sat up straighter. "What's he going to say?"

"I guess they expect him to say the same thing he told the police the night Juna died, that he was at work and when he came home, he found you with Juna and that Juna was already hurt when he got home. That way, the jury will think that it must have been you who hurt Juna."

"But Afa knows I didn't do anything," Kala said defensively. "When I talked to him on the phone, he told me he knows I didn't do anything."

"When did you talk to him on the phone?" I asked, surprised at the revelation.

"I called him from the jail."

"When was that?"

"During the couple of weeks after I was here at the jail I called him several times."

I said, "The jail records those calls. Let's make a note to subpoena those phone records. That way, if he testifies and claims that Kala did do something, we can use the tapes to impeach him, to show the jury that he previously admitted that he knew it wasn't Kala. And there's one other thing about Afa that we can use against him. A month ago, he was charged with terroristic threats. The probable cause statement filed with the charges says that he threatened to kill some renters at a house his father owns if they didn't pay up. We've sent a subpoena to get the police reports about that case. We hope to identify potential witnesses that could testify about how violent Afa can be. That'll support our argument that the only reason you didn't tell police the truth the night Juna died was that Afa had threatened you."

Kala frowned. "So now Afa is going to be at the trial? Afa told me he would kill me and my other kids if I told anyone what happened. If he's there at the trial, I don't think I'll be able to testify. I'll be too afraid."

We needed Kala to testify to establish our defense. We had tried but failed to get statements from Kala's daughters about what happened. It would be inadmissible hearsay for anyone else to testify about what the kids said about how Daddy did it. One more idea jumped into my mind to try to give Kala confidence.

"Mary, why don't you tell Kala about the domestic violence expert you found."

"Sure. We've decided to have an expert named Adya Singh testify in your case about the dynamics of domestic violence. I sent the prosecutor a notice of expert for her yesterday. She should be able to testify that women who are in abusive relationships do tend to lie about the abuse. It's very important that we explain to the jury why you didn't tell police what happened at first. But her testimony won't mean anything if you don't testify to say you're not guilty, if you don't explain to the jury what really happened."

Kala shrank back into her plastic chair and buried her head in her hands. "I can't."

Becoming more and more dispirited about our prospects at trial myself, I tried to give her, and myself, some encouraging news. "We also sent an investigator to the soap factory where Afa works to ask some questions. Afa's supervisor said Afa was always getting into arguments and fights, and they were about to fire him anyway. It's a long shot, but if the judge will let it in, that's one more little bit of evidence for our battered woman defense."

"Afa did get fired," Kala said. "My aunt Lovai said that Afa blamed your investigator for him getting fired, for nosing around and asking questions about him, making it look like he did something wrong. He was mad. Sione said Afa bought a gun."

I glanced at Mary. I was sure we were thinking the same thing without having to say it. Afa flattened my tires after I blamed him in court for the murder. Now he had a gun.

Bump, bump. The guard was knocking on the window, pointing at his watch. It was lunchtime, and morning visiting hours were over. Not wanting Kala to miss lunch, we gathered our papers.

"Thank you," Kala said. "You're the first ones who have ever been there for me. No one has ever stood up for me before."

As we got up to leave, I was grateful that Mia had persuaded Kala to tell us the rest of her story, but if Kala wasn't willing to tell that whole story to the jury, it was all for nothing. If we couldn't do something to change Kala's mind, we wouldn't be able to establish our defense.

Then, she would likely be convicted of murder.

Chapter Eighteen

Kala's trial was finally here, and my stomach was churning, a rarity for me after all these years, but I didn't know how in the hell we were going to make our case for Kala's innocence without her testimony and without the testimonies of her daughters. A life sentence awaited her.

Kala sat next to me wearing a simple flower print dress that Mary had personally selected from a well-equipped walk-in closet full of nice street clothes we provided for our incarcerated clients to wear during trials. Also, she didn't have any chains. For trial, unlike other hearings, defendants have a constitutional right to appear without chains. Otherwise, the jury has more of a tendency to convict.

We were back in Judge Russo's courtroom. The first thing on the agenda was to pick a jury. Given the challenges we were facing in our case, selecting a good jury was critical to having any chance at all of acquittal.

"Please stand for the jury," bellowed the bailiff.

As we stood, the bailiff held the door as some thirty potential jurors shuffled nervously into the courtroom, each wearing a number hanging from a cord looped around their necks. The bailiff guided them to sit in numerical order, seating them one row at a time until the courtroom's benches were all practically full.

Judge Russo addressed the jury first. He thanked

them for showing up at all, since we all knew that jury service was not at the top of the list of things they wanted to do this week.

The judge quickly covered some basic questions to ensure that the people who had appeared today were eligible to serve on a jury. He instructed them that to serve on the jury, they needed to be over eighteen, to live within the county limits, that they could not have any felony convictions, and that they must understand English.

"The defendant is charged with murder," the judge said a little more loudly than I thought necessary. Some of the potential jurors started shifting uncomfortably in their seats. That was fine with me because we didn't want anyone on this jury who was going to be shocked or overwhelmed emotionally by the nature of the charge. I tried to make a mental note of who they were.

"The trial is scheduled to last all this week," stated the judge. He asked the group if any of them had any compelling conflicts or medical problems that would prevent them from being able to sit and pay full attention to the trial for the full week.

One woman raised her hand.

"Yes, juror number fourteen," the judge said, "what is your concern?"

"I'm a doctor, and I'm on call in the ER this week. I don't see how I can miss the whole week."

"I'm sorry. General work responsibilities are not grounds for avoiding jury duty if you're selected to serve. Everyone who is selected will receive an official notice of service to give to your employers. Is there anyone else?"

No other hands were raised. Many probably had

work conflicts, but if the emergency room didn't count as a significant conflict, probably no job did.

Next, the judge asked if any of the potential jurors knew the attorneys, had already heard about the case, or if they or their family members worked for law enforcement.

Finally, the judge had agreed to let us, the lawyers in the case, ask some more specific questions. He addressed Randy Johnson first.

"Mr. Johnson," asked the judge, "does the State have any questions?"

"No, Your Honor," stated Johnson. "The State's satisfied with the qualifications of the jury." Then he sat down.

Johnson's ploy was clever. He signaled that he trusts *all* of the jurors, which tends to make those jurors more sympathetic to him. I didn't have the luxury to pass up the opportunity to question the jury, however. Our only chance was to get a jury that was supportive of our arguments.

Mary had done some extensive research and preparation and had come up with some good questions about what we had decided were the two most critical issues in the case.

Judge Russo. "Mr. Bravo, do you have any additional questions for the panel?"

"Yes, thank you," I said as I took a few steps closer to the potential jurors. "I do have a few questions to ask." I tried to make eye contact with all of them before I started.

"First, there will be evidence presented in this case that Ms. Tausinga was the victim of domestic violence. Some people feel that no woman should put up with violence and so they feel unsympathetic to a woman who has stayed in such a relationship. Please raise your hand if that's how *you* feel."

Confused expressions appeared on several faces, probably because we were painting a picture, quite intentionally, that the *defendant* in this case was a *victim*. I waited. No one raised a hand. We expected that. In group settings, some people are shy about giving their opinions, especially when it reveals a bias. I was ready with another question on the subject to dig deeper into the jurors' beliefs.

"Can you think of any reasons why a woman might stay in a bad or abusive marriage?"

Several hands went up. I called on them one at a time. Mary noted their answers on the cards we had prepared for each. We had anticipated the answers we got: "For the children's sake" was the number-one response. "Hope things will get better" was a distant second but was still not the answer I was looking for. I kept prodding.

"Who else? Give me another reason why a woman might stay with an abusive man."

"Fear," a woman said, finally.

I didn't see a hand, but I knew who had spoken. I saw it in her penetrating stare, like maybe she had personal knowledge on the subject.

I glanced at Mary, and she nodded as she put a star by juror number ten. That was the answer we needed. I had planned a follow-up, equally important.

"Now, along those same lines, can you imagine any circumstances where you might lie to police?"

Again, there was no immediate response. I expected none. Who was going to admit in public they might lie to police? Nevertheless, I persisted.

"I understand that under *normal* circumstances, *none* of you would lie to the police. What I'm asking you to consider is whether you can think of *any* circumstances, clearly *not* normal, where you or some other regular person *might* lie to police."

I waited. I was determined to keep waiting until I saw a hand go up.

"Fear."

This answer came from a different woman this time, juror number eight. She made eye contact with juror number ten and nodded. I didn't have to look at Mary. She was scratching out another star.

There were no other hands, but I was satisfied that *everyone* could understand the point. I let that answer sink in before moving on.

"Okay, on another subject...a child may testify in this case. I would try to avoid it if I could. She's only four years old. How many of you would find it difficult to rely on the statement of a young child?"

Mary and I were, of course, hoping to find jurors who would be willing to accept the statement of a young child, but it was equally important that we identified people who wouldn't. I saw hands and followed up.

"Why is that? Why would it be hard for you to accept the testimony of a young child?" I asked juror number six.

"They make up stories."

This was an answer we expected.

"Okay, anything else?" I asked.

"They have poor memories."

"Fair enough. I saw one other hand." I pointed to

juror number fourteen with my right index finger.

"They can be influenced by adults."

That's the answer we didn't want to hear but figured we would. Mary nodded. I knew she was marking an X by juror number fourteen.

Having drawn the bad answer, I immediately tried to create a more positive vibe in the courtroom. "Okay, now, under what circumstances would you find it *easier* to rely on a child's statement?"

The question was vague, and I didn't see any hands, but I did have some suggestions in mind. "For example, how about if it's clearly a spontaneous remark and so obviously not the result of suggestion by an adult? Any hands?"

Two hands went up.

"What if an adult authority figure questioned or challenged the child's statement, but the child stuck with the original statement? Wouldn't you agree that such a statement ought to be considered a relatively reliable statement?" I raised my own hand and was nodding my head because I wanted some hands on this one.

And I got them. This question was a setup for what we hoped would be Lei's testimony. When Amanaki said that Daddy did it, and Lei asked, "Don't you mean Mommy?" Amanaki didn't change her statement. It was an important point, but I had made it now. So, I thanked the jury and told the judge we didn't have any other questions at this time.

All that remained now was for Randy and me to pick the eight people who would be on the jury. *Picking* a jury is a misnomer, however. We don't pick who we want to be on the jury. We can only eliminate people we for sure did not want on the jury.

So that was what we did next. Johnson struck four names off the list of potential jurors. I struck another four names, and the first eight of the remaining names constituted the jury that would hear the case.

"Very well." The judge reviewed the list. He called out the numbers of those first eight remaining jurors and had them come sit in the comfortable chairs in the jury box, and then thanked and dismissed the other potential jurors.

"Ladies and gentlemen of the jury," said the judge. "It is 11:30 a.m. We will now take a lunch recess before we hear the opening statements of the attorneys. Meanwhile, you may wish to contact anyone who should know that you'll be in trial this week. Also, the bailiff will hand you a list of places where you can have lunch. Please be back to the courtroom by 1:00 p.m."

"Let's go compare notes before we take off for lunch," I whispered to Mary as the jurors filed out of the courtroom.

Mary and I took the list of all the people in the jury pool into the nearest empty conference room in the hallway outside of Russo's courtroom.

I pulled out my notepad. "Let's see if Johnson excluded any of the jurors who gave us good answers. I excluded number fourteen, the one who said children can be influenced by adults and the one who said children make up stories. But did we keep both of the women who said that fear would keep a woman in an abusive relationship?"

Mary double-checked her notes. "Well, yes, yes, we did."

"An oversight by Johnson?" I suggested.

Mary said, "I assume he was betting that women would be more likely to convict someone charged with injuring a child. So, he struck men. In fact, three of his four strikes were men."

"How about the ER doctor?" I asked. "Did we keep her?"

"No," said Mary. "Johnson struck her too."

"Maybe because she complained about missing work," I replied. "Sometimes I let those people go because I'm afraid they'll be checking their watches and not paying attention to the trial."

"But we did keep two jurors who raised their hands on your question about reliable statements from children," added Mary. "I think we did all right overall. What do you think?"

I pondered her question for a minute before coming up with an answer. "I think it's hard to predict what a jury will do. But I think we have a fighting chance with this one."

Chapter Nineteen

"Good afternoon, ladies and gentlemen of the jury."

Randy Johnson had a great voice and presence. Not only was he handsome and debonair, but unlike me with my bald head, he had perfect hair—blond and recently trimmed.

As he began his opening statement, I could tell that the jury was immediately mesmerized. This was important for Johnson since everyone had just returned from lunch, a time when people tend to want to nap.

Mary laid a yellow pad on the table, ready to take notes. We had decided that she would present our opening statement, and I, as lead counsel, would do the closing argument.

Johnson continued. "This is a sad but simple case. The evidence will show that on the day in question, Afa Tausinga Junior, a small sixteen-month-old toddler, was brutally killed by his mother, Kala Tausinga. She was home alone with Junior and her other two children while her husband Afa was at work. His timecard will show that he didn't leave work until 5:30 p.m. When he arrived home, he found Kala holding Junior in her arms. His baby was badly bruised and appeared to already be deceased.

"When interviewed by police, Ms. Tausinga made the claim that perhaps it was her two little daughters who hurt Junior. These little girls were barely age three and age four at the time.

"But Dr. Ed Schmidt of the medical examiner's office will explain that Junior had a massive subdural hematoma, or bleeding in his brain, that was so severe that it would not be possible for a young child to have caused the injury.

"Now I'm not saying that Ms. Tausinga set out to harm her son that day, but she was clearly overwhelmed. The house was a total disaster area. The other children were both dirty and developmentally delayed. Kala was pregnant and probably just couldn't keep up with everything. So, it must have been in a fit of desperate anger that she did what she did."

Johnson paused and tried to meet the gaze of each person on the jury. "And finally, we will review the contents of Ms. Tausinga's videotaped statement to police where she confessed that the reason she didn't call 911 until six hours later, after her husband came home, was because the baby was bruised, and she thought she would get into trouble if she called the police and would go to jail. Well, ladies and gentlemen, unfortunately, that's exactly where she belongs."

Johnson sat down, and Mary confidently took her turn at the lectern.

"Good afternoon, ladies and gentlemen. Researchers say that *some* jurors make up their minds early in a case, usually right after the prosecutor's opening statement." Mary chuckled and got some smiles in return as we had hoped she would with that line. In my experience, jurors who like you are less likely to convict.

"But of course, as the judge has instructed you, you

need to keep an open mind until you have heard all the evidence before deciding anything."

Mary paused to allow her words to sink in before continuing. "Right from the beginning of this case, I don't want there to be any question in your minds about our position, and that is that Kala Tausinga is absolutely innocent of this charge. She sits here with us today as a victim—*twice* a victim.

"First, Kala was subjected to years of repression and emotional and sometimes even physical abuse by a violent and controlling man, a man who never loved her child, which was, by the way, his *step*child," added Mary, pausing to let that fact sink in, "and who, in a fit of jealous rage, killed her child.

"Second, tragically"—Mary stared at Randy Johnson— "Kala is now being victimized *again* by the State, which has wrongfully accused her of the death of her own little baby.

"The State's version of events, which you have heard from Mr. Johnson, is based on a *one-day* investigation by police. In fact, most of the officers were involved only from midnight until 2 a.m. Only a couple of them did interviews the next day. So, we're being generous when we give them credit for a full one-day investigation.

"But *we* did a thorough investigation. And here's what we found out. Afa Tausinga was an angry, jealous man who used fear, threats, and violence to control Kala.

"In order to fully understand what happened, it's important for you to know that after Afa had an affair, Kala did leave him once. During that time, she got pregnant by an acquaintance of her husband named Vai.

Afa wanted to get back together with her and promised to be good to her. She had always hoped to have a family, so she took him back. She named her son Afa Junior, Juna for short, hoping that her husband would grow to love him. But he never did. And things soon got worse between Afa and Kala."

I took a moment and glanced at Johnson. Mary was about to drop a bomb on him and his case. This next part was all news to Johnson. I turned back to watch Mary.

"Then, on the tragic day of Juna's death, Afa came home from work angry. He was angry because he had learned that Vai was back in town. He told Kala that if he even heard that she was around him, he would kill her and himself.

"Kala tried to calm him down. She went to the store to buy a few groceries, including some eggs, to make him a cake since his birthday was the next day. But when she returned, she found Afa sitting in the living room with her two daughters. He was crying. Kala asked him what happened. He cried out, 'I'm so sorry!'"

"Objection," Johnson said, standing up quickly. "That is hearsay."

Judge Russo didn't wait for Mary or me to answer the objection.

"Mr. Johnson, as you well know, this is merely an opening statement. The admissibility of the actual evidence presented will occur only when the witnesses are called to testify. If you have any objections to Ms. Tausinga's testimony, you may make them when she testifies."

When she testifies? God help us, I don't know if she

will testify.

Johnson sat back down.

Mary continued and doubled down on the point Johnson objected to. "As I was saying, when Afa blurted out that he was sorry, it took Kala a moment to find out what he was sorry about. She hurried through the house and found Juna in his crib. He wasn't breathing. She wanted to call 911 for help, but Afa wouldn't let her. He threatened to kill her too if she did.

"As you might imagine, Kala was terrified. Five hours passed before Afa finally allowed her to call 911. He concocted a story and told Kala to go along with it. The story was not true. That false story is what you just heard from the prosecutor."

Mary turned to look at Randy Johnson and then back at the jury, letting her accusation against him sink in before continuing. "We will also present testimony from several other witnesses with important information we gathered from our own investigation that proves Kala is not guilty of murder. Among these several witnesses include Kala's children, a registered nurse, and the State's own medical examiner. So, remember, keep an open mind after you hear the State's case, and then we'll give you the rest of the story.

"Finally, let me say that we are glad that you are all here to protect Kala's rights today and throughout this trial and to prevent a terrible miscarriage of justice."

She walked back to our table and took her seat.

"Call your first witness, Mr. Johnson," boomed Judge Russo.

I stood up quickly. "Your Honor, I invoke the exclusionary rule."

"Very well," declared Judge Russo as he scanned

the courtroom. "I am ordering that anyone who may be a witness in this case must leave the courtroom and wait in the hallway until you are called to testify."

I turned to see who Johnson would bring in as his first witness just in time to see Afa getting up to leave the courtroom. I saw him frowning at Mary. *Shit.* He must have come in during opening statement and heard her accuse him of murder. Then I caught his eye, and we had a stare down. Could he see that I knew it was him that cut my tires?

Afa stared at me over his shoulder as he left the courtroom, and he bumped into someone coming in— my daughter Bella. My heart jumped. Bella had come to court to see the testimony of the medical examiner who was scheduled to testify today. As Afa pushed through the outer door, he scowled at Bella.

I motioned for her to sit on the back row. Mia smiled at Bella and waved her over to sit next to her. Bella and Mia had not met, but I had spoken to each of them about Bella coming to court and asked Mia to keep an eye on Bella while there, describing her so Mia would recognize her.

"Your Honor," Johnson said, as he led someone through the courtroom door, "the State calls Detective Terence Jenner."

An overweight, graying officer dressed in uniform ambled into the courtroom slowly behind Johnson. He was sworn in by the judge's clerk and settled heavily into the witness chair.

Randy Johnson stood in front of his table. "Detective Jenner, please tell the jury what happened last December second."

"Well, my partner and I were grabbing a snack at

the 7-11," the officer volunteered, quite unnecessarily, "and at about midnight, we got a call. As I approached the door at the address we were given, the door opened, and the baby's father, Afa Tausinga, was standing there at the door. He had a baby in his arms wrapped in a blanket. Inside the apartment, we also found the defendant, Kala Tausinga, and two young girls."

Johnson asked, "Did you examine the baby?"

"Yes. He had bruises and scratches on his face. I didn't examine him beyond that."

"Was he alive?"

"Oh no. I checked his pulse. He was definitely dead."

"Can you please describe the apartment?" Johnson asked.

"The apartment was messy, cluttered. There were stains on the carpets and writing on the walls. The dishes hadn't been done. There was clothing all over the place on the floors, and one of the cupboards was broken."

Johnson nodded. "I'd like to show you the State's Exhibits Nos. 1 through 10. Please tell us if you recognize them." Johnson picked up several large photographs and walked them over to the officer for him to review.

Detective Jenner examined each one. "Yes, these are photographs I took of the inside of the apartment."

Johnson turned to the judge. "Move for admission, Your Honor."

"No objection," I said, having planned on submitting them myself.

"When you went into the apartment, did you speak with Kala Tausinga?" Johnson asked.

"Yes," said the detective. "She stated she was home alone with her two children, well, the three children. She said that at about 4:30, she left the apartment to go pay her rent and that she was gone for about five minutes."

"Did she say where she left her son when she left?"

"Yes. She said she put him in his crib."

Johnson paused and glanced toward the jury.

"Now, Detective, please tell the jury, did Ms. Tausinga say if she noticed anything unusual when she returned?"

"Yes. She said that she found her son in the crib and saw that he was in physical distress. He had his fists clenched tightly, and he was shaking and having a hard time breathing."

Johnson asked, "So, the baby was alive when she found him?"

"Yes."

"And did she call 911?"

"No," the detective replied. "She said that she began to perform CPR on the child."

"Did the CPR revive the child?"

"No, it did not."

Johnson cleared his throat. Then, he asked his next question more slowly than the others. He was distinctly enunciating each syllable. "Now, Detective, did you ask Ms. Tausinga why it took her so long to call 911?"

Johnson was now laser-focused on the single most damaging part of his case against Kala. There was no avoiding it, given that Kala had given a videotaped interview to police. Because she was the defendant, the rules of evidence stated that the testimony about what she said to police was not hearsay.

Police officers frequently gave damaging testimony about the so-called "confession" of the accused. Most of the time, they overdid it, trying to make a big impression with the jury. Then, on cross-examination, we used the actual statements, which were typically far less damaging than what the officer had said, to point out the exaggeration to the jury. Not this time, though. Johnson must have reviewed the recorded interview with the officer because the officer absolutely nailed what Kala said in the interview—word for word.

"Yes," Detective Jenner said. "She said she was afraid."

Johnson asked, "Did she say what she was afraid of?"

"Yes. She said she was scared because the child had bruises on his face, and she thought she might go to jail. She said that she had heard that's what happens to parents who hurt their children."

Johnson glared at Kala before continuing, and several jurors followed his lead. "One last thing...you said earlier that the baby had bruises and scratches on his face."

"Yes. They were obvious," the detective confirmed.

"Did Ms. Tausinga say *how* her baby got the bruises and scratches on his face?"

"She stated that a couple of days earlier, she put the baby on the floor in the living room and that when the baby crawled over to the other children's toys, those children attacked the baby and caused the scratching and bruising."

"How old are these other children?"

"They were little girls, ages three and four, if I

recall."

"Thank you, Detective Jenner. No further questions for this witness."

"Detective Jenner," I said as I approached the lectern, "one point of clarification up front. You referred to Afa as the baby's father. I take it you are *unaware* that he is actually *not* the baby's father?"

"Oh, yeah. I'm sorry. I found out later that he is actually the baby's stepfather."

"Thank you." I like to thank witnesses to reward them for cooperating with me. It seems to make them more willing to agree with the points I need them to make. I started here with an easy question, one I knew how he would answer, just so I could thank him for doing so.

I motioned to the pictures that Johnson had given the detective earlier. "Now, let me redirect your attention to the photos that show that the apartment was messy. Is it fair of me to say that Afa appeared to you to be a strong and healthy young man?"

Detective Jenner nodded. "Yes, I guess that's fair to say."

I turned and tried to make eye contact with the women on the jury as I got ready to ask the next question, a question suggested by Mary.

"Strong and healthy enough to maybe help his pregnant wife pick up and clean up the apartment?"

I caught at least one of the women on the jury nodding.

"Uh, yeah. I guess so," the detective said.

"And you knew that Kala here was nine months pregnant?"

"Yes, she was very pregnant."

"And she told you that due to high blood pressure and diabetes, she had little energy and needed to rest?"

"She did say something about high blood pressure."

"Thank you. Now Mr. Johnson here made a big point of having you testify that Kala didn't call 911 until almost midnight, correct?"

"Yes, that's right," replied the detective.

"But isn't it true that Afa, Kala's husband, also said he was home before six p.m.?"

Detective Jenner paused, and his gaze fell before answering. "Um, yeah, I guess that's right."

"So, Kala's husband *also* waited for several hours to call 911, isn't that true?"

"Well, yes. I guess that's true," the detective admitted.

"Thank you. Detective Jenner, you're the case manager for this case, right?"

"Yes, that's correct." He sat up straighter in his seat, obviously proud of this important point.

"I need to double-check something. It seems like every report written by the West Valley City Police Department was dated December 3. Does that seem correct to you?"

"Yes," replied the detective. "That was the day immediately after we found the baby dead."

"So, I'm not exaggerating when I say your department did only a one-day investigation in this case?"

Detective Jenner shifted in his seat and didn't answer right away. He glanced toward Johnson for help but got none. His gaze faded away from the jury. Finally, he cleared his throat. "Um, well, you know, we were very busy." Jenner fidgeted in the witness chair. "We kept getting calls. That next day, we got a call for a home invasion robbery where someone got stabbed and—"

"That's okay," I said, interrupting him. "I understand. But isn't it true that at the end of your department's investigation, you hadn't decided on a suspect yet?"

"No, that's not correct."

I wasn't surprised that the detective was scrambling to defend his actions. He was testifying in front of a jury in a murder trial. But I prepared for this. I've done this too many times to let a cop get away with cheating on his answers. I made my move.

"Detective, let me direct you to your synopsis in the last paragraph in your report. You wrote that the child had injuries that required further explanation and that the matter remained active pending a postmortem examination of the body. Doesn't that indicate the case was still open? You hadn't arrested *anybody* at that time, correct?"

"Um, that's correct."

I decided to rub it in a little more. "I don't see any conclusion by you that Kala Tausinga committed a murder."

"That's right," replied the detective. "But it doesn't mean she wasn't a suspect."

"Thank you for bringing that up because speaking of suspects, didn't you also consider her husband a suspect at that point?"

"Yes."

I wasn't sure I was going to get that *yes* answer, but I decided to keep going with the positive answer.

"Why is that?"

"He had access to the child as well."

I asked, "Are you also aware of his history of domestic violence?"

"Objection," interjected Johnson. "Those matters are hearsay and not relevant to this case."

I turned my attention onto the judge. "Your Honor, I'm not asking for any specific statements made by Mr. Tausinga, which indeed would be hearsay. Instead, I'm merely questioning the detective about the scope of his investigation, whether he considered alternative suspects. To that end, whether he became aware of these sorts of incidents is relevant."

"I understand your point, Mr. Bravo, but I disagree," said Judge Russo. "At this point at least, without further foundation demonstrating relevance, the objection is sustained."

"Very well, Your Honor. I'll move on." I put my attention back onto the witness. "Detective, isn't it true that Afa also gave inconsistent statements about how he learned of the child's death?"

"Objection," Johnson yelled. "The question calls for hearsay."

"Sustained," ruled Russo without waiting for my argument.

I could see I was going to get totally shut down on this line of questioning. It hurts your credibility with the jury when the judge keeps sustaining objections against you, so I elected to stop the bleeding.

"Very well, Your Honor. I have nothing further for this witness anyway."

Judge Russo glanced at the clock on the wall. "I have to participate in a settlement conference on a civil case. It won't take long. Let's take a short recess." Russo raised a finger. "And then we'll have time for *one* more witness, Mr. Johnson."

Chapter Twenty

Grateful for the recess, Mary and I grabbed some file folders to go plan for the next witness. On the way out of the courtroom, I waved at Bella and Mia who were sitting close together. Mia had a hand on Bella's arm.

After the recess Johnson was going to call a key witness, the medical examiner. We used the break to review Mary's questions for him one last time because his answers could make or break our case. On our way back into the courtroom, I made eye contact with Bella and mouthed, "Now it's the medical examiner." She gave me a thumbs-up.

Once the jury settled into their seats, Judge Russo's clerk had the doctor raise his hand and promise to tell the truth. Johnson got right to the point.

"Dr. Schmidt, you conducted the autopsy of the child known as Afa Tausinga Junior, did you not?"

"Yes, I did."

Dr. Ed Schmidt was the epitome of how I had always imagined a medical examiner would look before the pretty actresses on the various CSI shows graced the airways. He was paunchy and had a gray beard. I had questioned him many times before. He was good at his job.

"Would you describe that body as you first observed it?"

Dr. Schmidt pulled his black-rimmed glasses from his jacket pocket and pushed them onto his straight nose. "It was a young child, clothed in a one-piece sleeper and disposable diaper. He had some obvious injuries to the face that were easily visible without even removing the clothing."

"And what was his weight?"

"He weighed 18.3 pounds."

"Doctor, did you compare that with growth charts used by doctors in evaluating the weight of children?"

"Yes. He was quite underweight. That weight puts him at the third percentile for his age."

While Johnson marked his growth chart as an exhibit and walked it over to the medical examiner to show the jury, Kala touched my arm. "That doesn't sound too good. Is it important?"

"Don't worry about that," I whispered. "That's the least of our problems."

Still standing near the witness stand, Johnson handed several eight-by-ten-inch photographs to the doctor. "Let me also show you what has been marked as State's Exhibits eleven through twenty, and ask you what these are?"

Dr. Schmidt methodically reviewed the photos. "Those are all photographs taken as part of the autopsy."

"Your Honor," said Johnson, "I move for the admission of these exhibits."

"Counsel?" queried the judge, looking at Mary and me.

"Your Honor," said Mary as she stood, "we have no objection to exhibits eleven through eighteen, but we do believe that numbers nineteen and twenty are legally inadmissible for reasons described in detail in our pretrial motion regarding the admissibility of evidence."

The reasons "described in detail" to which Mary euphemistically referred for the benefit of the jury were that photographs nineteen and twenty were bloody nightmares.

"Numbers eleven through eighteen are admitted," said the judge. "Mr. Johnson, I don't think I want the jury to see the other photographs."

The judge had finally made a ruling that went in our favor, but the way he did it would leave the jurors speculating about what they didn't see and probably conjuring up their own gruesome images in their minds.

The M.E. was going to lay it all out in words for the jury. The autopsy photos wouldn't come in, but the words still would. It would be bad.

"As part of the internal examination of the head, we reflect the scalp forward," said Dr. Schmidt in a comfortingly clinical tone. "In doing so, I saw that the bruising on the inside of the scalp was more diffused or widespread than the bruise on the outside."

I glanced sideways and saw several jurors frowning at Kala with obvious disgust during Dr. Schmidt's description of this injury. Exactly what we were hoping to avoid.

Johnson continued, "In addition to reflecting the scalp, did you also examine the inside of the skull?"

"Yes." Dr. Schmidt turned toward the jury. "As I removed the cap of the skull, I saw a hemorrhage inside of the head beneath the dura, which is a membrane that coats the inside of the skull. This blood would be called a subdural hematoma."

Johnson glanced at the jury, appearing to assess their responses to the M.E.'s testimony. "Now, let's go down farther on the face, particularly the eyes. Did you notice anything unusual externally on this little baby's eyes?"

"Yes. There was a little bit of bruising on the upper eyelids on both sides."

"Why is that significant?"

"Given the absence of skull fractures on the base of the skull, those would be bruises as a result of direct impact to those areas."

To my left, Kala made a whimpering sound. Choking back tears, she had both hands covering her face. How would the jury interpret that? Remorse for killing her child?

Johnson made a check mark on his notepad. "Now, going farther down the body, did you find other injuries?"

"Yes, a clustering of faint bruising on the left side of the abdomen below the ribs but above the hip bone."

"Is it consistent with something as large as a fist?" Johnson suggested.

"Yes," the doctor said. "Or perhaps a foot."

A woman in the jury gasped out loud. Johnson paused, letting that emotion echo in the courtroom.

"All right," Johnson said finally, "are there any other significant injuries that you noted?"

"Yes. To the legs."

"Please explain."

"There were large bruises, light blue in color like the others, that wrapped around each of the legs."

"Is that consistent with something in your experience?"

"Yes. To me it's consistent with a grab mark, with somebody grabbing and squeezing, with the upper extension of the bruise being related to fingers grabbing onto the child in that area."

"Could you tell if that was consistent with an adult's hand or a child's hand?"

"It's quite obviously not a child's hand," asserted the medical examiner as he turned again to the jury, apparently to emphasize the point. "In one of the photographs we took as part of the autopsy, I placed my hand in that particular area, and that bruising would fit the size of my hand."

"Thank you," said Johnson, obviously pleased with his carefully crafted and thorough questioning. "I have one last question for you, Dr. Schmidt. What did you list as the cause of death on the death certificate?"

"Homicide."

"No further questions," said Johnson as he walked away from the lectern.

Judge Russo asked, "Will there be any cross-examination by the defense?"

Mary stood. "Your Honor, would you please give us a minute to discuss that?"

"You may have a minute."

Mary whispered, "The jurors seem upset, and they're staring at Kala like they're ready to convict right now. Should we ask to continue until tomorrow? Or at least ask for a recess so that they can calm down a bit?"

"I don't think so. We need to try to change their mindset as soon as possible. The M.E.'s testimony was bad for sure. But we need to try to present our defense that these injuries, horrific as they are, were simply not caused by Kala."

"You're right," Mary said. "I know exactly what to do."

Mary scooped up her notes and strolled up to the lectern with the calmness that comes in a murder trial only after meticulous preparation.

"Dr. Schmidt, based on the objective criteria in your pathology report, do you have any opinion as to the time of death?"

Mary knew the answer to this question. We had discussed it at length. It was the key to our defense. She started out with it on purpose. Primacy and recency have been found to be significant in the attention span of jurors. The first thing and the last thing you say sticks in their minds more than anything else. We knew Dr. Schmidt's answer to the time of death question from the autopsy report. Schmidt didn't know the time of death.

His head jutted back as his forehead furrowed. "I can't say."

Mary was developing this point in some detail. Our rule was that if you had an important point that you wanted the jury to get, you had to hammer it home. And then hammer it again. "Dr. Schmidt, what are the physiological indicators used to determine time of death?"

"The things that we use to determine time of death are rigor mortis, or stiffening in the joints, lividity, which is the settling out of blood in the body after circulation has stopped, and body temperature."

Mary nodded. "What can you tell, if anything, from those indicators in this case?"

"Not much. With infants, anything that's written

about them in the textbooks, you can pretty much throw out the window because they're so small that they don't follow the rules usually."

"Nevertheless," persisted Mary, "would it be fair to say that rigor could set in within a short time where an infant is involved, perhaps as soon as one hour?"

"Possibly an hour, maybe two, no more than three," the doctor agreed.

"Is it also correct that no one ever attempted to take a body-temperature reading in this case?"

"That's correct," Dr. Schmidt replied.

"Because of that, we don't know the time of death," said Mary, more as an assertion than a question.

"Yes, that's true."

Mary nodded and waited a moment, wanting to make sure the jury got that point before continuing. "Now, Doctor, let's turn to the subdural hematoma. What can you tell from the subdural hematoma regarding the time of death?"

Again, Mary knew the answer to this question. She had a background in pathology from helping her father with autopsies and had studied up on the subject during our preparation for trial.

"The hemorrhage was recent," Schmidt answered as expected.

"And what is it exactly that you do to determine if a hemorrhage was recent?"

"I take a slice of the brain and do a histological microscopic analysis, to see if there are any reactive changes present in the brain, such as fibroblastic infiltration, endothelial proliferation, or hemosiderin-laden macrophages."

"In layman's terms, Doctor?" Mary chuckled and

glanced toward the jury, some of whom were obviously relieved by her request.

"Yes. Sorry. Those are changes that occur in the brain when the body is trying to heal itself after an injury."

"Were these indicators present in this case?"

"No. This indicated to me again that the injury was recent."

"I have one final question on the subject of time of death, Doctor. Are all of the medical and physiological indicators you've described consistent with the child's injury and subsequent death both occurring *after* six o'clock p.m. on December second?"

"Yes. That's certainly possible under the circumstances."

Mary glanced at me. It was a signal we had talked about. She was wondering if she needed to work that time-of-death issue any more than she already had. I gave her an unobtrusive thumbs-up to indicate that she had done the job.

She came over to the table anyway. Whispering, she said, "I need to talk to you about something Schmidt said. I need time. Can we get a break?"

I checked my watch. It was only 4:15. But if Mary said we needed time, we needed time. I stood up.

"Your Honor, given that we've been going all day, and given that it may be difficult for the jury to digest much more of this medical testimony, we would suggest and request that the court adjourn until tomorrow morning."

"I agree," said the judge without waiting for input from Johnson. "Court is adjourned until 9:00 tomorrow morning."

Chapter Twenty-One

Mia and Bella stood waiting for us as we left the courtroom pulling our rolling file carrying cases. I gave Bella a hug and asked, "Did you like court?"

"I'm not sure *like* is the right word," Bella said, making a face, "but yes, the medical examiner's testimony was especially interesting. But is he finished testifying? I wasn't sure by the way it ended."

"No, he comes back tomorrow morning."

"I don't think I can get off school two days in a row," Bella said, frowning.

"Don't worry about it. I'll fill you in later about how it goes, and if you're interested, I can get you a recording of the hearing."

"That sounds good. I've gotta go do some homework now."

I leaned in and kissed Bella on the forehead.

"Love you, Daddy," she said as she turned to walk away.

"Love you too, sweetheart."

"Bye, Mia," Bella added with a smile.

"It was nice to meet you," Mia said, waving at Bella before turning back to me. "She's sweet. And smart too from the conversation we had."

"Yes, she is," I said. "She'll have completed all of the Advanced Placement classes at her high school by the end of her junior year. I'm happy to take all the credit."

Mia and Mary glanced at each other, and both turned back to me at the same time, but before either could speak, I quickly held up my hands. "Okay, okay, she may have had something to do with it too."

As I grabbed the handle of my rolling file case and turned to go, Mia said, "Frank, please wait a minute."

Mia had been watching the afternoon court hearing even though her official clients, Kala's husband and children, had not come.

"I need to talk to you."

"What is it?" I answered cautiously. Mia somehow convinced Kala to open up to us, but she still played for the other team.

Mia pointed to the conference room door next to the court's door. "It's probably better if we talk in here."

Mary followed behind us. Once we were all seated, Mia got right to the point. "I'm convinced that Kala's innocent. What can I do to help?"

Mary's eyebrows arched high on her forehead.

"Um, you can talk to Johnson. He totally disregarded what *we* told him about the case. Maybe he'll listen to you and end this trial. Tell him what you think. He's the only one who can stop this train from crashing into the station."

"I did talk to him," Mia said.

"What happened?" I asked.

"Johnson threatened to have me fired. He told me to shut up and do my job. He ordered me to be like the other victim advocates who stay with the family members *he* says are the victims."

159

Mia paused, pressing her lips together. "But I don't care what he says. I have to do what I can. I *have* to do something."

"Mia," Mary said, after a pause. "There is one thing you might be able to do. The prosecutor's investigator found Afa. They're bringing him in to testify. Kala is so afraid of Afa that she's saying she won't testify now. But we need her to tell her story to the jury, to tell them everything that happened. If we can't get her story out, the jury could easily convict her."

Mia leaned forward as Mary described Kala's fear.

"Would you be willing to talk to her again?" Mary asked. "Go see her at the jail. Try to persuade her to testify and reassure her that she can be protected? That's what you do, right? Can you please help Kala find the courage to testify?"

Mia set her jaw. I could see the veins in her neck. "Afraid of Afa you say?" She made a fist in her lap. Her demeanor changed. "Yes," she replied, firmly. "I need to speak with some friends first. But I'll go talk to her. I told her I would continue to visit her."

I wasn't sure what Mia meant about her friends, but clearly, she would try to help. I gave her the business card that included my cell phone number. "Text me at that number. That way, I'll have your number too. I want you to follow up with me as soon as you know anything more."

Mia stood up to leave.

"Wait," I said. "Mia, I want to know how grateful I am that you're helping us. Helping Kala. I don't know how to thank you."

Mia nodded. "Don't worry about that. This is just

something I have to do."

As I pushed my own chair back to get up, Mary put one hand on my forearm and held the other one up, which I took as a sign to wait.

"While we're here, let me run an idea by you I've got for tomorrow. It's a way to demonstrate our point that Kala didn't hurt her baby. It also supports what the other kids are saying about *Daddy* hitting Juna's head on the wall."

"Yeah, yeah, go ahead. Tell me what it is."

"Dr. Schmidt said during his testimony that the bruise on the baby's thigh was the size of *his* own hand. So, if we could compare Schmidt's hand with Kala's hand somehow, maybe we could show that her hand is smaller than his. Then, when Afa testifies, we compare his hand too. I had the idea in court but couldn't think quickly enough of a way to do it."

"That would be great," I responded, liking the idea. "Jurors love concrete evidence. We could do our own O.J. argument in closing: *if the glove don't fit, you must acquit*."

"The thing is *how* to do it." Mary's voice carried an undertone of excitement. "We'd need to make imprints of everyone's hand and mark them all as exhibits. The jury could take them when they go to deliberate. With something concrete to review, I think it'd be easier for them to get past Kala's original statement to police of finding Juna injured before Afa came home."

"Yes. I see your point." Joining in her excitement. "The jury can play CSI. There's a reason why there are so many CSI shows on the air. People love to see facts and solid evidence to solve the case."

Mary said, "You have most of the rest of the

State's witnesses on cross tomorrow. I only have the nurse who examined the other children, and I'm ready for her. So, I'll see what I can come up with tonight while you get ready for your witnesses."

"Okay," I said. "I'm planning to go back to the office to do some prep. I still need to organize my notes to cross-examine Afa and prepare some arguments for the judge about the admissibility of Afa's terroristic threats arrest. I also have to prepare to cross-examine Alicia Simpson. I found an article she wrote about interviewing children, and I want to pick through it to see if there's something I can use to question her."

"Sounds good," Mary said while writing on her yellow pad.

"But there's one other problem with the hand evidence." I gazed up at the ceiling. "How do we know how big everyone's hands are? I wasn't paying attention to the size of Schmidt's hands. What if Afa has some weird midget hands or something? What if we end up proving that Kala did commit the crime?"

"Well, if that happens, the appellate lawyers could always argue that she had ineffective assistance of counsel at trial." Mary chuckled at something we both knew wasn't very funny because that meant that we as her lawyers had fucked up and that Kala was convicted because of it.

Chapter Twenty-Two

I yawned and pushed my cup of coffee to the back of my office desk. More caffeine was the last thing I needed right now. Rest would be my priority tonight after a long day in trial.

I clicked the print button to get my notes for the next day's critical testimony and shut down the computer. Slipping on my suit jacket, I grabbed my keys with one hand and my file for the next day in the other and headed out to the parking lot to go home.

The sun had set about an hour or two earlier. It was dark now. I tossed my notes onto the passenger seat, fired up my Jeep, and headed for the exit from the parking lot to the narrow side street that connected with 500 South.

It was late, and I wasn't much of a cook anyway, so I decided to get some takeout for dinner. As I turned left and started west on 500 South, a large white commercial truck that had been parked just east of the office turned on its lights and pulled out from that parking spot, also heading west on 500 South.

Is that truck following me?

After a few seconds of staring at it in my rearview mirror, I figured I must be paranoid because I had been thinking about and talking about Afa Tausinga so much. I couldn't see the driver because the truck's high headlights blazed right through my rear window.

Confident that this truck pulling out behind me was merely a coincidence, I signaled to turn left toward my favorite Thai restaurant. The white truck's left-hand turn signal came on immediately too.

Maybe it was going to turn left anyway.

Okay, so it turned left. I still didn't think it was following me. But just in case, I decided to put the theory to the test and got ready to turn left again at the next intersection. As I pulled into the left-hand turn lane, the truck changed lanes again as well and pulled in behind me.

Now I was getting pissed, probably for no reason at all of course. The truck could have needed to go back in the direction from which it must have come. When I turned left, the truck waited for an oncoming car to pass before turning. After I made the turn, I glanced back over my shoulder and could see the side of the truck. *No.* The streetlights in the intersection clearly illuminated the logo of the soap company Afa worked for on the truck's door.

Okay, I had to admit that now I was getting nervous for good reason. Afa's threats to Kala, the damage to my Jeep at the golf course, and Kala saying Afa had bought a gun all flashed across my mind.

As the truck turned the corner behind me, I stepped on my gas pedal to put some space between it and me. But as I picked up speed, so did the truck. *Shit.* I reached to try to wrestle my cell phone out of my pant pocket to call 911 but looked up to see that the light had turned red. I braked hard. The truck caught up and stopped behind me, before lurching forward again and crashing into my rear bumper.

Now what? Get out? And then what? Tell the

driver we have to call the police about the accident? Wait for the police to arrive?

This was no accident. Whoever was driving the truck wanted me to stop and get out of my vehicle.

I jerked open my door and stepped out. The driver of the truck also got out and slammed its door. As he started striding toward me, the truck's headlights revealed his identity—Afa, with fire in his eyes.

I was in good shape, but he was bigger than me and his fists were clenched. I remembered the knife in my tire and the gun I was told he had bought, so I made a quick decision.

"Fuck off, asshole," I shouted as I jumped back into my Jeep, thankful I had left the door open. I pulled it closed with my left hand at the same time I jerked the shifter into drive and pushed the accelerator to the ground. Afa caught up in time to pound hard on my window as I pulled away into the intersection.

Shit, cars coming! It had slipped my mind that the light was red. I swerved around one car whose horn was screaming at me and floored the accelerator again.

I saw that the next light was red too. Not wanting to take a chance with having to stop at another intersection, I decided to take a hard right. As I approached the next corner, I could see that Afa's truck had followed me into the intersection despite that red light but hadn't had as much luck as I did. Two cars screeched and honked as they approached him. Hard metal crunched. Afa was blocked in.

I turned my full focus back to the road as I sped around the corner to the right. Taking advantage of Afa being stuck in traffic, I yanked my steering wheel hard right to enter the parking lot of an apartment complex. I sped toward the back, pulled into a parking stall, and turned my lights off to hide out for a while.

No, this was no good. Gotta call the police. Afa had an accident at that last intersection. Gotta go back and make sure they get him.

I punched in 911 on my phone and sat it on my lap waiting for the operator to answer. After turning my lights on, I backed out of the parking space and accelerated toward the exit to the street. Not wanting to waste any time, I didn't stop as I approached the street. I quickly glanced to my left as I entered the roadway. The last thing I remembered seeing was the grill of that big white truck approaching my driver's side window.

Chapter Twenty-Three

"What's your name?" came a voice from the darkness. "*Sir*, can you tell me your name?"

I opened my eyes and saw a young woman in scrubs with a stethoscope around her neck. *Must be dreaming.* Then, darkness again.

"Sir. Sir!"

I opened my eyes and tried to focus on the voice. The woman in scrubs again. A nurse?

Her face hovered above me; her forehead furrowed with concern. "Can you tell me your name?"

"Yeah. Sure. I'm, ummm, *shit*, I don't know."

"Well, my name is Dr. Emery," the woman said. "Don't worry. Short-term memory problems are common in this kind of accident.

"How about today's date?" the doctor asked.

The left side of my head throbbed as I searched the inside of my head for the date. "Dammit. Unh uh."

"Do you know where you are?"

"Hospital," I answered with confidence this time.

"No. Sorry, I mean where—as in which city?"

I thought hard before answering this time. Not confident now, I said, "Salt Lake?"

"Yes. Good," the doctor said. "By the way, we found a couple of identifying documents in your wallet. I hope you don't mind that we looked. Here they are. They should help."

A young Hispanic man with shortly trimmed hair and dressed in full police gear entered the hospital room. A nametag above his badge read *Officer Rios*. "I heard he was awake," the officer said, a little more loudly than necessary, at least to my ears.

Turning my attention to the driver's license the doctor had given me, I tried hard to focus, and saw my name and address. The other ID was my Utah State Bar card. It all came back to me in a rush.

"Ohhh. Yeah. Truck hit me." I rubbed the side of my head again and was happy not to feel any blood.

"How long have I been out?"

"For several hours. You regained consciousness a couple of times but were incoherent. So, I gave you something to help you sleep. It's morning now."

"I have some questions," the officer said.

"Me first," I insisted, focusing my attention the best I could from my prone position on the hospital bed. "Did you get the driver of the truck?"

The officer said, "No. It was a hit and run. Another driver reported the accident to police. He didn't get the plate number but saw a man driving and did see a business name on the side of the truck as it sped away from the accident."

"Yeah, not an accident, I think," I said.

"Anyway," the officer said, "we found the truck damaged and abandoned a couple of miles from the scene. The driver had fled. And the truck had been reported stolen, so we don't know who he is or where he is."

"Afa Tausinga," I said. "Lives with his father."

"Are you sure?" asked the officer.

"Yeah. He got out of the truck at the intersection. It

was him."

"Do you know his address?" Officer Rios asked, pulling out his pen and note pad.

"No. Maybe in my notes," I answered, pulling my covers off and putting all my effort into swinging my feet to the floor. "Where's my file?"

"Nooo," Dr. Emery said quickly as I got to my feet. "Please lie down. You're not ready to get up."

The room spun around me. I turned and steadied myself by putting both hands back on the bed. The breeze on my backside made me realize I had a hospital gown on but nothing else. Dizzy and a little embarrassed, I flopped back down onto the bed and dragged up the covers.

"Officer, please give him a break for a minute," Dr. Emery insisted. "We don't want his blood pressure to spike. We're monitoring him for a possible hematoma."

"Yeah, okay," Officer Rios said. "But I'm going to wait right here."

When the room quit spinning, I said, "Hey, Doc. I'm happy to rest, but I need to call my friend Mary to come pick me up. I'm a lawyer. We're in a murder trial this week. I have to be back in court this morning."

"Your phone is in your pants over here on the chair with your jacket," Dr. Emery said. "I'll get it for you, but I have to tell you no one can pick you up right now. The good news is you have no broken bones. But your head impacted the window of your car. We want to hold you at least another day for observation."

The doctor handed me my phone. I couldn't think of Mary's number, but I replied to the last text she had sent me. "I'm in hospital. Call me."

Mary arrived quickly. I told her that Afa had

followed me and had T-boned my car. I assured her I was fine, but she cornered the doctor and asked her a question. Something about brain injuries.

After a moment, Mary came over to my bed. "Dr. Emery said she thinks you'll be fine but insists on keeping you here at least until this evening."

"Can you call the court? Tell them what happened?"

Mary called the court clerk, and she quickly set up a conference call with Judge Russo and Randy Johnson. Mary put it on speakerphone.

"Go ahead, Ms. Swanson." I recognized Judge Russo's voice. "I understand that you have a motion."

"Yes sir. Last night, my co-counsel Frank Bravo was injured in a hit and run. He's at the University Hospital under observation for a concussion. They're holding him today and possibly overnight or longer. So, I'm making a motion to continue the trial until he's available."

"I see," the judge replied cautiously. "Mr. Johnson, what is the State's position on a continuance?"

"The State opposes any continuance," Johnson declared in a strong voice. "The jury has been seated. Jeopardy has attached. If we had to start over, the defense could move to dismiss based on the Double Jeopardy clause. Moreover, my witnesses have taken time off from work to appear on my subpoenas. I believe we should go forward."

"Ms. Swanson, I'm inclined to agree with the State," Judge Russo said, "for the reasons stated by Mr. Johnson. But for the record, if I were to agree to continue your case, would you be willing to waive any defect in the proceeding and stipulate that seating a new jury would not constitute double jeopardy?"

After staring at me for a moment, Mary said, "We're not willing to waive any of our client's constitutional rights, Your Honor."

"That's what I thought you'd say," the judge replied.

"Well, Your Honor," Mary said, "we request a one-week continuance? By then we should be ready to go forward."

"Sorry, Ms. Swanson," said Judge Russo quickly, "I have another in-custody trial scheduled to begin later next week. My clerk is telling me that the next available date for a five-day jury trial would be at least two months out. If I recall correctly, your client asked for a speedy trial. The best I can give you is one day."

"Very well, Your Honor, we'll try to be ready."

"Make it work, Ms. Swanson," replied the judge. "Make it work."

Chapter Twenty-Four

Mia had just found a parking spot at the courthouse when she got the text from Mary that court was cancelled for the day because Afa had injured Frank, and Frank was in the hospital.

Mia put her car in park. *Oh no.* Worried about Frank, Mia called his cell number immediately. It rang several times. *Maybe…*

"That you, Mia?" came the familiar voice on the other end.

"Yes, it's me." Mia could tell Frank's voice was weak, and he was speaking more slowly than usual. "I just got Mary's text. She said Afa hurt you. What happened?"

"He crashed his truck into my car. I was totally knocked out. I don't remember anything until I woke up in the hospital this morning."

Mia remembered all the violence that Kala endured at Afa's hands and now *this*. "Oh, my God, Frank. Are you going to be okay?"

"Not sure. I think so. Doctor said no bleeding in my brain. That's good. Have a bad headache, though. Not so good. Get dizzy when I stand up. So, lying down. Except to go pee."

Mia smiled at the way Frank shared such personal information with her. He was growing on her. He wasn't so bad after all, for a defense attorney anyway.

"Oh sorry," Frank said. "Too much information. On meds. You know."

"Don't worry about it. Hey, I'll come by and see you later. Can I bring you anything? A snack or something?"

"Not hungry. Probably the meds. But thank you. Very kind of you."

"You're welcome. By the way, did they arrest Afa?"

"No. Police say he abandoned the truck. Ran away. I told police he might be at his father's house. But I don't know if he'll go back there."

Mia wondered whether The Sisterhood would decide to help Kala and stop Afa. Maybe they could find Afa.

"Mary told me that there's no court today. When will it start up again? I don't want to miss Kala's testimony."

"Tomorrow. Judge wouldn't give us more time. Hope to see you there."

"I'll be there."

"Hey, Bella's calling," Frank said. "Gotta take it. Talk to you later."

Mia terminated the call with Frank, switched to Bluetooth, and called Victoria. The phone rang as Mia backed out of the parking spot at the courthouse to go back to her office.

"Hello, Mia."

"Hi, Victoria," Mia said urgently. "Is there a decision? Will The Sisterhood help Kala? Things are getting worse. Afa just hurt Frank, one of Kala's lawyers."

"Yes. The decision was final yesterday," answered

Victoria. "Sounds like it was none too soon."

Mia gave a sigh of relief. "Great. What do you do next?"

"Well, Mia, it's more like what do *we* do next," Victoria said. "Given your close connection to Kala and your background and preparation, Xtina said to tell you, to *ask* you, to help."

Mia's phone buzzed. She glanced at it in its holder on the front of the dashboard and saw that it was an incoming call from Randy Johnson. She didn't pick it up.

"In fact," Victoria added after a pause, "as you must recall, Xtina spoke of making you a part of The Sisterhood. If that's something you want, you'll have to prove yourself."

Mia had been thinking about what Xtina said and asked tentatively, "What is it that I am supposed to do?"

"This isn't the sort of discussion we have over the phone," Victoria said. "I have assigned Zena and Sally to help you with Kala's case. You'll meet with them to discuss what to do. We've brainstormed some ideas about how to proceed and when. But there is some preparation for you to do. Can you meet with Zena and Sally the day after tomorrow, in the morning?"

"I have trial all this week," replied Mia. "It's Kala's case. It's part of my job to attend and be with the family."

"Well, Mia," Victoria said, "Kala is your case. It's up to you, I guess. Is it important to you or not?"

Mia's phone buzzed again. A text from Randy Johnson. Mia pulled over.

"I'm sorry, Victoria. Kala's prosecutor has just

contacted me twice. Can you hold for a minute while I see what it's about?"

"Sure, Mia. I have a minute."

Mia pulled into a strip mall and stopped in the first available parking spot. She grabbed her phone and opened Randy Johnson's text message.

"Mia, you didn't answer my call, so I am putting this in writing. I wanted you to know that I checked the visitor's log at the jail and saw that you visited Kala again after I instructed you not to do so. Well, now you can do whatever you want to because you are fired. Your fob has been disabled, so you cannot even come into the office. Call the victim advocates' secretary if you have any personal items you want, and she will ship them to you."

"Are you still there, Victoria?" Mia asked, feeling a weird combination of hurt, anger, and a sense of destiny too. "I will make time to meet with Sally and Zena. Just say where and when."

Chapter Twenty-Five

I made it to court the next day, but Judge Russo had already taken the bench when I pushed through the courtroom doors. I was on a mixture of a pain reliever for my headache and a stimulant to help me focus. Still woozy, I was glad that Mary had the first witness today—the ongoing cross-examination of Dr. Schmidt, the medical examiner.

Mary must have heard the courtroom door open because she turned around as soon as I came in. When I sat down between her and Kala at the counsel table, she glanced down at her watch. "Right on time, Frank." Concern wrinkled her forehead.

Kala touched my arm and leaned over to talk in a low tone. "Mary told me what happened. I am so sorry. Are you okay?"

"I seem to be fine, Kala. Thank you for asking."

Judge Russo cleared his throat. "It's good to see you, Mr. Bravo."

"Glad to be here. As opposed to the possible alternative."

"I understand," said Judge Russo, with a wry grin. "For the record, is the defense ready to go forward today?"

"Yes. Yes, we are," I replied.

Judge Russo nodded approvingly and told the bailiff to go bring the jury into the courtroom.

Mary said, "By the way, I reviewed the witness notes that you forwarded from your phone yesterday, and I'm ready, willing, and able to take over for you on your witnesses today."

"Thank you. But I think I'll be able to manage."

She searched my face. "Well, please at least let me know if you need help or a break or something. I'm sure the judge will cut us some slack under the circumstances."

The bailiff led Dr. Schmidt from the hallway up to the witness chair. Mary picked up where she had left off two days earlier.

"May I approach the witness, Your Honor?"

"Of course, Counsel. You needn't ask again."

Mary walked up to Dr. Schmidt and extended an eight-by-ten photograph toward him. "Now then, Dr. Schmidt, I'd like to show you what has been marked as State's Exhibit No. 14. Please describe what it shows."

Dr. Schmidt studied the picture. "A door that's been damaged."

"Specifically, it has a crescent-shaped indentation in it toward the top, right?"

He nodded. "Yes, that's right."

"I'd like your opinion on something. Considering the size of the indentation, as indicated by the ruler in the photo, is the size and shape of the indentation consistent with the child's head impacting on the door?"

Eyes still on the photo, the doctor answered, "Head impact could potentially produce that damage, I suppose."

"And could that head impact result in the subdural hematoma you found?"

"I couldn't rule it out." He shrugged.

"Thank you," said Mary. "Now let me focus your attention on one final matter, the bruising on the leg you've already described."

Mary walked to the prosecutor's table and selected another photograph. Johnson frowned, apparently oblivious to her purpose. In his direct examination of Dr. Schmidt, he had made it a point to show that the bruises on the child's thighs could not have been made by his three- and four-year-old sisters, thereby effectively rebutting the explanation Kala had given to police in her original statement, that the other children must have hurt Juna.

Mary was now about to use one of the simplest of CSI techniques to engage the jury's attention and to actively illustrate her own point. She was about to exploit the critical detail that Johnson had overlooked.

"Now, Dr. Schmidt, I'm showing you what has been marked as State's Exhibit No. 16. Is this the photograph you described earlier showing the bruises on the child's thighs?"

He examined the photo for a few moments. "Yes, this is the same photograph."

Mary walked back to the defense table, opened her case file binder, and pulled a twelve-inch ruler from the inside pocket.

"Your Honor"—Mary turned from Schmidt— "I would like the court's permission to create a new exhibit for the jury."

Johnson stood up behind the prosecution table and opened his mouth, but no words came out. Mary paused to watch him to see if he were going to interrupt. After a moment of his not saying anything, Mary turned back to the judge.

"We would like to have the bailiff take Dr. Schmidt back into the secretarial staff's area and photocopy his hand. After that we'll measure it with this ruler and mark it as a defense exhibit."

Johnson said, "This is very unusual, Your Honor."

"Do you have some specific *legal* objection to make, Counsel?" Judge Russo asked.

"Well, no, I guess not," Johnson replied, frowning.

"Then carry on, Counsel."

Mary left the courtroom with Dr. Schmidt and the bailiff as the rest of us waited. Several jurors exchanged glances, fascinated by what was occurring.

When Mary and the doctor returned, Dr. Schmidt testified that the photocopy labeled Defense Exhibit No. 1 accurately depicted his hand. Mary got him to confirm that in his prior testimony, he said that the bruises on the child's leg were the same size as his hand. Mary took the ruler and measured the length and width of the hand and wrote the measurements on the exhibit with Johnson standing over her shoulder as she did it.

Mary asked for and obtained permission to show the exhibit to the jury immediately instead of having them wait until after the trial to examine it. Mary waited for the jury to pass the exhibit around. She didn't want to interrupt them or distract them by talking to the judge. Eventually, she indicated to the judge that she had no other questions for the doctor and sat down.

Johnson sat fumbling with papers at the prosecution table. We appeared to have taken him by surprise with the hand-size issue. He scribbled a note and stood up.

"Dr. Schmidt, I have one question regarding the bruising on the child's thigh. Is it possible that the bruise could have been made by an adult *female*?"

"That would depend on the size of her hand, but I couldn't rule it out."

"Thank you," Johnson said, having made the only point he could about the bruise on the child's thigh. "Now, Dr. Schmidt, I'd like to return to the issue of time of death. Yesterday, uhm, sorry, the day before yesterday in cross-examination, you indicated that the injury resulting in the child's death could *possibly* have occurred after six p.m. What I would like you to tell the jury is whether the physical evidence is *consistent* with the injury having occurred at about 4:30 p.m. *instead of* 6:00 p.m."

"Yes, the evidence is also consistent with the injury having occurred at 4:30 because we cannot determine the exact time of death."

Johnson was sharp. In two questions, he had substantially undone most of Mary's work. The hands could be those of a female, and the injury could have occurred at 4:30 instead of 6:00. Both of those facts, if accepted by the jury, pointed back to only one conclusion, that Kala killed her baby.

Johnson's gaze followed Dr. Schmidt as he made his way out of the courtroom and then switched to track a well-dressed young blonde woman who entered at the same time.

"The State next calls Alicia Simpson to the stand."

Alicia Simpson was the expert about whom Johnson gave us late notice. His Notice of Expert had said that Alicia Simpson would be going to testify that the disclosures by the Tausinga children may have been coached. We suspected that Johnson would later argue that Kala's aunt and uncle had somehow taught the children to say that their father hurt Juna in a desperate attempt to save Kala from a murder conviction. It was a good argument—one the jury might accept. I found myself nervously clicking my pen over and over.

Simpson testified that she was the Director of the Children's Justice Center or the CJC. Johnson had her explain to the jury that the CJC was where Kala's two girls were taken to be interviewed the day after Juna's death. She went into extensive detail about the training, education, and experience that she and her staff had in the field of interviewing children properly.

Then Johnson asked, "Ms. Simpson, are children prone to suggestibility from adults?"

Several jurors perked up at this question. They must have remembered the issue from jury selection and were waiting for it to come up.

"Yes. Until about age ten, children are likely to accept statements by adults as true. I should clarify that this is particularly true if the adults are authority figures for the children, such as adult family members."

"Do the children then repeat the stories suggested by the adults?"

"Objection, Your Honor," I interjected as I stood up. My head was swimming from the quick movement. I put both hands on the table in front of me for a second to steady myself. "Speaking of suggestion, that's a leading question."

"That's true, Counsel." Judge Russo nodded. "Objection sustained."

Grateful the judge had so quickly agreed with my objection, I sat back down.

Johnson glanced from me to the judge and then back to Ms. Simpson to whom he produced a charming smile. "How do children respond to hearing suggestions from adults?" he asked, rephrasing the same question.

"Children will tend to adopt the suggestions and may repeat them later," she said, dutifully adopting Johnson's earlier suggestion.

"Now, Ms. Simpson, given that you are an expert in conducting interviews, please explain to the jury the proper way to do it."

"Certainly." Ms. Simpson took Johnson's directive literally because she physically scooted her chair to her left and faced the jury.

"To avoid contaminating a child's disclosures, we always start with free recall questions or invitation questions, such as 'Tell me everything you did this morning.' Then, we might follow up with a cue question, such as asking them to tell us more about some specific thing the child mentions."

"Thank you," Johnson said. "Now, can you give us an example of the type of questioning that is suggestive and should be avoided?"

"Yes. On the other end of the spectrum are leading questions such as 'Your uncle Tommy touched your peepee, didn't he?' Forced choice questions are also suggestive such as 'Did he touch you in the bedroom, in the basement, or in the garage?'"

"Thank you. Now Ms. Simpson, will you please explain to the jury why is it that you are so careful in conducting these interviews with children?"

"It's simple. Children who are not interviewed properly can end up telling stories that are simply not true."

Johnson paused. It was exactly the answer he wanted. A few jurors were nodding in agreement.

"Ms. Simpson," Johnson said, "are you also aware of statements reportedly made by the children while in the custody of their aunt and uncle?"

Johnson had taken the bait. We might get the children's statements in after all.

"Yes, I am."

"What is your opinion about the reliability of any statements made by the children?"

"The disclosures I'm aware of were not given to a trained interviewer, and they lack detail and context. They were also apparently not made until several days after the incident, which causes me some concern.

I glanced at the jury, who seemed engrossed by Ms. Simpson's testimony. That testimony was bad for us. Mary sighed and shook her head almost imperceptibly.

"Finally," Johnson said to ensure he kept the jury's attention, "as an expert in child interviewing, please tell the jury if you find the children's statements to be reliable."

"No," Ms. Simpson replied, "I would not rely on such statements to begin legal action against an adult."

The jurors' eyes widened some in response.

"Thank you. I have no further questions at this time."

Johnson scooped the loose pages of his notes together from the lectern and started back to his table to sit down. But as I stood up, a juror raised her hand and asked the judge if we could take a short break.

The judge glanced at me with concern and then nodded. "Court will be in recess for fifteen minutes."

Chapter Twenty-Six

The recess, while unexpected, gave me a chance to update my notes for cross-examination based on Ms. Simpson's testimony on direct examination. Johnson had managed to get his expert to discredit the children's statements implicating Afa Tausinga as the murderer without discussing the actual statements. Clever. That would make it more difficult for me to get the statements in, but I had to try.

I approached the lectern and laid down an article I had found that was written by Alicia Simpson about interviewing children. I used it to prepare specific questions for my cross-examination, and it was what kept me late at the office two days ago. I was determined to transform Ms. Simpson into a witness for the defense.

Pulling the article open to my first yellow tab, I asked, "Ms. Simpson, you said that *free recall* questions are the most reliable because there is no suggestion made by the interviewer, right?"

"Yes, that's right."

"Along the same lines, would you agree that a *spontaneous* statement, one not made in response to any question, would tend to be reliable for the same reason?"

"Yes, unelicited reports of abuse are the most reliable," Simpson said, almost quoting from the article

I had on the lectern in front of me.

"Thank you. Now you have said that children can be influenced by adults and will tend to adopt suggestions made to them by adults. Is that right?"

"Yes. That's the most serious problem we see. We see it all the time," Simpson responded, seizing the opportunity to re-emphasize a key point that Johnson got from her.

"Okay," I replied. "I'm willing to *accept* that statement as true." I turned and saw puzzlement on Johnson's face. He had to be wondering why I seemed to be supporting his witness, not attacking her. I was about to show him why.

I turned back to the witness. "So, based on your testimony so far, I would like you to assume the following hypothetical situation—instead of a situation where a child hears a suggestion from an adult, let's assume a situation where a child makes a *spontaneous* statement reporting some abuse. Then an adult in authority challenges that statement and suggests a contrary alternative. Would you agree that if the child maintained his or her original report, despite a specific contrary suggestion by an adult in authority, it would be an indication that the child's original spontaneous disclosure was reliable?"

Ms. Simpson hesitated before responding. "Yes, I believe that it would."

Ms. Simpson's answer helped me. I could stop here and use that answer to argue that the Daddy-did-it statements were reliable according to the State's own expert. I pushed past my instinct to stop with that base hit and decided to swing for the fences.

"Thank you. Now let's take a more specific

example. Let's say an adult in authority tells a young child, 'Your daddy's coming to visit.' Then, the young child spontaneously says, 'No, Daddy stupid. Daddy hit Juna's head on the door.' "

"Objection!" Johnson leapt to his feet, knocking his rolling chair into the aisle in the process. "May we approach, Your Honor."

"Very well."

I followed Johnson to the bench self-consciously, a bit worried that I had overreached.

"Your Honor," whispered Johnson, "Counsel's trying to introduce the statements of his witnesses, the statement about Daddy hitting Juna's head. That's hearsay."

"Your Honor," I replied quickly, "Mr. Johnson elicited some examples of suggestive questions and answers from Ms. Simpson. And he asked her opinion *specifically* about the statements the Tausinga children made while in the custody of their aunt and uncle. By asking his expert about the children's statements, he *opened the door* so that in fairness, the *actual* statements should be put into evidence at this time."

"No, Your Honor," said Johnson, not waiting for the judge, "I specifically avoided talking about the actual statements and only elicited general principles of interviewing and reliability from Ms. Simpson."

"That's enough," said Judge Russo, raising his hand. "Mr. Bravo, I am going to deny your request to introduce the children's actual statements at this time. They are hearsay at this point. You may ask only general questions to Ms. Simpson. Do not go past that limitation. Do you understand?"

I nodded and walked back to the podium as

Johnson sat down. I couldn't end my cross-examination here right after the judge shut me down. That's the last thing the jury would remember. I needed to remind the jury what we were talking about and try to finish with something good. I scanned my notes to find something.

"Now, Ms. Simpson, I believe you were saying that a spontaneous statement made by a child which withstood a challenge and contrary suggestion from an adult in authority would be considered reliable. Is that correct?"

"Yes," she said again.

"Thank you. Now regarding what you said about there being a delay in disclosure by the children, did you know that the children have been exposed to both the Tongan and Samoan languages, as well as English?"

"That's what I understand."

"So, is it possible that a language barrier impeded an earlier disclosure?"

After a pause, she said, "I suppose that's possible."

"What about trauma? Isn't it fair to say that a young girl who had just witnessed the violent death of a sibling and then had been dragged away from her mother by strangers with guns might be in shock, and for that reason, might not be talking much?"

"I suppose that's possible also."

Ms. Simpson's level of cooperation with my examination had allowed me to finish on a positive note. I decided not to press my luck again.

"Thank you. No further questions."

Alicia Simpson's direct testimony hurt our case. But finding her article had kept us in the game.

Judge Russo scanned the jury apparently to make

sure they were all still actively following the lengthy testimony. "Counsel, it's been a long morning. May I inquire as to how many more witnesses you intend to call before lunch?"

Johnson and I turned toward each other at the same time. I took a step closer to him and spoke in a quiet voice. "What do you think?"

"It seems like the judge is suggesting to us that we wrap things up for this morning," he said. "But I have one more witness out in the hallway that I'd like to get to, if possible."

I nodded and shrugged. "That's okay with me."

Johnson turned back toward the judge. "Your Honor, if it please the court, I'd like to call one more witness if I may."

The judge frowned. "I guess you can call *one* more witness, Mr. Johnson. Then, we'll break until the afternoon."

"Very well," said Johnson, "the State calls Janet Willis."

A heavy-set middle-aged woman lumbered into the courtroom, was sworn in by the clerk, and settled into the witness chair.

"Ms. Willis," Johnson said, "please explain to the jury what you do."

"I'm a family nurse practitioner. I work at the Children's Medical Center with the Child Protection Team. My primary duties include performing medical evaluations of children when sexual or physical abuse is suspected."

"How long have you been doing this kind of work?"

"For about twenty-eight years."

"Did you have occasion to examine Amanaki and Emeni Tausinga on about December 4 of last year?"

"Yes, I did."

"Under what circumstances?"

"It was reported to me that an autopsy had determined that the children's little brother had died of an abusive head trauma. The Department of Family Services and law enforcement requested the medical examination of the children as siblings at risk."

Randy's eyes darted between Ms. Willis and the jury. "Please tell the jury what you found."

"Amanaki was extremely dirty. To differentiate the dirt from the bruises, the areas needed to be wiped clean. Many areas were suspected to be possible bruises; however, cleaning the areas showed them to be only dirty. There was also an increased amount of smegma in the genital area and fecal matter around the anal area. An examination of the ears revealed cerumen oozing out of the ear canal."

Johnson asked, "Did you do anything else with Amanaki?"

"Yes, I attempted to do a developmental assessment, but she was uncooperative."

"Did you also examine and make findings about the younger girl, Emeni?"

"Yes. The physical evaluation revealed extremely poor hygiene. Her hands and feet were especially dirty as well as the folds between the scalp and the ears. After we cleaned her, we found a purplish bruise on the edge of her ear approximately one-half centimeter in diameter. She also had a yellow discharge from her nose."

Johnson scanned the paper he was reading.

"Finally, regarding the hands of each child, did you notice any offensive wounds, or in other words, any injuries to their hands that would indicate either of them had hit someone or something with their hands?"

"No. Other than being dirty, there was no injury to their hands."

"Thank you. No further questions." Johnson walked away from the witness and sat down at his table.

"Ms. Willis," began Mary as she shuffled through a couple of pages of notes on the lectern, "first, I have a question about the scope of your assessments. As I understand it, you did a physical exam on each girl and after that attempted to do a developmental assessment?"

"That is correct," the nurse replied.

Mary said, "In your report of the physical exam, you talked about bruising quite a bit. But to be clear, is it correct that Amanaki was determined to have no bruises whatsoever?"

"That's correct."

"And Emeni had only one bruise, on her ear?"

"That's right."

"Otherwise, and let me read directly from your report, physically you found both of the girls to be *normal, healthy, and well-developed*?"

"That is true," replied the nurse. "Other than being extremely dirty, they were physically healthy."

Mary made a check mark on her notes. "Okay, now your examination was conducted some two days after the death of the children's little brother, correct?"

"That's what I understand."

"And the person who had custody of the children during that time was not Ms. Tausinga, right?"

"I only know that the paternal grandfather of the girls is the one who brought them in."

Mary continued. "Fair to say that this dirt could have accumulated during the two days during which he had custody of the children?"

"I don't have the information to answer that question. I only know they were dirty. I think they were too dirty for only two days."

Mary asked, "Did you know the children have a father who could have cleaned them?"

"Yes," the nurse said. "I understand that there is or was a father in the household."

"Now, according to your written report, you also conducted a sexual assault examination on the girls?"

"Yes, I did," the nurse replied.

"Was there any allegation or accusation or even suspicion brought to your attention that these girls had been sexually assaulted?" Mary asked, her tone of voice making clear that she was personally offended by such a thing.

"No, not that I know of."

"Yet you undressed them and examined their vaginas?"

"Yes," the nurse admitted.

"And found them to be completely normal?"

"Yes."

"And I see from your report that you noted no anal spasm or laxity," Mary added. "Doesn't this mean that you stuck something in the anus of each of these little girls?"

"Yes, that is part of the examination, to see how the anus responds. If there has been sexual assault, we expect either laxity or sphincter spasms."

"So, is it fair to say that it should be no surprise at all that after you conducted your *anal* examination, these little girls were, what did you say, *resistant* to participating in your developmental assessment?" Mary had raised her voice to emphasize her outrage.

"I'm not sure what you mean." Ms. Willis acted confused, but her face flushed.

"Your report says that Emeni was upset and screaming and that Amanaki, and I quote, 'sucked her thumb throughout most of the assessment and cried when she was not sucking her thumb.' Isn't that right?"

Nurse Willis didn't answer right away, clearly flustered. Mary remained silent and let her soak in the discomfort of the moment.

"Let me ask you one more question," said Mary after a while. "The prosecutor asked if the girls had offensive wounds on their hands from hitting. Isn't it true that a child could hold a weapon, such as a wooden block, and hit someone with it without injuring their hands?"

"Objection," interjected Johnson. "Calls for speculation."

"The State's whole case calls for speculation, Your Honor," Mary blurted out.

Judge Russo scowled at Mary's argumentative outburst and opened his mouth as if to berate her, but Mary quickly sat down without waiting for Russo to make any ruling on Johnson's objection.

Russo paused for a second and checked his watch. Instead of responding to the warring lawyers in front of him, he simply said, "That's all we have time for this morning. Ladies and gentlemen of the jury, thank you for the close attention you paid during a long morning of testimony. You are free to go until court resumes this afternoon at 1:30 p.m."

Chapter Twenty-Seven

As she had been instructed by Victoria, Mia drove around to the back of one of several nondescript warehouses in the industrial zone on the west side of town and parked. A door opened, and Victoria appeared and waved Mia inside.

"Hi, Victoria. I didn't expect you to be here. I thought it would be Zena and Sally."

"You can call me Vic. I was tired of being cooped up in the office. And don't worry, although Zena isn't here today, she still has her part to play."

The closing door echoed into the mostly empty space of the large steel and aluminum building. Mia saw only a few offices, a conference room, and what appeared to be a big storage unit.

Victoria led Mia into the conference room. Sally, who Mia remembered was the CIA operative, was already there. Both Victoria and Sally were in comfortable jeans and jackets.

The warehouse was clean, but the conference room was immaculate. The sparse furnishings included a small flowering cactus on top of a filing cabinet, and on the wall a painting of a flamenco dancer and a framed photograph of a woman on a mountain peak.

Mia stared closely at the photo. "Is that you, Sally?"

Sally smiled broadly. "Yes. Trekking in Nepal.

Something I wanted to check off my bucket list."

"That's pretty awesome," Mia said, nodding enthusiastically. She glanced at Sally with admiration, grateful to find there was a more friendly side to her than what Mia had experienced when being questioned by her at the meeting with the board of The Sisterhood. Then remembering what she had come for, she turned back to Victoria and Sally. "Now, were do we start?"

"Sally will lead this meeting," Victoria said, nodding at Sally.

Sally turned to a whiteboard behind her and picked up a marker. "We need to determine the mission parameters and define our strategy and tactics. First, the mission. Our target is Afa Tausinga, correct?"

"Yes." Mia nodded in agreement.

Sally put a check mark by Afa's name.

"Now, let's talk about time frames. Have system options failed?"

"What do you mean?" Mia asked.

"The Sisterhood has a strict rule. We only intervene when the system has failed to get justice for our clients. So, what I mean is, has the judicial system failed to resolve the matter? Is there still a possibility that justice can be served without our intervention?"

"I don't think so," Mia said. "I told the prosecutor he should be prosecuting Afa for murder, not Kala. But he said he wasn't going to do it. Afa didn't even get arrested for any of the four prior domestic violence incidents against Kala."

Sally turned to the whiteboard and drew a big X through the words System Options. "Game on, then. How about urgency? When do we need to move?"

"I don't know," Mia said. "Soon, I think. Afa has

also threatened the lawyers now and put one of them, Frank, in the hospital a couple of days ago. He needs to be stopped."

"Got it," Sally said. "Next, we need to find Afa and track him. See where he goes, where he sleeps, where he shits, and what his routines are. I understand he didn't go back to his father's house after the hit and run in the stolen soap company truck. We tried his phone number, and he's not answering. For starters, though, I'm thinking we should monitor his father's house and place a tracker on Afa's car."

"Sounds good," Victoria said. "What do you have in mind?"

"The cable-guy ruse," Sally said. "Victoria, you go in as the cable guy, so to speak, to investigate signal problems in the neighborhood, or to do a complimentary upgrade of the box, something like that. While you're there, you plant some audio devices."

"Consider it done," Victoria said simply. "And I'll take Mia with me, for some on-the-job training."

Mia turned toward Victoria. "I thought you were the executive director now and didn't go out and do fieldwork."

"Working in the office is interesting, but I can't let everyone else have all the fun," Victoria's eyes danced with mischievous fun. "Besides, you and I go way back. I feel a connection with you. I want to help. Help you."

Mia nodded and smiled, her eyes softening. "Thank you. I'm glad you're here. With me."

Sally's eyes darted back and forth between the two. With a tinge of annoyance in her voice, she said, "Sorry to interrupt your mutual admiration society, girls, but we still have some planning to do." When Mia and

Victoria had turned their attention back to her, she continued. "When you two find Afa's car, put a LoJack on it. And to help find his car, I'll ping his phone."

"Don't we need a warrant for that?" Mia asked, remembering conversations she had heard in court.

Sally stared at Victoria with a raised eyebrow.

"Don't you worry about that." Sally waved that idea away with her hand. "By the way, do you have a gun, Mia?" Her tone return was now all-business.

"Me?" Mia's heart leapt into her throat. "Why do I need a gun?"

"Listen to me carefully," Sally said, annoyance turning to an unmistakable bit of frustration in her voice. "You remember Zena, right?"

"How could I forget? The Amazon warrior I met at The Sisterhood meeting, right?"

"You could call her that. Anyway, Zena is Option A to deal with Afa. But sometimes, things do not go as planned, so we must make contingency plans. We need to be prepared with options, okay?"

"Okay," Mia replied, tentatively.

Sally's eyes bored into Mia's. "And Afa is a killer with a gun, right?"

"Yes."

"Come with me." Sally walked out of the conference room while Victoria held open the door. Mia followed closely behind, observing her surroundings along the way. Sally led them straight to the internal storage unit Mia had seen earlier. She punched in a code and opened the door.

Inside was another storage area with guns, guns of every type Mia could imagine—long rifles with scopes, assault rifles with giant clips, and numerous handguns.

"What's this one?" Mia pointed to something that resembled a shotgun. "What's this big round thing around the barrel?"

"That's a Streetsweeper shotgun. Lots of extra shells fit in that big clip. The mechanism quickly reloads the next shells, making for fast firing. Great for clearing a house full of targets."

Mia nodded, impressed.

"But that's not what we're going to give you, dear," Sally said, with satisfaction as she admired the artillery in the room like most women admire jewelry. "That's definitely overkill for our situation. And hard to carry around with you without attracting unwanted attention. Find yourself a handgun instead."

Mia carefully perused the assortment of pistols.

"Go ahead. Pick one up. See how it feels."

Mia picked up a Smith & Wesson .45 caliber pistol.

"Wow," Mia said. "Feels powerful. It's heavy, though."

"Bring that one, and I'll choose another for you. Come with me. We have a shooting range downstairs."

Mia followed Sally through another door and down a flight of stairs. Sally flipped a switch and illuminated a long and narrow room. Near the entrance stood wood-framed stations with waist-high shelves. The air smelled to Mia like the Fourth of July after the grand finale of the fireworks display.

She couldn't see the far end of the room very well. Some rectangular sheets of paper with circular red targets draped down from a wire attached to a track on the ceiling that ran the length of the room.

Sally picked up two boxes of ammunition from a

shelf on the front wall and placed them off to the side in one of the partitioned shooting stations.

"Watch me," instructed Sally. She pushed a button on the side of the Smith & Wesson, and the ammunition magazine popped out. She pushed several cartridges from the ammo box into the magazine one at a time and then slammed it back up into the gun handle.

"Now, go ahead, and try shooting. But let me move the target a bit closer." Sally pushed a button and activated an electric pulley system which moved the target closer.

"Go ahead." She nodded her head toward the target.

"Won't someone hear me shooting?" Mia asked.

"No. We're underground in an industrial park, and the room is soundproofed. Don't worry."

Mia nodded, took the Smith & Wesson in her right hand, lifted it in the direction of the target. She aimed carefully and pulled the trigger.

Click.

"Lesson one," Sally said, nodding her head and clearly expecting this result. "Most guns have a safety latch. If you don't release the safety, bad guy wins. You're dead."

Mia's heart beat faster, and her armpits were wet now. *What am I doing?*

Sally stood a little behind her but close enough to point at the gun in Mia's hand. "On this gun, the safety's right here." She pointed at a little lever. "Push it upward, and you'll see a red dot. Now you'll be able to fire the gun. Try again. I'm going to put some headphones on you. You'll need them this time." She placed the muffs on Mia's ears from behind.

Mia took the gun in her right hand, aimed toward the target, then pulled the trigger again.

Blam! A bullet ricocheted off the floor as the gun recoiled upward. Mia barely held on to it.

"Lesson two," Sally said, apparently still unsurprised, "it's important to pick the right weapon for you. This .45 is too big for you. Heavy. Big recoil. You shoot the floor. Bad guy shoots you. Bad guy wins. Easier to show you than tell you.

"Now, try this one." Sally handed Mia a five-round .38 revolver with a pink handle. "It's only about twelve ounces and has a small handle."

Mia took the gun in her hand. "Yes, it fits my hand. I like the feel."

"Put these bullet cartridges in it and try again. The cylinder opens with this button here," said Sally. "Two helpful hints: use two hands, like this, for better control, and don't jerk on the trigger, just squeeze it."

Mia loaded the cartridges in the cylinder as Sally had instructed and picked up the gun in her right hand. She put her left hand on the other side and somewhat underneath the gun as Sally had shown her. She stared at the target, took a deep breath, aimed, and fired once. The paper target flapped backward.

"There you go," Sally said, encouragement in her voice. "That's the gun for you. Let me show you some holsters for it. But it fits easily in a purse as well. And, if you live through this case," added Sally, laughing now, "I'll show you my 007-ish stash of cool weapons and spy toys."

Mia was getting into the excitement of the moment. "Spy toys? Can't you show me some now while I'm already here?"

"Yeah, don't tease her," Victoria said. "Show her something."

Sally raised an eyebrow. Then, cocking her head to the right, she said, "Okay. Follow me."

Sally led Mia and Victoria out of the shooting range and down another hallway to a dead end. But Sally waived a ring on her right hand near the wall, and machinery whirred.

A door swung slowly backward into a large room. The lights came on automatically as they entered and illuminated white tables in the middle of the room and black metal cabinets all around the sides.

"Okay, I'm going to show you some of the fun stuff." Sally opened one of the cabinets and pulled out a drawer. "Here is part of my lipstick collection. At least they *appear* to be lipstick cases. And some of them do have a bit of lipstick packed in at the top of the tube to camouflage the rest of the contents."

Mia said, "They seem like regular lipsticks. Here's one that's even a name brand."

"Actually"—Sally peered over to look more closely at the lipstick Mia was examining—"that one's mine. I don't wear lipstick often, but here is where I keep it if I need it."

"What about these?" asked Mia, pointing to the other sticks.

"Well, let's see." Sally started at the left of the row of lipsticks. "This type carries a pressured dart, which can be filled with either a knockout drug or a poison that kills. The next one contains poison in the lipstick itself. It is potent. If you wear it and kiss someone, they'll die within minutes. So, before you put it on, remember to take the antidote that's in a tablet hidden in the bottom of the tube."

Mia reached for it, but Sally grabbed her hand. "In due time, Mia, but not before a little training."

Sally reached for the next one. "This one has a spring-loaded razor in it. The case is a metal that shields the knife from view if you need to go through a metal detector. It's small, but a slice along the carotid artery is all you need. And the last one in *this* drawer is the best. It contains two separate compounds that will explode soon after you stick them together."

"Wow. Can I see?"

"Not here, Mia," said Sally, shaking her head. "I don't want you to blow up my favorite room."

"Show her some jewelry," Victoria said.

"Yes. Good idea. Much safer." Sally led Mia and Victoria to a cabinet on the other side of the room. Inside, Mia observed a large assortment of rings, earrings, and necklaces with pendants.

"Most of these are audio-visual or transmitting devices," Sally explained. "These fancy earrings loop into your ear to allow for two-way communication with other sisters. And these dangling spheres have a piece that can be slid off and slipped into a purse or jacket pocket to allow us to track targets."

"And they're beautiful," Mia said.

Sally nodded. "Looks can be deceiving. Check out these necklaces with pendants. This large shiny pendant is filled with those same two explosives that are in the lipstick but in much larger quantities, enough to destroy a house."

Mia took a step back from the cabinet.

"Don't worry," Sally said. "They're not dangerous unless mixed."

Sally pointed to a necklace with a shiny black stone pendant rimmed with ornate silver. "This is one of my favorites. The chain can easily be used as a garrote if you need to strangle someone."

Mia cringed.

"But the pendant itself is what's special. It has a long-range GPS transmitter that's activated by turning the silver rim a centimeter clockwise and a video recorder that can be activated by turning the rim another centimeter. It's great for my spy work. And Victoria here even used the video recorder once to catch a cheating husband for one of the sisters."

Victoria caught Mia's eye and winked. Mia nodded but thought that using Victoria to catch a cheater was unfair. Her beauty and charisma made it easier to take any man down. And perhaps most women.

Sally saw Mia staring longingly at the black pendant, picked it off the hook, and offered it to her. "I have several similar devices. Go ahead and take this one."

"Oh, my God. Thank you, Sally." Mia took the pendant and reached her hands behind her neck to connect it. She rubbed the smooth black stone for a minute and peered into it, trying to see the camera. *Nope.*

Victoria also wore a small pendant around her neck. Her open blouse revealed a silver tube on the end of a chain.

"Is that silver tube a weapon of some kind?" Mia asked, nodding toward Victoria.

Victoria gave Sally a nod, and Sally pulled a similar pendant out from beneath her own shirt. Mia inspected both pendants and concluded that they were identical.

After a moment Victoria said, "To answer your question, no, it's not a weapon. Inside the titanium cylinder is...a gift, from Xtina, given to the members of The Sisterhood who do the group's work in the field."

"Will I be getting one of those?" Mia asked.

"I don't know," Victoria said. "It's up to Xtina. If you're accepted into The Sisterhood, there will be a ceremony. That's when you would get it."

Mia quietly wondered to herself what the future held for her. Would she become a full-fledged member of The Sisterhood?

After a while, Sally stood up. "I think we're done here. At least for today. But there is one more thing I'll give you." Sally pulled a document out of a filing cabinet. "This is an official gun safety class certificate of completion. If you want to make it official, you can take it to the Bureau of Criminal Investigation and get yourself a concealed carry permit. Then, you're good to go."

Mia thanked Sally and placed the certificate plus the gun and a box of ammunition in her purse. *Good to go? Where am I supposed to go with a gun?*

Chapter Twenty-Eight

After lunch, the jury shuffled back into their seats slowly. They seemed weary. A long morning of medical and expert testimony could do that to you.

Johnson approached the lectern.

"Who are you calling next?" I asked as he passed by me.

He ignored me and addressed the judge. "The State next calls Rich Donaldson." Johnson gestured with an open hand toward a middle-aged man with oddly gray skin and unkempt hair. He haltingly stood and slowly ambled up toward the clerk standing and waiting with her arm up ready to swear him in as a witness.

"Hey, that's one of our witnesses," Mary whispered urgently, grabbing my arm.

It was true. Donaldson was on the witness list we provided to the State and the court. We were planning to call Donaldson to talk about the damage that Afa caused to the walls in apartment 305 where Kala had lived with Afa prior to them transferring to apartment 105. The neighbors in 306 had complained to the apartment manager about frequent shouting matches.

Donaldson was the one who had gone in to make repairs in 305. We figured that evidence of significant damage would corroborate Kala's testimony about the domestic violence she had endured. Johnson had blindsided us.

"Mr. Donaldson," Johnson said, "do you recognize the defendant here, Kala Tausinga?"

"Ummm, yes, I reckon I do," he said, nodding. "She is, was, a tenant in the apartment complex I work at."

"Do you recall being asked by the apartment manager to do some maintenance work in her apartment, number 105?"

"Yes. I went into her apartment to fix the dishwasher."

"Approximately when was that?"

"I'm not exactly sure. I'm thinking it was sometime in November of last year."

All the jurors were focused on Mr. Donaldson. Why had Johnson called him to the stand? What testimony would he give? How badly would it hurt our case?

"Did you observe anything that concerned you when you were there?"

"Objection, Your Honor, on notice and relevance grounds," I announced as I stood.

"Counsel, please approach the bench," Judge Russo directed.

I glanced at the jury as I walked up to speak to the judge. Several frowned at me. "Your Honor, the State has not given notice of this witness, and we haven't received any reports regarding his testimony."

"I'm sorry about that, Your Honor," Johnson responded in a conciliatory tone, "but my investigator only spoke to Mr. Donaldson for the first time yesterday and hasn't prepared a report yet. Besides, I didn't think I needed to give notice. Mr. Donaldson is listed as a witness by Mr. Bravo himself."

"Mr. Bravo," whispered Judge Russo as he leaned forward with a smirk on his face. "I have a question for you. Why are you objecting to your own witness?"

"Mr. Johnson is asking about something that happened well before the incident in question. I don't see the relevance."

Judge Russo took his eyes off me and placed them on the district attorney. "What evidence are you trying to elicit, Mr. Johnson?"

"Mr. Donaldson will testify that when he went in to fix the dishwasher, the child, Juna, walked into the kitchen where he was working. Ms. Tausinga came and jerked his arm violently and threw him onto the couch in the front room."

"Judge, that is a prior bad act, and so it's not admissible," I asserted, more forcefully now. "Mr. Johnson is only trying to show bad character. Besides, like I said before, it is irrelevant. It doesn't have anything to do with the homicide at issue."

"I disagree," said Johnson, obviously prepared for this discussion. "According to the plain language of Rule 404(b), prior conduct is admissible if it's offered to show things like motive, intent, plan, identity, or absence of mistake. In this case, it goes to show intent and absence of mistake. That makes it relevant. I have a case on point in a file on my desk. The Court of Appeals has held that evidence of a parent who has acted violently toward a child is admissible in a trial against that parent alleging that the parent had killed that child. If you like, Your Honor, I can go on..."

"That won't be necessary, Mr. Johnson," Judge Russo interrupted and took in a deep breath. "Even if the evidence were not otherwise admissible, the defense's claim that the father committed the murder opens the door to evidence showing a violent propensity toward the deceased child by the mother. Your objection is overruled, Mr. Bravo."

Feeling the sting of that rejection, I walked back to our table, quickening my pace somewhat so I could whisper something to Mary before Johnson continued.

"While I'm focusing on Donaldson's testimony," I whispered, "I need you to ask Kala about this dishwasher incident."

"Now then, Mr. Donaldson," said Johnson, gloating, "please tell the jury what you saw when you went into the defendant's apartment to fix the dishwasher."

"Well, I was in the kitchen fixin' the dishwasher and the little feller came toddlin' in to see what I was doing. You know how curious kids are. Well, first she yelled at him saying, 'Come out of there. Don't bother that man,' that sort of thing."

"And did he leave the kitchen?"

"No. And when he didn't, she came into the kitchen, grabbed his arm, and *yanked* it. I was shocked. I thought his little arm was going to come out of the socket. No one should be allowed to treat little children like that." He shook his head.

"I object, Your Honor," I said loudly as I stood. "This doesn't have *anything* to do with the homicide at issue."

Johnson was about to respond, but Judge Russo raised his hand. "Duly noted, Mr. Bravo," the judge replied, understanding that I was only making sure the record reflected the objection I had made at the bench that he had already overruled. "You may continue, Mr.

Johnson."

"Now, Mr. Donaldson, a moment ago you said *she* yanked his little arm. Would you please tell the jury to whom you are referring?"

"Mrs. Tausinga there," said Donaldson, pointing at Kala.

A lot of eyes opened wide in the juror box. Some jurors openly glared at Kala in disbelief.

"Anything else, Mr. Donaldson?"

"Well, one last thing," he said, sitting up a little straighter. "After she yanked his arm, she dragged him by the arm and threw him onto the couch in the living room. I could see him through the archway from where I was. He looked at her with sad eyes and then laid his little head down on the couch."

"That's all for now, Mr. Donaldson," Johnson said, his tone seemingly reflecting sorrow. The jury watched him as he returned to his seat wearing a frown.

"May we have a brief recess, Your Honor?" I stood and asked, hoping for some time to consider this damaging surprise testimony.

"Yes, but keep it to fifteen minutes," the judge replied, without requiring me to state on the record the obvious explanation that I didn't want the jury to hear—that this new evidence hurt our case and we needed time to figure out what to do about it.

I found myself at the end of the fourth-floor hallway with my hands firmly clutching the brass railing that encircled the vast rotunda of the courthouse. They say no one has ever jumped to his death from here. I was surprised. Lots of bad things happen to people in court.

Johnson's surprise calling of Rich Donaldson as his

witness had put us in a tough position. Kala told Mary that she remembered him fixing the sink and that she had pulled Juna into the other room by the arm, but she was sure she had not hurt him. She said she was in the habit of keeping Juna away from Afa when Juna would go to him because Afa would shout at him.

Mary said, "But Kala insisted that Donaldson was exaggerating what happened."

That gave me an idea as to one small point I could make regarding Johnson's direct examination. Back in the courtroom, I approached the lectern and laid a page of hastily scratched notes on it.

"Mr. Donaldson," I started after I saw that the jury was reseated, "you said a minute ago that you were, um, *shocked*, I think was the word you used. Did you report this so-called shocking incident to the police?"

"Well, no." His eyes widened a little.

"Did you report it to the apartment manager, or anyone else?"

"Um, no," he answered in a softer voice than he had during his testimony with Johnson.

"Is it possible that you are exaggerating a little bit?" I asked while using my index finger and thumb to demonstrate the words "little bit."

"No. I said what I saw," Donaldson said defensively while jutting up his chin.

"Well now, his arm didn't come out of its socket, right?"

"Well, no I guess not."

"And from what you've said, he didn't even *cry*?"

"Um, I don't remember." He shook his head. "I guess not."

"Thank you."

I switched subjects and got Donaldson to talk about the damage to apartment 305 he found and repaired after Kala and Afa were transferred to apartment 105. Then, I took a deep breath and sighed as I sat down, trying not to be obvious about how much Donaldson's testimony hurt our case. This surprise was a bad one. Our defense was based on showing what a loving mother Kala was and what a bad husband Afa was.

This arm-jerking incident put a big smudge on the picture we were trying to paint. We should have seen it coming. Johnson should have told us ahead of time. The judge shouldn't have let it in. But there it was. Sometimes things happen in trial that are totally unexpected. Witnesses exaggerate, forget, or testify to new or different things than what they said in earlier statements. Or one judge lets in evidence, damaging or helpful, that another judge would have kept out.

Occasionally, even after all the witnesses have testified, and a trial is over, I have still had significant questions about what had happened. Regardless of what a jury decided, one of the questions in such cases was always *was justice done*?

It was time for Johnson to call his next witness. He stood but didn't introduce anyone for questioning. He was facing back, staring intently at the door to the courtroom. After a moment Detective Jenner came striding through the doors and went straight to Johnson. They whispered and gestured.

"Your Honor," Johnson said finally, "the State requests a recess. Our next, and perhaps last, witness is not present yet."

"Who are we waiting for?" Judge Russo asked.

"Afa Tausinga," Johnson said after some

hesitation.

I saw that the jurors all perked up at the name of the missing witness. Afa was clearly a key witness for the prosecution. But we had been painting Afa as the murderer all along.

What were the jurors thinking? Did he decide not to testify against his wife? Was he avoiding court because he was guilty? Or—and the jury couldn't know this—did Afa fail to appear in court because he assumed that I would file a police report against him for putting me in the hospital?

"Can the defense proceed at this time, Mr. Bravo?"

"No, Your Honor, we didn't expect to call witnesses until tomorrow."

"It's a bit early," Judge Russo said, "but we'll break until tomorrow. Mr. Johnson, let me be perfectly clear with you. If your witness is not here first thing in the morning, he won't be testifying."

"Yes, sir. I understand."

I was pleased to have this break and intrigued to discover that Afa was still missing. *What did all this mean for the prosecution's case?*

Afa's failure to appear for court today obviously concerned Johnson, but it also created a dilemma for Mary and me. On one hand, we had been counting on getting a photocopy of Afa's hand for a comparative exhibit. In fact, I had been practicing in my head how we would surprise Afa with the question.

First, I would start with his motive and opportunity: "Mr. Tausinga, isn't it true that every time you looked at Juna, you were angry because he was not your son but the result of an affair your wife had with another man? And on December second, when you heard Juna's father, Vai, was back in town, your rage boiled over, and you picked Juna up and slammed him against the wall?

"And your daughters saw it too, right? And when you heard that your daughters were telling the Alekis that Daddy did it, you quit going to visit them?

"By the way, did you know that the medical examiner did an autopsy and it showed that the medical evidence was consistent with the injury having occurred right after you got home from work, at around 6:00 p.m.?

"And did you know the medical examiner already testified about the size of the hand that made the bruise on Juna's leg? He said it was the size of his own hand, which is significantly larger than Kala's hand, and more like yours?"

Then, after carefully setting the stage and making him nervous, I would spring the trap on him. "Now, Your Honor, I would like to create an exhibit for the jury. Would you instruct the bailiff to escort Mr. Tausinga to the copy machine?"

I could see it in my mind, the elusive Perry Mason moment! Afa would either confess or make a run for it instead of going to the copy machine with the bailiff to get his hand photocopied. And Kala would be found not guilty by the jury.

I smiled at the imagined scenario.

Conversely, Afa's nonappearance could benefit our case in a few ways. First, he wouldn't be there to swear to the jury that he didn't hurt Juna. That would be good. And maybe Kala would be now willing to testify after all. In addition, we could argue to the jury that his failure to appear was due to knowledge of his own guilt and fear that he would be found out. I would be ready for him, but would he show?

Chapter Twenty-Nine

"Frank, we have a problem," Mary said urgently, as she came striding into my office as we each reviewed our trial notes after returning from court.

"Only one? That's a relief."

"No, actually, not only one," Mary said, chuckling. "But I just got off the phone with Kala's aunt Lovai. I was going to review with her and the other family members the main questions we'd be asking them tomorrow. But she told me that they were not coming to court, that they didn't want to get involved."

Leaning forward with anticipation, I asked, "Did you tell that because we served them a subpoena, they're required to come?"

"Of course," Mary said. "But Lovai said that the little girls are starting to do better now and are sleeping through the night. She was afraid it'd be harmful to them to try to make them testify at trial."

"Shit," was all I could think to say. I tossed my pen onto my desk.

"I asked her what about Kala? Didn't they want to help her? She said that every time Kala calls from the jail and talks to the girls, they cry as soon as she hangs up, and they say they want to see her. The Alekis are trying to adopt Kala's children, and they think that Kala's influence is bad because it makes the girls cry."

"Are you kidding me right now?" I rolled my eyes

and shook my head.

"No. That's what she said."

"I've had a bad feeling about having Amanaki and Emeni testify ever since we tried to talk to them when we first met them, and Amanaki hid under the table in our conference room."

"I know, Frank." Mary sounded resigned. "That's why I didn't specifically refer to their possible testimony in my opening statement."

"So, what are we going to do?" My eyes searched Mary's face as if the answer could be found there.

"Well, I begged her to reconsider. I tried to put a plain-cold guilt trip on her. I told her how much Kala needed their testimony, that her whole life is at stake here. She seemed sympathetic to that argument. I said that we would not try to make Emeni testify, only Amanaki. And I told her that we would help arrange for counseling sessions for Amanaki and Emeni if necessary. In the end, she agreed to think about it."

"Well, that's something," I said, feeling a smidgeon of hope.

"But," Mary added, "I should also tell you...the last thing she said was that her husband, Sione, had forbidden it."

I flopped into the back of my chair and took a deep breath. Maybe it was time for some incense and my meditation pillow.

Chapter Thirty

"Mia, it is you," Kala stated excitedly, smiling as Mia settled into the plastic chair across the table in the contact visit room at the jail. "I was wondering who would be visiting me. Nowadays, it's only Frank and Mary or you. I am so happy to see you. Thank you for coming again."

"Well, the jail knows me," said Mia, returning Kala's smile, "and I'm still able to use the badge the DA's office issued to me to get in to see you. At least they haven't cancelled it so far."

"Cancelled it?" asked Kala. "What do you mean? Why would they cancel it?"

"Oh. I guess I didn't tell you. Randy Johnson found out I visited you after he ordered me not to, and he fired me." She shrugged and turned her palms facing upward.

"No, Mia. I feel like it's my fault." Kala's eyebrows raised in the middle.

"No, dear sweet Kala." Mia reached her hand across the table. "It's definitely not your fault."

"Well, I'm so sorry about it."

"Don't be sorry about *that.*" Mia waved her hand to shoo away Kala's concern. "Now, if I had remained in a job where I was forced to sit back and watch injustice and do nothing about it, *then* you could feel sorry for me. But that's not who I am. That's not why I became a victim advocate. So, don't worry about me.

I'll find another job. Staying in this one would have cost me my soul."

Mia leaned forward over the table. "Until I do find another job, though, I'm here to help *you*. Speaking of which, Mary told me that you don't want to testify now. Is that right?"

"Yes," Kala said quickly. "Mary said Afa was coming to court to testify. If he sees me testify or if he even hears that I told on him, I'm afraid...I'm afraid he will kill me or hurt our children. He said he would."

"Kala, you need to be brave. You need to be strong and stand up against him and say what he did."

Kala shrank back into her chair. "I'm not strong. He is too strong. After he killed Juna, he would not let me call 911. He threatened to kill me and my kids." She put a hand to her forehead for a minute. "At first, he cried at lot and said he was sorry." She fixed her eyes on Mia's hand holding hers. "He acted like he was not mad at me at all. So, I thought it would be okay to call 911. But when I picked up the phone, he totally flipped out. He grabbed the phone and threw it. He grabbed me by the neck and threatened to kill me. I could see in his eyes that he would do it too. I can't testify. I'm too afraid."

Mia sat thinking, unsure of how much to tell Kala about The Sisterhood. She had sworn not to speak that name and not to name anyone who was a member of The Sisterhood.

"Kala, do you trust me?"

"Well, yes. Of course, I do."

"Then trust me when I say that I will protect you from Afa."

Kala scanned Mia's face, arms, and shoulders as if

assessing her ability to do that, to protect her. Mia sensed that Kala doubted her because of her small physical size. Most people underestimated her, but she needed Kala to trust her on this.

"I have friends," Mia decided to add. "Lots of friends. Women who are strong. Smart. Capable of helping you. That's what they do. They help women who've been abused, women the system has failed to protect."

Mia repeated what Xtina had told her. "A woman alone may be weak, but women together are strong. With their help, I can protect you."

Kala shifted back in her seat and sat up straighter now, perhaps sensing Mia's rising passion. Still, she said nothing.

Mia understood Kala's fear better than most. Abuse changed you. People could tell you not to be afraid. They could give you reasons not to be afraid. But once you had faced death, or the constant fear of harm, reasons were merely words you heard. But you *felt* fear. Felt it in your bones. And fear blew words away like leaves in a storm.

With Mia's continuing encouragement, eventually Kala said, "Okay. I'll do it. I'll testify."

Mia sighed and nodded. But she wondered if Kala's much-needed agreement was just words.

Chapter Thirty-One

Mary and I had arrived at the courthouse early the next day to meet with Kala. A lot was at stake. Afa didn't come to court when he was expected yesterday. But would he appear today? Would he testify? Would she?

Kala gave Mary and me the good news that Mia had visited her last night and encouraged her to testify, to tell the truth about what happened. If Afa didn't come today, we could put Kala on the stand and present our defense. But if he did come?

"Good morning," said Judge Russo after the jury was seated. Turning toward Johnson, he asked the one question that everyone in the courtroom was wondering— "Does the State have a witness this morning?"

"No, Your Honor." Johnson shrugged. "The State rests."

"Very well," Judge Russo said. "Then we'll hear from the defense."

"Give me a moment, Your Honor," I said to the judge.

Although it was an obvious breach of courtroom decorum, I couldn't help myself. The police had given up the search for Afa after he sent me to the hospital. Whatever else Afa was guilty of, he was guilty of that. I took the two steps between my chair and where

Johnson was still standing, and I whispered in his ear. "Tell your investigators to find that motherfucker, and you charge him. Do you hear me?"

To his credit, and to my benefit, Johnson didn't make a scene. He simply frowned at me. But I couldn't afford to waste any more time. Right now, it was our turn to call witnesses, and the judge and jury were waiting. But who we could call as witnesses was totally up in the air. Afa hadn't shown up, so I wouldn't be able to do the cross-examination I had rehearsed nor photocopy his hand for the jury. And we wouldn't be allowed to call Afa's supervisor at the soap factory or Lisa Miller, the woman Afa had threatened to kill this past summer over past-due rent. They were both impeachment witnesses who could give evidence of Afa's bad character, but only if Afa or another State witness first gave testimony claiming that Afa had good character or that he wouldn't commit crimes. They were both waiting in the hallway, but apparently for nothing.

The Alekis had not shown up either. And the Daddy-did-it testimony was critical to our case. An empty ache filled the pit of my stomach. Because they had been served with subpoenas to testify, we could ask the judge to hold them in contempt for not appearing or send the police to arrest them and bring them to court in handcuffs. But that would make them even less likely to want to help us.

The only other defense witness present at the time was Patricia Poulson, one of the nurses who treated Kala at the Granger Medical Clinic when she was pregnant. We would try to elicit testimony from the nurse that Kala was afraid of Afa, and that he threatened her.

Mary placed her hand on my forearm. "Hey, it's still early. He could still show up."

But we had no choice now.

"The defense calls Patricia Poulson to the stand," I announced as I approached the lectern.

"How are you employed, Ms. Poulson?" I asked after she was sworn.

"I'm a licensed nurse practitioner at the Granger Medical Clinic."

"Do you know Kala Tausinga?"

"Yes. I was one of her prenatal nurses for her last two children, Junior, or Juna as she called him, and Malohi her youngest son. And I was present at the birth of Malohi."

Nodding, I asked, "Do you also know Kala's husband, Afa Tausinga?"

"Not well," she said. "I've seen him a few times at the clinic, and he was with her at the hospital when she gave birth to Malohi."

"Do you normally allow spouses to be present throughout the labor and delivery?" I walked closer to the witness stand.

"I leave that to my patients. Kala asked me to tell him to wait outside of the delivery room, but he refused to leave the room."

"Do you recall how long Kala was in labor?"

She nodded. "She came into the hospital around six p.m., already in labor. She gave birth around midnight."

"During that time, did you have any discussions with her?"

She glanced over to the jury. "Yes. Perhaps it's because we're helping them through such a personal and intimate thing as childbirth, but our patients confide in us about everything. Kala described something of a personal nature."

"What was this other thing of a personal nature about which she talked to you?" I too glanced at the jury. Good, we had their attention.

"Objection," yelled Johnson, again doing his best to interfere with every attempt we made to slow down his buzz-saw prosecution. "The question calls for hearsay."

"Your Honor," I replied, "we're not offering the statement for the truth of the matter asserted but as background for something else."

"Then by definition it's not hearsay, Mr. Johnson," said Judge Russo. "You may continue, Mr. Bravo."

"Go ahead, Ms. Poulson, tell the jury what happened."

"During the evening when I was checking Kala's blood pressure, she started whispering to me. She has a quiet voice anyway, but she was actually whispering. She peeked over at her husband and then asked me if I knew what had happened to her son Juna."

"Did you know at the time what had happened to Juna?"

"No."

"So, she didn't tell you?"

"No, not at that time. But her husband must have heard her because he sat forward in his chair and glared at her."

"What happened next?"

"She quit talking. She didn't say anything."

I turned around to scan the courtroom audience and scanned the jury as I returned my focus on the witness.

"Ms. Poulson, was there any other time before or after Juna's birth that Kala did try to speak with you again?"

"Yes. Kala gave birth at about midnight. There were no complications. Then she went to sleep. The next morning, I went in to check on her and to bring her some food. Her husband was asleep. She waved me close to her and started to tell me about her son Juna, that he had been injured and died a week earlier. She asked me if I thought she was the sort of person who could do such a thing."

"Objection," said Johnson again, "there is inadequate foundation for such an opinion."

"That's true, I suppose," agreed Judge Russo, "but Mr. Bravo hasn't asked the witness for her opinion at this point, so your objection is premature." He gave me a brief nod. "You may continue, Mr. Bravo."

The opinion testimony would have been good, but I had something better than a mere opinion from this witness. Now was the time to get it out where the jury could see it.

"Ms. Poulson, while you were talking with Kala about what happened to Juna, did anything out of the ordinary happen?"

"Yes. Her husband woke up. He came out of his chair right up over the bed and doubled up his fist."

The jurors were all staring intently at the nurse. So was Johnson. I planned to take full advantage of their attention.

"Now, Ms. Poulson, the jury wasn't there, so please try to describe what happened in enough detail so that we all understand. First, how would you describe him physically, his size?" I took a step back to give the jury full view of her.

"He was huge, over six feet tall, maybe 250 pounds."

"And please describe his emotional state at the time."

"Objection," Johnson said, "she can't speculate about his state of mind."

"Just describe what you saw," I interjected without waiting for the judge. I wanted this out while the emotion was high, without further interruptions. "What was the look on his face?"

"He had a scowl on his face," the nurse replied. "But the fist said more than the face."

Out of the corner of my eye, I could see several of the jurors leaning forward. "How did you react?"

"I was frightened. I backed up against the wall. I didn't know if I should run out."

I let that answer hang in the air for a moment. "How about Kala? How did she react?"

"She became small," replied the nurse, her eyes landing on Kala. "She shrank back onto the bed and curled up. She turned away from me and him and became quiet."

I stopped again and allowed the emotion in the room to continue simmering. Now the whole jury was leaning forward.

"Did you speak with Kala again after that time?"

"I spoke to her, but she didn't answer. She wouldn't say another thing to me the rest of the time she was there. Whenever I asked anything, even questions about how she was feeling, *he* would answer me, not her."

"How much longer was Kala there?"

"We kept her one more day."

"What about Kala's husband? Did he stay too?"

"Yes, he did."

"No further questions." I walked back to the defense table, feeling that I had made some good points.

Johnson stood up and walked quickly to the lectern.

"Ms. Poulson," said Johnson in a derisive tone that the jury could not have liked, "I *assume* that you *immediately* called the police after this frightening event?"

"Well, no, I didn't call the police at that time." She stared at Johnson.

"Perhaps you called hospital security?"

"No, I didn't."

"I have a copy of the hospital records from the birth you're testifying about. At least I *think* I have all the records. There's nothing in them about this frightening event. Or am I missing something?"

"All I wrote is a note saying that the husband was controlling." Her voice sounded as if it may have had some regret in it.

"So, this whole thing must not have been that frightening after all?" Johnson retorted, sneering.

"I *was* frightened. But nothing happened. Her husband just sat back down in the chair. So, I went about my business."

"Thank you, nothing further." He walked away.

"Any redirect, Mr. Bravo?"

"Yes, briefly, Your Honor." I knew something Johnson didn't know, and now he had opened the door wide for me to inform the jury about it too.

"Ms. Poulson, Mr. Johnson tried to make a big deal

about you not calling the police right away." I gave Johnson a contemptuous glare. "But did you at some *later* time call the police?"

"Yes," she said, her eyes regaining some hope.

Johnson perked up.

"When?"

"When I saw on the TV a few weeks later that Kala had been arrested and charged with murder, that's when I called the police."

"Why did you call the police?"

"To tell them they must have made some mistake."

Johnson stood up. This testimony hurt his case badly. He must have wanted to object. But apparently, he couldn't come up with any specific objection. I glanced toward the jurors. All eight of them seemed completely engrossed by the nurse's testimony.

"Did you call 911?"

"No," the nurse said, "I called the West Valley City Police Department."

I paused, hoping the jury would remember that the West Valley City Police Department was the same one that did the one-day investigation on this very case.

"To whom did you speak?" I asked.

"I don't know. I didn't talk to anyone. They transferred my call to some detective, I think, but he didn't answer. I had to leave a voice mail."

"Did anyone call you back?" I asked with a raised eyebrow and tone of curiosity.

"No." Nurse Poulson shook her head. "So, I called them back, two more times. Again, I had to leave messages, but no one ever called me back."

I checked the jury again. They still seemed to be hanging on to the nurse's every word. The emotional impact of this type of testimony can be more persuasive than the words a witness says. I tried to keep it going.

"So, then what did you do?"

"I called the District Attorney's Office."

"What happened?"

"Again, I had to leave messages. In the last message, I asked if someone could at least tell me the name of the defense attorney. But again, no one called me back." She sounded frustrated and shrugged.

"That's no wonder, I suppose." I scowled at Johnson. He put his hands on his table as if he were going to stand up to object again, but I quickly moved on.

"Did you do anything else after that, Nurse Poulson?"

"No. I assumed that *someone* would do *something*."

I shook my head, allowing the anger and frustration building up inside of me to peek out. "Thank you, Ms. Poulson. No further questions."

As Patricia Poulson came down from the witness chair, Kala smiled and mouthed "Hi" to her. The nurse stopped briefly to say hello and to wish Kala good luck in the trial. The jury watched the unusual process with apparent interest. I suspected that the kindness displayed to Kala by the nurse would have a positive effect on the attitude of the jury toward Kala as well.

As my first nurse left, my second nurse arrived. Right on time. Melinda Ramirez introduced herself as a nurse at the Granger Medical Clinic. She was wearing her nurse's uniform, adding to her credibility.

I asked her, "Do you know Kala Tausinga?"

"Yes. She was a patient of mine for prenatal care."

"Did she have any issues that caused you concern?"

"Yes," replied the nurse. "She had gestational diabetes."

"Objection," said Johnson. "She's just a nurse. I don't think she's qualified to give a medical opinion."

A woman in the jury box glared at Johnson. He didn't appear to see her. The diabetes diagnosis was frankly a minor point. We didn't need the testimony. But now that Johnson had objected, I didn't want to give him the satisfaction of winning the point. Plus, I wanted to back up my witness to emphasize her expertise.

Facing the judge, I said, "Your Honor, I can elicit some foundational testimony."

"Go ahead, Mr. Bravo."

"Ms. Ramirez, are you qualified to diagnosis diabetes?"

"Yes. I'm not only a nurse. I'm an LPN. The study of diabetes was part of my basic medical training in school. In addition, I've had a great deal of experience testing for and treating diabetes in my practice."

I peered at Johnson and tilted my head to see if she had given enough foundation to keep him from interrupting with another objection. He shrugged, so I figured I had enough to go on.

I went back to my witness. "How do you diagnose gestational diabetes?"

"We draw blood and check the glucose levels."

"Did you get a test result in this case?"

"Yes. Kala's glucose levels were too high, over 120. That puts her at risk for birth defects or miscarriage or overdevelopment of the fetus."

"What, if anything, did you do?"

"We put Kala on a diet. She followed the diet and controlled the diabetes, so we didn't have to put her on insulin."

"Thank you. Is the emotional health of the mother also a concern in prenatal care?"

"Yes, of course," she said, nodding.

"During Kala's prenatal care, did you have any concerns about her emotional health?"

"Yes. She reported depression."

"Objection," Johnson said again, "I don't believe this witness, nor Ms. Tausinga, are qualified to diagnose depression."

The same woman in the jury glared at Johnson again. He saw it this time and sat back down, apparently giving up on the objection.

Judge Russo nodded at me, so I continued.

"Ms. Ramirez, do you have any training or experience that would qualify you to testify about depression?"

"Yes. Courses in psychology and mental illness were part of my training, and I have had much experience as well. Besides, in many circumstances, depression is circumstantial and not necessarily the result of a chemical imbalance."

"Did Kala report symptoms consistent with depression?"

"She told me that she felt depressed and frustrated."

"Objection," Johnson blurted, "that's hearsay."

Taking an exaggerated breath, I said, "It's a statement given for medical diagnosis, Your Honor, which, of course, is a recognized exception to the hearsay rule."

"I'll allow it," ruled the judge.

The woman in the jury was absolutely rolling her eyes over that objection by Johnson. She had folded her arms and frowned.

I smiled. "Ms. Ramirez, for the benefit of us men in the room, what sorts of things do pregnant women talk about with their nurses?"

"Everything, including their health, their children, their husbands…"

"Did you discuss these subjects with Kala?"

"Yes."

"What did she say?"

"Kala said that she was having problems in her marriage but had no resources to deal with them. Her mother was sick and too far away to help. She went to her church for help, but that didn't resolve her problem. Her husband wouldn't let her work, so she didn't have any money to leave with, and she couldn't take her children without money to take care of them."

In my peripheral vision, I saw Mary scoot back her chair and leave the courtroom.

Refocusing on my notes, I asked, "Are you saying Kala seemed concerned about the welfare of her children?"

"Yes, I would say so. More than anything else she was concerned about them."

"Thank you. Now, Ms. Ramirez, given your experience with and knowledge of Kala, and your discussions with her about her children, about her husband, and about her problems, and being familiar with her general emotional state and demeanor, have you developed any opinion about whether she's the type of person who could hurt her own children?"

"Objection," Johnson said again, "due to lack of foundation."

"Sustained. Counsel, I've let you go as far as I can with this opinion testimony. Move on."

Too bad. I was scoring a lot of points with the jury until that objection was sustained. I did have one more area to get to, though.

"Ms. Ramirez, during your physical exams of Ms. Tausinga, did you ever see bruises on her?"

"I don't recall." She closed her eyes and then popped them right back open. "Wait, there was one time she showed up with a black eye."

"Thank you. No further questions." I walked back to the table, Mary's absence creating curiosity.

Johnson now stood up but stayed behind his desk. I was close enough to see that he was holding Ramirez's medical reports about Kala in his hand. I quickly surmised what he was about to ask. It was not good for us.

"Only one question, Ms. Ramirez. Did Kala say how she got that black eye?"

"She said it was an accident."

"No more questions," said Johnson, sitting down.

At that same moment Mary returned and sat in her seat. She waved me close as Nurse Ramirez stepped down from the witness chair. She leaned forward. "Lightning has struck. The Aleki family has come after all. And they'll testify."

Suddenly a light had appeared at the end of the long dark tunnel that led to our Daddy-did-it defense! Before this moment, our initial exultation to hear what the children disclosed about their brother's death had been slowly and effectively crushed as if by an industrial-strength trash compactor.

The Alekis declared time and again that they wanted nothing to do with the case, that they wanted nothing to do with Kala, except to exclude her from her children and from their family. They insisted they weren't coming to let Amanaki testify. Plus, Johnson had effectively blocked our other various efforts to get the testimony in. But finally, this morning, albeit two hours late, they arrived with Amanaki in tow. The seeds planted by Mary's emotional pleas had sprouted overnight.

"A brief recess, Your Honor?"

A couple of the jurors glanced my way, seemingly grateful for a break. But I hadn't asked for the recess for their benefit. I wanted to see the Aleki family with my own eyes.

Judge Russo glanced at his watch. "Granted."

Chapter Thirty-Two

"The defense calls Amanaki Tausinga," I announced firmly after the recess. I found myself holding my breath at the podium as Mary went out to the hallway to get Kala's four-year-old daughter, Amanaki.

Lovai Tausinga walked into the courtroom, holding Amanaki by the hand. But when they got inside the packed courtroom, Amanaki froze. Lovai pulled her forward by the arm a step or two farther, but Amanaki dug her heels in and pulled back with all her little might, fear filling her dark eyes as they darted around the room.

Despite the Alekis' initial refusal to come to court, we had eventually persuaded them that Kala may go to prison for life if we didn't win the case, and that Amanaki's testimony was critical to our victory. They had reluctantly agreed to help. Lovai set her jaw now and picked Amanaki up in her arms to carry her forward to the witness box. Amanaki twisted her little body and stretched both her arms back toward the courtroom door. But after another step or two, she let out a bloodcurdling high-pitched scream at the top of her lungs.

I reached out my arm and stopped Lovai, shaking my head. I told her not to worry as the worry was plain on her face. "Go ahead and take Amanaki back outside."

Ever since the first day we tried to speak to Amanaki, I had been afraid that we wouldn't be able to get her to testify. That was the day that she slid off Lovai's lap onto the floor under the conference table with her thumb in her mouth.

I was disheartened, but I still had one last, thin hope.

Lovai Aleki herself was our next witness. She came back into the courtroom and sat in the witness box, visibly shaken. Still, she outlined for the jury all the family names and relationships. We made a diagram so that the jury could see the spelling of the names, and partly to re-emphasize that Juna, or Afa Tausinga Junior, was *not* Afa's son at all. Afa's jealously about Kala having had an affair was important. It was our explanation for Afa's anger at Kala. It was the reason for Afa's neglect and disdain toward Juna. It was motive.

Lovai explained that she and her daughter Lei were the primary caretakers of the little girls. Lovai watched them during the day, and Lei watched them after she got home from work. I had tried to anticipate Johnson's possible cross-examination as I framed my questions for Lovai.

"Lovai, did you try to get the children to talk about what happened to Juna?"

She rapidly shook her head. "No, I never say anything. I never ask. We don't talk about it."

"Did the subject of what happened to Juna come up anyway?"

"Yes. One night we were waiting for Afa. He was supposed to be visiting the children, but he didn't come.

This night he said he was coming, so I told the girls that he was coming. But when I said that Daddy should be coming soon, Amanaki said, 'No, Daddy stupid.'"

"Objection!" Johnson jumped to his feet this time as I had anticipated, and he spoke urgently. "This is *blatant* hearsay, Your Honor."

"Counsel, this does appear to be hearsay," said Judge Russo.

"Actually, I believe that Amanaki's statement is admissible through this witness. The State filed a Notice of Expert for Alicia Simpson of the CJC in which they asserted that the child's statements are recent fabrications, and Ms. Simpson gave testimony earlier toward that point. In such circumstances, testimony that the statements were made long before the allegation of recent fabrication is admissible as a prior consistent statement under Rule 801."

"I would agree with you, Counsel, *if* she had actually testified," said Russo without waiting for Johnson to answer. "But without a *current* statement or actual testimony, I don't see how you can have a *prior* consistent statement."

It was my bad luck that Judge Russo had been a trial attorney for many years and was an expert about the rules of evidence. Some judges would have accepted that argument. I tried another.

"In the alternative, Your Honor, Amanaki Tausinga was legally *unavailable* as a witness today given that, as you just pointed out, she could not be made to testify. Consequently, prior statements made by her are admissible under Rule 804 if they are reliable. As I'm sure you'll recall, I took some pains to have *the State's own expert* describe the circumstances in which statements by children are most reliable."

"Yes, Counsel, I do recall that. It struck me as unusual at the time," said Russo, with a sly grin. "Somehow, I think you must have anticipated this problem."

"I do my best," I said. "In any case, Ms. Aleki can testify that Amanaki's statements were made under the circumstances deemed reliable by the State's own expert witness. Specifically, the statements were spontaneous and not the result of any leading questions by an adult. Also, the statements actually withstood an attempt by an adult in authority to make an alternative suggestion."

"But that testimony would be completely self-serving," said Johnson, interrupting.

"That is perhaps an issue for cross-examination, Mr. Johnson. Your objection is overruled."

Returning to my witness, I tried not to let the jury see my astonishment that my novel Hail-Mary argument worked. "Now, Lovai, please go ahead and tell the jury what Amanaki said when you told her that her daddy was coming to visit."

"She said, 'No! Daddy stupid. Hit Juna on door, bump head.'"

Wanting the jury to envision that picture for a moment, I paused before asking the next question. "What was your reaction when she said that?" I asked after a brief pause.

"Shock."

"When was it that Amanaki said that it was Daddy who hurt Juna?"

"In January, a little while after they gave us Kala's children."

"Had you received any information about Kala's case from the courts at *that* time?"

She stared at the jury and replied, "No, we didn't know anything about it."

I followed her stare and started asking my next question before focusing back on her. "You said that Afa didn't come to see the girls that day. Did he come to the house at any other time?"

"Yes, he came one other time."

"How did the girls react to him when he came?"

"They both ran into the front room. But when they saw that it was Afa, they both turned and ran away."

They ran away was a great answer for us. That kind of spontaneous reaction is often more persuasive than any words a witness might utter. I decided this was a good place to stop. The jurors sat on the edge of their seats, concerned by the information they were now learning.

I thanked Lovai and sat down, confident that we had finally established our defense, at least well enough to argue it in closing.

Johnson jumped up quickly without even taking his notepad.

"Mrs. Aleki," Johnson stated in an accusatory tone, "you are Kala's aunt, her mother's sister, isn't that true?"

"Yes, that's true."

"And truth be told, you are here today specifically to help Kala, isn't that right?"

"Yes, I want to help her," said Lovai, oblivious to Johnson's point. The point was an important one, though. Blood is thicker than water. People will lie early and often to protect their own. I see it regularly.

Jurors have a gut feeling about that too. That's why I would always rather have a stranger, a bystander, an outsider be a witness for my case than a member of my client's family. Johnson enthusiastically exploited this truth.

"You're trying to keep her from going to prison, isn't that true?"

"That's true."

"Now then," said Johnson with an air attempting to convey that *he* at least rejected Lovai's testimony out of hand, "you did not report this so-called statement by Amanaki to the police, did you?"

"No. Was I supposed to?" she asked, her eyebrows raised in concern.

Johnson faced the jury and asked the next question, ignoring her question. "And you did not report it to the District Attorney's Office either, did you?" he asked in a menacing tone.

"Um, I, no."

Johnson turned to the judge. "I think that's all the jury needs to know from this witness. No further questions."

Johnson had exposed Lovai's inherent bias as a family member, but I hoped the jury could see that he hadn't challenged the facts I had elicited from her. It was hard to read the jury. Maybe they had mixed feelings about Lovai's testimony.

"Mr. Bravo," said the judge. "You can call one more witness, and after that we'll break for lunch."

I nodded. "Very well. The defense calls Lei Aleki.

"Please tell the jury your name and your relationship to our last witness," I began after Lei was sworn in and settled into the witness chair.

Lei smiled at Kala. "My name is Lei. I am Lovai's daughter."

"Lei, there's been testimony that Kala's young daughters have been staying with you in your mother's house recently. Do you ever help watch them?"

"Yes. I watch the children in the evenings after I get home from work."

"Did the subject of what happened to Juna ever come up while you were at home watching the children?"

"Yes. One time. We were looking at a collage of family pictures. Amanaki was pointing at everyone in the pictures and saying their names. When she got to Juna, Amanaki said, 'I love Juna.' That's what she calls Junior. She said, 'Daddy hit Juna's head. Juna in Heaven.' "

"Objection," said Johnson. "That's hearsay."

Judge Russo didn't wait for me to respond. He had already ruled on this same objection during Lovai's testimony. "The record will reflect your objection. Please continue, Mr. Bravo."

I nodded and said to Lei, "How did you react to Amanaki's statement that it was Daddy that hurt Juna?"

"I was confused, so I said, 'Amanaki, don't you mean Mommy?'"

"What did she say?" I watched the jury for their reaction.

"'No, not Mommy! Mommy not stupid.'"

"Objection," said Johnson again. "For the record, Your Honor, I still believe this is all unreliable and inadmissible hearsay and so should not be admitted as evidence."

I figured that Johnson objected this time solely for

the benefit of the jury. He must have known the judge would rule against him again. But he also knew that jurors don't like hearsay. They think it shouldn't come in. They've heard on law dramas on TV that hearsay is not admissible. So, they discount or disregard it. Johnson played that card now and took away the momentum I had been developing with Lei.

"Overruled."

Johnson had interrupted during the most important part of Lei's testimony, so I needed to get her to say it again without quite telling her to say that again. It would be a strong question to end with.

"Lei, sorry for the interruption. To be clear with what you meant to say, let me ask that last question again. You testified that Amanaki said that *Daddy* hurt Juna. Please tell the jury what Amanaki said when you asked, 'Don't you mean Mommy?'"

Lei took me literally when I told her to tell the jury. She turned towards the jury. "She said, 'No, Mommy not stupid.'"

Johnson jumped up quickly to cross-examine. "What about Emeni? What does *she* say about Juna?"

Damn, I sat there thinking, *Johnson is good*. He picked out the single most problematic thing from Lei's interview transcript to ask her about.

"Emeni repeats whatever Amanaki says."

"As if someone *told* her to say that same thing?" Johnson asked, more loudly than necessary.

"Um, I don't know," was all Lei could say.

"You don't know," Johnson said. It wasn't a question. He wasn't trying to ask a question at all. He was emphasizing the point for the jury. He was trying to leave that one last negative impression in their minds about Lei's testimony, successfully I feared.

"No further questions."

Judge Russo adjusted his microphone. "Ladies and gentlemen, this is a good time for a break. The court is in recess until 1:30."

Mia was waiting for us in the hallway. She had come with the Aleki family and watched their testimony.

"Good to see you, Mia," I said. "Can you walk with us? We're going downstairs to the court's deli on the first floor to grab a bite to eat. Would you like to join us?"

"Thanks," Mia said. "I'd like that. But let me take a rain check for another day. Today I need to go meet with some friends over the lunch hour to make some plans. But I will be back in time to support Kala when she gives her testimony."

"Sounds good. Thank you again for helping her."

Mary said, "Mia, in the hallway you said you were waiting for Afa? Is he coming?"

"I don't know," Mia replied. "It was just in case he did show up. My friends and I are trying to find him."

"What friends?" asked Mary as we got into the elevator.

"I'll tell you a little bit more about it another day," Mia answered, glancing at the other people on the elevator.

None of us spoke while the elevator descended. Mia clearly didn't want to speak about her friends, and we as lawyers can't talk about our case in public to avoid having a juror overhear us or maybe another prosecutor report back our strategy to Johnson.

We said goodbye to Mia in front of the deli and

went in, ordered some sandwiches, chips, and iced tea, and sat down at an empty table.

Tearing open a couple packs of sugar, I said, "I have a question for you, Mary. Now that it seems Afa isn't coming, is there any reason for us to call Katie Foulger, the guardian ad litem in Kala's parental rights case?"

"I have mixed feelings about that," Mary said. "One thing we could get from her is that Afa didn't even show up to try to keep his parental rights. I think it reflects badly on him. After all, what kind of father would abandon his children at the time of their greatest need—after they had been taken from their family, their mother incarcerated, and their little brother killed brutally right in front of them?"

I stirred my tea with a straw while the visions of all those consecutive tragedies flashed through my mind.

Mary sipped her soda. "Katie Foulger could also testify that the court ruled as a matter of law that Afa was an unfit father and that his rights were terminated forever."

"It would be great to get that evidence in," I said, "but Johnson might object on the grounds that Afa's parental rights case is not relevant to the murder charge. And he would probably be right."

Mary held up a finger. "I've considered that. Even if she were allowed to testify about Afa, Johnson might be able to get her to say that Kala's rights were terminated also. That would eliminate any benefit we would get from the fact that Afa's rights were terminated." She shrugged. "It'd be a wash at best."

"Then let's skip Foulger and focus on witnesses that help our case for sure," I suggested.

"I agree," Mary said. "Hey, is that Ms. Foulger entering the deli?"

I followed Mary's gaze. "Yes. At least she showed up."

"I'll go tell her that we're not going to call her so she can go somewhere better for lunch. And you go get our sandwiches. We need to choke them down and get back to court."

Chapter Thirty-Three

We beat Judge Russo back to the courtroom after lunch. He arrived and called the court to order. "Good afternoon, everyone," he said, cheerfully. He must have enjoyed his lunch. He must have eaten somewhere other than the court's deli.

Fortunately, Kala's bishop had come to court this afternoon without the lawyer who had substantially blocked our attempt to interview him previously. Hopefully, he would cooperate this time. I called him as our next witness.

"Bishop Kimball," I started, "how are you employed?"

He sat straight and stiff in the witness chair. "I'm an accountant."

"Do you also have responsibilities in your church?"

"Yes, I am a bishop in The Church of Jesus Christ of Latter-Day Saints."

I cocked my head toward the defense table. "Do you know Kala Tausinga here?"

The bishop smiled at Kala. "Yes." It was a nice touch. If the jury can see that he has warm feelings for her, it could help us on the verdict. The jury, however, showed no emotion either way.

"How do you know her?"

"She has been in my ward for the past three or four years."

"Do you know who else is in her family?"

"Yes. She has a husband and four children," the bishop replied. "Oh, sorry, she now has three children." He looked at Kala, and his eyes softened as the corners of his mouth turned down.

Kala wiped a tear from her eye.

"Has Kala come to you in your role as bishop for advice and counsel?"

"Yes."

"For what purposes?"

"For one thing, she came for assistance from the Bishop's Storehouse."

"Can you please explain what the Bishop's Storehouse is?"

"The church helps needy members with the basic necessities like food and clothing."

"Has Kala Tausinga received such services?"

"Yes," the bishop said. "When Kala had her third child, Juna, she said she needed money to buy him food and clothing, that her husband's income was insufficient to care for him."

"For what other purpose did Kala come to seek help?"

"She came to seek marital advice," the bishop replied.

"How did you advise her?"

"I told her to try to work it out. I recommended that she and her husband go to marriage counseling with LDS Social Services. It's an organization with professional counseling services for marriage, substance abuse, and people with mental health issues. The counseling is free for members."

My next questions had been carefully chosen. They

were the same ones I had asked him during our first interview. His answers then had caused me to lose my cool and yell at him. I needed to maintain a professional demeanor with him now to get him to answer my questions, but I hoped that at least some members of the jury would have the same reaction now that I had previously.

"And why did you feel it was so important to try to save the marriage?"

"In our church, we like to say that families are forever. We believe that families can stay together in the afterlife and live with God the father and his son Jesus Christ."

"Can everyone achieve that goal?"

"No," the bishop said, shaking his head. "The covenant of eternal marriage is necessary for exaltation. A woman needs to be married to her husband in the temple."

"Otherwise, she can't live with God?"

"That's right."

As I expected. I checked the jury to gauge their reaction. Some of jury members must be Mormon because they seemed completely willing to accept the bishop's assertions about what women had to do to get into Heaven as gospel, but others seemed appropriately bewildered.

Mary and I believed this religious angle was important. We had presented various parts of our case to numerous people, both inside and outside of the office. Most people we talked to got caught up on the fact that Kala had not left her husband. Mothers were especially concerned about this fact. *If* indeed she was being abused, *why* didn't she leave?

Or even more important, if any of her children were being abused, how could she possibly *not* leave? Their assumption was that since she didn't leave, it must not have been as bad as we were telling them it was. The bishop's explanation about his church gave us at least *one* compelling reason for her not having left. She went for help, and he told her to stay.

There was one other religious angle that resonated with some of the people we talked to. Most traditional Christian churches are based on patriarchal authority— the men are in charge. The Bible says something about how wives should submit themselves unto their husbands and that he is the head of the wife, even as Christ is the head of the church. Many religious people, especially older people, understood that a woman might stay with a man and submit herself to him merely because of her Christian beliefs.

"Thank you. No further questions." I turned and walked back to our table, passing Johnson as he made his way to the lectern without any notes.

"I have only one question," said Johnson. "Did Kala ever tell you that her husband had beaten her or threatened her or anything of the sort?"

"No, she never said anything like that."

"Thank you," said Johnson, sitting down with a smug sneer on his face.

Johnson was a bulldog. He always got every bit of useful evidence that he could from his witnesses, and he did this now with the bishop too by drawing the attention of the jury to something that Kala did not say.

If the jury wanted to know what Kala had to say about all of this, they were about to find out. At first, Mary and I had planned to call Kala to testify last. But in the end, we decided that Adya Singh from the YWCA would testify after Kala so that Adya could give her expert opinion based on what Kala had said. And unlike lay witnesses, Ms. Singh, as an expert witness, was able to stay in the courtroom and listen to Kala's testimony.

I patted Kala on the shoulder. "It's time, Kala."

Her body stiffened, and her eyes opened wide. She nodded at the inevitable.

"Call your next witness," said the judge.

Mary stood up. "The defense calls Kala Tausinga."

Undoubtedly, we had the juror's full attention. Behind us, the audience started murmuring.

Kala stood up but didn't move. Mary stepped away from the lectern and took her gently by the arm and led her to stand in front of the court clerk. Kala complied with Mary in an almost robotic manner.

"Please raise your right hand," the clerk said. "Do you solemnly swear to tell the truth, the whole truth, and nothing but the truth?"

Kala nodded. "Yes. Yes, I do."

Mary waved her arm in a half circle directing Kala to go around the wall in front of the witness chair and up the stairs.

While Kala settled nervously into her seat, she scanned the courtroom. I craned my neck to see if Afa had snuck into the back seats. Fortunately, he wasn't there. I breathed a sigh of relief.

Mia was there, however, sitting on the back row. She raised her hand and gave Kala a small wave and mouthed the words "You can do this."

With Afa absent and Mia present, Kala relaxed, enough to tell her story to the jury I hoped.

Mary stood patiently at the lectern until Kala's eyes met hers. "Please state your full name for the record."

"My name is Kala Tausinga."

"Please tell the jury a little bit about yourself."

Kala and Mary had rehearsed her response to this question. "Well, my family is Tongan, but I was born in American Samoa. I have one sister. My dad worked at a market selling fish and worked part time at a plantation."

"Kala, did something happen to your dad?"

"Yes." Her voice was soft, maybe too soft. "When I turned ten, my dad passed away…" Mary motioned with one of her hands, palm up, to speak louder. Kala nodded. With a louder voice, she said, "When I turned ten, my dad passed away, and I came here to America to live with my uncle, Sione Aleki, and his family."

Mary smiled and nodded at her. Kala's body relaxed from the encouragement.

"When did you meet your husband, Afa?"

"During high school. Afa was different from the other guys I had dated. He said that I was his first love. He treated me with love and respect, well, at first."

"What do you mean at first?"

"When I found out I was pregnant, I was so happy. I dropped out of high school, and Afa and I moved in together in Afa's aunt's house. But finally, I saw Afa's true colors. He would call me nasty names, and he slapped my face whenever he got mad. One day Afa's aunt came into my room to talk to me. She told me that Afa said I could not have our baby because he was not ready to be a dad."

Johnson stood up as if he were going to object.

Mary stopped her questioning and glared at Johnson, waiting for him to say something...do something. But, after a moment, he sat and waved at Mary to continue.

Mary turned back to Kala. "When Afa's aunt told you that you shouldn't keep the baby, how did that make you feel?"

"I was hurt. I told both her and Afa that it was my baby too, and I would never give up my baby. I was seven months pregnant, and I could feel the life inside of me. We argued, and I told Afa I didn't want to be with him anymore. When he saw me putting some things in my suitcase, he got so mad that he kicked me in the stomach. I had bad pain and some bleeding. I called the doctor, and they sent me on a life flight helicopter to the hospital. When they asked me what happened, I said I fell down the stairs."

Mary's voice softened. "Which of your children were you carrying at that time, Kala?"

"Amanaki. I gave birth to my princess Amanaki Tausinga two months early. She was so beautiful. My best Christmas present ever."

Mary waited a moment for everyone to digest Kala's words before she moved to the next point. "Kala, did you leave Afa after that?"

"No." Kala dropped her head. "I wanted to leave, but the bishop of our ward always told us we should do the right thing and get married. So, we got married, and a year later, I had my second child, my beautiful Emeni."

"After your marriage, how was your relationship with Afa?"

"It was good for quite a while. But one day, Afa asked me to please promise him that I would never leave him. He started crying and told me he was sorry for the way he treated me and that he loved me. I wondered why he was being so nice to me. Then he told me that he had cheated on me with Mele, my first cousin." She fidgeted with her hands in her lap. "I remember him always complaining about my thing not being tight enough and about me being fat. He's right about that, so in a way I don't blame him for cheating on me."

"Your Honor," said Johnson, standing up again, "I'm afraid I have to object to this line of questioning. It's not relevant to the question at issue. And these long narrations...they're not responsive to the questions."

Judge Russo turned to Mary. "Well, Counsel?"

"Judge, I'll move this along. I have only a little more to cover." She used the index finger and thumb to form the universal sign of "little." "Then I suggest we take a recess. After that, we'll focus on the present charge."

"Very well," the judge said as he sat back in his big chair. "You may continue. But please move this along."

Mary asked, "Kala, what did you do after Afa cheated on you?"

"I told Afa that I didn't want to be with him anymore. He got so mad. He slapped me and said he loved me and that's why he told me the truth. But I still told him I didn't want to be with him. So, he went to stay at Vai's house, a guy he worked with."

Mary glanced at the judge. "Without going into all the details, after you and Afa separated, did something happen between you and Afa's friend Vai?"

Kala hesitated a moment before answering. Her eyes dropped back to her fidgeting hands. In almost a whisper, she said, "Yes. Vai and I had sex together, and I got pregnant."

Mary nodded and scanned the jury. Disapproval emanated from several jurors. But that couldn't be helped. The fact that Juna wasn't Afa's child was the key to our defense.

"Did Afa find out about Vai?"

"Yes. One night while we were still separated, Afa came back to our apartment to see if I would have sex with him. I said no. He said that he found out that I had been with Vai, and he slapped me hard on the face. He said that Vai was going to die, that he was going to kill him. I told Vai about Afa's threat, and Vai moved to Alaska, and Afa moved back in with me."

Mary asked, "Vai made you pregnant with Juna, is that right?"

"Yes."

"Kala," Mary said, her voice sympathetic, "how was your relationship with Afa after Juna's birth?"

"Afa controlled my life. I never had any money, so I said I wanted to get a job. When I did get a job, he refused to watch the kids so I could go to work, and I lost the job. After that he wouldn't let me even look for a job because he said that I only wanted to meet guys at work. And when sometimes he did give me money, I had to always show him a receipt for what I bought, even for a candy bar. I wanted to leave him so many times, but he always said he would take the kids if I left. I love my kids so much I could never leave my kids."

Mary's eyes darted between Kala and the jury. "Kala, did you ask anyone for help?"

"Yes, a few times." She raised her head with

pleading eyes. "I went in and talked to the bishop to ask for advice. The bishop called us both into his office and said he would help us get marriage counseling. When we got home, Afa slapped me and called me a slut and a stupid fat bitch. He said counseling was only for white people, and he tore up the referral paper the bishop gave us."

Johnson started to clear his throat, apparently as a warning to Mary about the length and nature of the testimony she was eliciting from Kala.

Mary nodded at Johnson. "Let me ask you one last question. Was there ever a time you considered giving up Juna?"

"Only one time," Kala said quietly. "My sister called and told me that she was unable to have children. My sister knew that Afa was mad about Juna and asked me if I would please let her and her husband adopt Juna."

Kala paused, so Mary prompted her. "What did you decide to do?"

"At first, I was going to do it. I love my sister, and she said it would help her marriage. But I saw Juna's little face, and I loved him too much to let him go." She burst into tears. "But I *should* have. I *should* have let him go!"

Kala sobbed uncontrollably, and Mary let her cry until the judge himself called for a recess.

I, myself, was a veteran of many courtroom battles. I had watched a hundred witnesses cry. But now, for the first time, tears streamed down my face too.

Chapter Thirty-Four

Judge Russo went to his office and let the recess continue until we reported to his clerk that Kala had finally calmed down. Before Russo called the jury out, Johnson again raised his complaint about the length and scope of Kala's testimony not being relevant to the case.

Mary glared at Johnson and assured him that she would get right to the point. Johnson backed off, perhaps realizing that having Kala testify about the most critical facts of the defense's case was not going to be a good thing for his prosecution.

But there was one important thing we had planned to do before Kala's testimony. After the jury had settled in, Mary had the bailiff take Kala to photocopy her hand. Mary measured the height of Kala's hand with a ruler, marked the paper as Defense Exhibit number 2, and offered it to the jury to view. We hoped that the jury would remember the size of the medical examiner's hand. But if they didn't now, they would have both exhibits to compare when they went to decide the case after closing arguments.

Mary waited until each juror had the opportunity to view the photo before addressing Kala again.

"Now, please tell the jury what was going on in your life during the time right before February of this year."

"I was pregnant again, and I was almost due. I was having a boy."

"Now, Kala, what happened on December second of this year?"

"Afa came home from work mad. He said that one of his friends at work told him that Vai was back from Alaska. Afa said that if he heard anything about me and Vai, he would kill me and Vai. I was so used to him always saying that if I do this or do that he would kill me that I didn't think much about it. But he was so mad. I told him I would go the store to get some things to make a birthday cake for him because the next day was his birthday. That calmed him down."

"How long were you gone?"

"About forty-five minutes, I think."

"Kala, what happened when you got back home?"

"I came home and found Afa sitting on the couch, holding my daughters on his lap, and silently crying. But I didn't see Juna. I could tell something was wrong. I ran through the apartment looking for my baby until I found him in his crib. He was shaking with his eyes rolled back in his head. I cried and asked Afa what happened to Juna. Afa was crying and said he was sorry and that he didn't mean to do it."

"Objection," Johnson almost shouted. "That's hearsay!"

"Your Honor," Mary calmly responded, ready with a carefully preplanned answer, "we offer that statement from Afa as an excited utterance, which is a recognized exception to the hearsay rule. The startling event is the injured child. Afa was clearly still under the influence of the event because he was scared and crying. That makes his statement admissible."

"I agree," said the judge. "Objection overruled."

Johnson didn't sit down immediately. Kala's testimony was crushing his case. But Judge Russo held his hand up and slowly brought it down in front of him to indicate that Johnson should just sit down.

Mary continued. "What did you do when you found Juna like that?"

"I kept asking Afa to call 911, but he wouldn't. I told him to give me the phone, but he said that if I tried to call 911, we would all die with Juna." Her eyes were opened as wide as they probably could go. Even from where I sat, I could see how tears flooded them.

"Objection." Johnson shouted it this time. "Again, Your Honor, this is hearsay. Even if his first answer was an excited utterance, assuming he said anything like that at all, that doesn't mean that the whole of an ongoing conversation is admissible."

"Actually, Your Honor," Mary said patiently, again as we had carefully planned, "we're not offering the threatening statement for the truth of the matter asserted but merely for its effect on the person who heard the statement. Consequently, by definition, under Rule 801, it's not hearsay at all."

The judge said, "I understand your objection, Mr. Johnson. It's a close call, but I believe the rules allow this testimony. Your objection is overruled."

Johnson remained standing at his table, jaw clenched and red face revealing his frustration at his inability to stop Kala from telling her story.

Turning to Mary, the judge said, "Having said that, Ms. Swanson, I am going to direct you to avoid eliciting any further testimony from this witness regarding statements made by her husband."

Mary nodded. "I understand."

Johnson finally sat down.

"Go on, Kala," said Mary, "but let's try to limit your testimony to what *you yourself* said and did from here on, okay? Please tell the jury what happened next."

"It was like a bad dream to me. I held my son as if he were sleeping. I cried and asked Juna to please get up, and I said, 'Mommy promises that I will leave Afa and take you with me.' After five or six hours, Afa finally called 911, but only after I agreed to tell the police that Juna passed away in my care while my husband was at work. The detective asked why I didn't call 911, and I told him because of the bruise on Juna's face, I was scared to go to jail."

"Did you tell the detective the truth, Kala?"

"No." She cast her eyes down.

"Why not?"

"I was afraid," she responded in a soft voice.

"Afraid of what?"

"That Afa would hurt me or the other children."

Mary stopped her questioning and glanced to the right. I followed her gaze. All the jurors were transfixed by Kala's testimony. One of the women wiped a tear from her eye. We had discussed Kala's testimony at length and decided that we should bring out during our direct examination the two conflicting statements she made to police the night Juna died. That way, when Johnson brought the statements up on cross-examination, it would have less of an effect.

"Kala, one last thing, please tell the jury—did you hurt Juna?"

"No, I didn't. I couldn't. I swear on my father's grave." Tears dropped down on her cheeks.

Johnson got up to cross-examine Kala. He didn't waste any time.

"So, you admit you're a liar?"

"What?" Kala's head jerked back. She adamantly shook her head back and forth, but eventually answered. "I... I admit I did lie to the detective."

We had anticipated Johnson's first question correctly, and we had prepared Kala to make that admission. There was no other option. It was always the worst fact of the case that our client was going to testify to something totally different than what she told the police. After all, who lies to the police? Only a guilty person is the prevailing wisdom.

"Yes. You've stated two completely different things. The first was that Juna died in *your* care while your husband was still at work. You made this statement on the very night Juna died while what it was still fresh in your mind, correct?"

"Yes."

"And in that first statement you said you were only gone five minutes, and now you say you were gone forty-five minutes. Is that correct?"

"Yes," she whispered.

"In that first statement, you explained why you didn't call 911—because you were afraid of going to jail."

"That is what I told the detective." Kala nodded.

"Now you're making this second statement, which is completely different, after you have had several months to come up with a different story, right?"

"Objection," said Mary, interrupting Johnson to help Kala. "That's argumentative."

"Overruled," said Russo. "You must answer the

question, Ms. Tausinga."

"I'm telling the truth now." She glanced between Johnson and Judge Russo.

"Now that you are on trial and don't want to be convicted, isn't that right?" Johnson spat out the question in an accusatory tone.

Kala fixed her eyes on Johnson. "You are right that I don't want to be convicted."

"That's what I thought," Johnson responded dismissively. "No further questions." He sounded disgusted. Mary and I both met Kala as she came down from the witness stand. I put my hand on her shoulder and whispered, "You did well, Kala." Mary gave her a little hug. This was definitely not standard courtroom procedure.

Before sitting, Kala looked to the back of the courtroom and mouthed "thank you" to Mia, who smiled back at her warmly.

I glanced at Judge Russo to see his reaction and saw him patiently watching the kindness we showed Kala, but after a moment he interrupted and asked, "Does the defense have any other witnesses?"

I held up my index finger toward the judge, and Mary and I huddled. "Do we call Adya now?" Mary whispered. "Or do we ask for another recess?"

"Which is best for the jury?" I asked. "To let sink in what Kala said or to move on?"

"I don't know. We were on a great roll until Johnson stopped it cold with his cross-examination. *That* is the last thing the jury will be thinking about if we give them time. So, let's move on, I guess. Let's call Adya right away."

I nodded my agreement, and Mary stood to face the

judge.

"The defense now calls Adya Singh, Your Honor."

Ms. Singh was the elder stateswoman of the local YWCA, having spent the last twenty years of her long career there. It was a coup for us to get her to testify, and her appearance and demeanor reflected it. Black pants suit. Contrasting white hair. Air of total seriousness. She approached the witness stand with confidence and was sworn in.

"Ms. Singh," Mary began, "how are you employed?"

"I'm Director of the YWCA's Family Justice Center and have been for the last ten years. The purpose of the center is to help women who are victims of domestic violence."

"What is your formal education?" Mary glanced down at her notes.

"I have a bachelor's degree in psychology, and a master's degree in social work. I am also a licensed clinical social worker." She directed her answer to the jury as experienced experts do.

"Have you had any additional training specifically in the area of domestic violence?"

After acknowledging Mary with this question, she turned to the jury with her answer. "Yes. I have hundreds of hours of postgraduate training and conferences on that subject."

Mary followed her focus momentarily before referring again to her notes. "Did you have any prior work experience in domestic violence prior to your current position?"

"Yes." She nodded. "I worked for the YWCA as supervisor of counselors and case workers. I also worked as a crisis counselor myself and as a clinical caseworker."

Going from dramatic testimony to controlled exposition changed the atmosphere within the courtroom. One juror fidgeted in his seat. Another picked imaginary lint off his jacket. Regardless, establishing this witness's credentials was crucial.

"Have you previously testified as an expert on domestic violence issues?"

"Yes, numerous times, in this state as well as in California."

Hurry this up, Mary, before we lose them all.

"So, Ms. Singh, generally speaking, based on your education and experience, can you explain to the jury the dynamics of domestic violence?"

She turned her body to emphasize her support of the jury. "Yes," she said. "We used to talk about domestic violence in the context of what we called battered woman syndrome. But over time, experts in the field have come to describe domestic violence in a broader sort of way, to include all behaviors that exert physical force to injure, control, or abuse an intimate partner or family member, forced or coerced sexual activity, destruction of property, as well as nonphysical acts that threaten, terrorize, or personally denigrate or restrict freedom."

The jury seemed tired and ready for a break. We needed to shake things up a bit. As if reading my mind, Mary put a graphic on the projector.

"I'm going to show you what has been marked for identification as Defense Exhibit number 3. Do you recognize it?"

The visual brought the jurors back to life. They all

took their minds off whatever they were thinking and doing and focused on the screen.

"Yes," Ms. Singh responded. "We call it the 'Wheel,' or sometimes the 'Wheel of Misfortune.' It is a pie chart that lists the most common categories of conduct that we classify as domestic violence."

"Please describe it."

"Certainly. In one category you have physically aggressive conduct, including violence, threats of violence, and destroying personal property, for example. In another category you have verbal or emotional abuse, such as putting a partner down, name-calling, belittling. Next is using male privilege, in which a woman is told that the man is in charge of the household and that she is subject to his control." Ms. Singh turned briefly to the jury. "This is quite common in the Polynesian community and in many religious organizations." Then, pointing back to the screen, she continued. "Another category is using children, such as threatening to take sole custody of the children. Isolation is the next category, where the abuser acts to cut his victim off from her friends and family. Next is economic control. Here, a woman is typically prohibited from having a job and must ask for money. This of course makes her dependent on her abuser and makes it more difficult to leave."

Mary said, "Your Honor, we offer this Defense Exhibit number 3 into evidence."

After a moment, Judge Russo announced, "There being no objection, it is admitted."

"Now, Ms. Singh," Mary said, "why do victims of abuse stay in abusive relationships?"

"They stay for many reasons. Fear is a big one—

fear for their own lives and for the safety of their children."

Mary stopped her questioning to see if the two female jurors, who during jury selection had mentioned fear as a reason a woman might lie, were paying attention. She made eye contact with each of them who nodded at her.

Mary asked, "You said there are other reasons why victims of abuse stay in their relationships?"

Ms. Singh nodded. "Yes, many victims hope for change. Their partner apologizes and promises to change. They want to keep their families together if possible. Often, all they have, at least in their minds, is their family. Also frequently, there's family or cultural or religious pressure to keep the family together, all of which can be powerful forces in a victim's decision-making process."

Mary paused to allow the jury to digest this critical testimony. Kala put her hand on my arm and whispered to me, "That's right. That's what happened to me."

"Thank you, Ms. Singh," said Mary when she was ready to continue. "Now, on another subject, based on your education, training, and experience, do you know if there are any differences regarding incidences of domestic violence to children by a stepparent as opposed to a natural parent?"

"Yes. Stepparents are significantly more likely to sexually or physically abuse children who are not their own."

"Objection!" Johnson said, standing. "There is no foundation for that assertion."

The electricity in the atmosphere had returned. The jurors were fully engaged as the drama intensified, thanks to Johnson.

"Counsel," Judge Russo said, "the objection seems to be well taken. Do you have any response?"

"Yes," Mary answered, "Ms. Singh's foundation is based on her education, training, and long experience, none of which was challenged by Mr. Johnson. Plus, I would argue that her testimony is admissible under the same rule that Mr. Johnson cited when we objected to his expert, Rule 702."

Judge Russo stared at Johnson, who gave up on the objection. "Objection overruled. You may continue."

"Now, Ms. Singh, are you familiar with Kala Tausinga and her circumstances?"

"Yes. I have reviewed extensive documentation associated with her case, including police reports and witness interviews. I've also met personally with Ms. Tausinga and heard her testify today as well."

"Based on your review of the case, have you determined whether the indicators of domestic violence that you have described are present in her case or in her life?"

"Yes. There has been a pattern of physical abuse increasing in severity and frequency, a pattern of emotional abuse, a pattern of coercive controlling behaviors, failed attempts by the victim to leave the abusive relationship, and significant threats by the abuser that increase the fear and serve to control the victim and keep the abuse a secret, which further traps the victim in the abusive relationship."

"What is the practical result of being in such a situation?"

"The abuse is kept a secret. According to the American Psychological Association, women are six times more likely to report a violent crime that is committed by a stranger than violent crime committed by an intimate partner. Often victims fear the abuser's actions toward them will intensify if they report."

"Did you find this effect of domestic violence in Kala's case?"

"Yes. Ms. Tausinga reported several visits by law enforcement in which she did not tell them what was happening because she did not want them to take him to jail for fear of what he would do when he came out."

"Other than merely not disclosing abuse, is there any other victim response that can be expected when confronted by law enforcement?"

Ms. Singh nodded once. "Yes. Victims of domestic violence will frequently lie to police about the abuse. It's not uncommon for a victim to make some excuse for injury, such as having fallen down the stairs or having been in an automobile accident."

"Why do they lie?"

I saw the facial muscles of the two female jurors who seemed to have a clear understanding of domestic violence tense as they shifted in their seats.

"Typically for protection. It can be either to protect themselves or others."

Mary closed her folder and leaned forward onto the lectern. "Knowing what you know about Kala, is it surprising that she did not report to police that her husband had killed her child?"

"Objection," interrupted Johnson. "That question assumes certain facts that have not been proven. The jury is to determine the facts of the case."

"Ms. Swanson," the judge said, "what is your position?"

"Ms. Tausinga has testified to this conduct. The facts *are* in evidence."

"I will instruct the jury that they are to determine the facts, but I will allow the witness to testify as an expert as to the *hypothetical* circumstance of what a victim of domestic violence might do in such a circumstance," the judge ruled.

"Very well, Your Honor," Mary said. "So, Ms. Singh, would it be surprising for a victim of domestic violence to fail to report that her spouse had killed a child?"

"I think not," she said. She again addressed the jury with her explanation. "While it may certainly be difficult for the average parent to imagine the circumstance where they would fail to report such an incident, it would not be unusual for a victim of long-term domestic violence to do so. Over time, a victim becomes so controlled and dependent as to lose his or her will and self-esteem. They're *not* like normal people. They do not *act* like a normal person would act. Plus, given a death threat such as reportedly occurred in Kala's case, it becomes—"

"Objection," yelled Johnson from his seat. "Again, Your Honor, there's another assumption of fact."

"I've already instructed the jury on that point," said Judge Russo. "But again, I will allow the testimony as a hypothetical circumstance."

I could see Johnson's antics were beginning to irritate Mary, to ruffle her normally cool, calm, and professional demeanor. I had rarely seen her like this before. But I could tell her blood was starting to boil, and the pressure was rising inside her. I found myself holding my breath.

"All right, Ms. Singh," said Mary in a biting tone of voice, "assuming the *hypothetical* circumstance of a woman who had been *dominated* by an abusive husband for several years, who had been *strangled* by her husband on more than one occasion, who had found that he had just *murdered* one of her children in a violent fit of jealous rage, and then threatened to *murder her* and her other children as well if she told the police what he had done, would it be unusual for *that* woman to fail to tell police what had just happened?"

Johnson, the judge, the jury, and everyone in the courtroom were stilled by Mary's question and by the sheer intensity of the emotion in the room. No one interrupted Ms. Singh this time.

"No, it would not be unusual. Such a woman would likely do *anything* necessary to protect her other children, and herself."

"Thank you, Ms. Singh. No further questions."

"Mr. Johnson," said Judge Russo with an atypical hint of menace, "I assume you have nothing further for this witness?"

Johnson hesitated and began to speak but stopped short. "No, Your Honor."

"In that case," Mary said, "the defense rests."

"Okay. That's enough for today. Tomorrow, we'll reconvene at 9:00 a.m. to hear the closing arguments of counsel. Members of the jury, do not discuss or try to decide this matter until tomorrow after I've instructed you as to the applicable law, and you have heard closing argument. Court is now in recess."

After the jurors had filed out of the courtroom, the judge turned and said, "Counsel, I'd like you all to be here at 8:30 to discuss jury instructions."

Chapter Thirty-Five

The next morning Mia met up with Victoria. The two of them were on a mission to find Afa Tausinga. Earlier, Frank had told Mia that he sent the police to look for Afa at his father's house, but he wasn't there when they checked. Today, Mia and Victoria were going to try to plant some electronic listening devices in the house so that they would know if and when Afa showed up again.

Victoria drove the cable company truck that she had borrowed from a company employee The Sisterhood had previously helped and parked on the street near the house of Koloa Tausinga, Afa's father. Victoria was assigned this duty because of her extraordinary beauty. The theory was that no man could resist her charms.

Mia tagged along as her trainee. Sally had shown Victoria and Mia how to replace a standard cable box with the enhanced cable-ready spy box.

From where they were parked Victoria confirmed via her mini laptop that the car in front of their target house was registered to Koloa Tausinga. Afa's car was nowhere to be seen.

"Let's do this," said Victoria as she grabbed her tools.

She walked up to the front door wearing a cable company uniform with her hair tucked under her cap.

After setting down her case of equipment, she knocked. Koloa Tausinga answered the door.

"Hello. My name's Molly." Victoria held up her nametag with her picture. "My trainee and I are in your area today fixing some signal problems and doing some upgrades." Victoria flashed her perfect teeth. "May we come in to test your equipment?"

Mr. Tausinga stared at Victoria, more mesmerized with Victoria than interested in her nametag. His gaze strayed to Victoria's intentionally too-small shirt whose buttons strained to contain her ample breasts.

"We don't have a signal problem here," he finally said, still fixated on her chest.

"I'm happy to hear that," Victoria said.

Mia and Victoria had planned a response to this reaction. They needed to get inside, and walk-ins were almost always preferable to break-ins.

"In that case I'll just do the complimentary upgrade for you," Victoria said, assertively picking up her bag. "We have a new box that has more memory and provides better picture quality. It'll only take me three minutes to swap out your old one."

Victoria stepped forward confidently and essentially forced Koloa to step back out of her way. "Show me your main TV," Victoria said with a charming smile.

Mr. Tausinga led Victoria and Mia into his living room and stood watching as Victoria replaced his old box with a new one. To ensure his continuing cooperation with her plan, Victoria turned to give him a good view of her butt as she bent over to take out the old box. When she sensed that Koloa was indeed staring at her butt, Victoria turned her head a bit and gave Mia a quick wink.

The new box Victoria quickly hooked up included a feature that she hadn't mentioned. It had a built-in microphone pickup and hidden wide-screen camera. Victoria executed the next step in the plan, which was to call The Sisterhood's contact at the cable company.

Victoria told the contact, "Send a signal to the new box, please."

"This will take a minute," Victoria said to Mr. Tausinga. "Our records show you have a second box downstairs. I might as well replace that one too while we're waiting, okay?"

"There is a box downstairs, but my son isn't home right now."

"That's actually better," Victoria said. "That way I won't bother him."

She said to Mia, "You wait here with Mr. Tausinga to make sure the new box is activated properly while I quickly swap out the one downstairs."

"Of course," Mia replied as Victoria grabbed her bag and went down the stairs. After a few minutes, Victoria returned from the basement and checked the TV. "I see the reboot worked. Well, we've gotta run. Our next appointment is across town."

Mr. Tausinga asked, "Is there going to be any charge for this?"

Victoria shook her head. "No, sir. Don't worry. I promise that *this* visit won't ever show up on your bill."

Mia and Victoria climbed in the cable van and headed toward the garage where The Sisterhood kept an assortment of vehicles for the work they did.

As they drove off, Mia said, "Hey, that was fun."

"Yeah. *Some* of what we do is fun."

"It must be great to have such control over men the way you do," Mia commented. "You have such a hot body. You could probably have any man you wanted."

Victoria raised an eyebrow. "Thank you, Mia." She appraised Mia from head to toe. "But I prefer women."

A hot flash washed down Mia's spine. Her heart started to pound, and her face blushed. She cleared her throat and decided to change the subject. "By the way, what about the basement? Was there any sign of Afa?"

"The basement seemed lived-in for sure," Victoria said, gracefully accepting the change of subject. "There were men's clothes on the floor. And a pizza box on a coffee table by the couch in front of the TV. I checked it. The leftover pizza wasn't too old. It could've even been from last night. Afa's father may have lied to police. Afa may be on the run, but he was definitely staying there with his father recently. While you were entertaining his father, I not only swapped out the cable box, but I had time to hide a few audio bugs too. If Afa goes back to that house, we'll know about it."

Mia asked, "What do we do next?"

"The plan to get to Afa still includes putting an electronic tracker on his car. Sally will ping Afa's phone to find him. His car will probably be nearby. Zena will take care of that. You remember the one we call the Amazon from your meeting with The Sisterhood? If Afa sees her or something goes sideways, she can take care of herself, or maybe have a chance to take care of him."

Victoria continued, "And, Mia, if you're going to join The Sisterhood, you should learn how to install trackers too. Sally will show you how to install the device, and she told me she may have some other things to show you too."

Excitement mixed with anxiety within Mia. "That sounds tricky. We don't want to get caught."

Victoria glanced over at Mia and then back to the road. "Installing trackers and spy equipment is the easy part. Finding and stopping a motivated person who has already killed, that will be the hard part."

Chapter Thirty-Six

Before the lawyers' closing arguments, the courts instruct juries on what the law is. The jurors try to decide what the facts are in the case, what actually happened, and apply the law to determine if a crime was committed and if it was the defendant who had committed it.

In this case, we had reached that part of the trial. Kala was the defendant, and this jury would determine her fate.

Yesterday, the last of the witnesses had testified. This morning, we were meeting with the judge in his courtroom to talk about the instructions he would give our jury when they arrived this morning.

Mary and I were amazed at the run of luck we had had with the evidence and the judge's rulings. We would be forever grateful to Mia for convincing Kala to testify. We had a fair chance at acquittal on the murder instruction we had submitted. Victory was within reach.

Johnson must have thought the same thing because just then he handed me a new instruction—Guilt by Omission. I quickly read the short paragraph. *No*. If the judge were to give the jury this new instruction, the jury could believe that Kala did not kill Juna but find her guilty of murder anyway solely on her failure to act to protect Juna.

Mary and I had prepared and presented our case on

the theory that it was Kala's husband, Afa, not Kala herself, who killed Juna. Our entire case was based on that point.

We were prepared to support that point in a dozen different ways: the children said that Daddy did it; the medical examiner said that the bruises on Juna's thigh were the size of a man's hand, and Kala's hand was smaller; plus by Kala's own testimony and other helpful witnesses.

I knew about the omission statute, but it had never come up in this case until now. It had not been relevant in Kala's case because Johnson had been arguing all along that Kala killed Juna, not that she failed to stop Afa from killing him.

Judge Russo asked, "Are the parties ready to discuss the jury instructions?"

Johnson stood and quickly walked up to Judge Russo and handed him the Guilt by Omission instruction. "The State is offering a new instruction based on our theory that Kala Tausinga can be found guilty of murder because she failed to protect her child from injury."

I stood. "Your Honor, we object to the State's proposed instruction on omission. Surely for a murder charge, more is required than to do nothing. Giving the instruction would be especially unfair on the facts of our case as they have been proven during trial. We have shown that Kala's husband was the real killer."

"Mr. Johnson," said Judge Russo quickly, "I'm inclined to agree with the defense here. I don't see how Ms. Tausinga could be found guilty of murder if she didn't actually cause the injury to the child."

Feeling empowered, I interjected. "Speaking of

instructions, Your Honor, may we have you instruct the jury on *that* point?"

"Wait a moment," said Johnson insistently, determined to stop me from getting *that* instruction. "First of all, I believe there is sufficient evidence for the jury to conclude that Ms. Tausinga actually *is* the one who inflicted the injuries on Juna. Her own statements to police were that the baby died in her care while her husband was still at work. And regardless of Mr. Bravo's own opinion on the omission instruction issue, we have done some research on the issue, and it's the State's position that the instruction is justified under the case law. If you like, I can cite some cases."

"Very well," said the judge, "but let's take a recess. I want to check out these cases myself. But I must tell you, Counsel, at this point, I have some misgivings on the issue."

As the judge walked out of the courtroom, I turned to Johnson. "Man, that's a dirty trick. Changing theories after all the evidence is in?"

"Look it up," Johnson said. "Guilt by Omission is in the code."

"I know it is." I shrugged. "But that's not what this case has been about. We would have elicited different evidence from witnesses. Developed different theories."

"Well, the judge hasn't decided whether to give me the instruction or not. So, let's wait and see, shall we?"

I was about to continue arguing when Mary interrupted. "Frank, let's talk." Mary must have seen my stubborn stance because she added, "Right now."

Mary led me out into the hallway and opened the door to a conference room. "We may not have much time," she said. "Let's strategize. I'm glad you objected to that Guilt by Omission instruction. If the judge gives that instruction, all our arguments so far were for nothing. I recently had a law clerk research that issue for another case. Let me show you her answer."

Mary pulled up the file of the case she was talking about on her laptop and selected a document helpfully labelled "Research on Guilt by Omission." In the clerk's devastating answer, he wrote: "A court will likely find that the defendant is guilty of murder if she knew that her husband had abused the child, and she failed to seek medical help when the baby was in distress."

"Oh no," I said. "That is exactly our case."

Mary said, "Too much was at stake to rely on anyone else's interpretations, so I decided to question the clerk's conclusions and read the case law myself. In the case cited by the clerk, a seven-year-old girl was found dead with extensive bruising from her scalp to the bottoms of her feet. Her brain was bruised and bleeding. Red marks where the surface of her skin had been scraped away were evident on her butt. The tissue around her vagina was also red and swollen.

"The defendant and his wife both told the police that their daughter had fallen down a staircase earlier that day and that her two-year-old sister had hit her with a doll. But, during the search of a closet, police found a cat-of-nine-tails whip and a leather strap with brass rivets as well as some leather restraints. They also found a videotape of the defendant's wife and another woman engaged in sadomasochistic sex. The defendant's wife was strapped down naked on the bed while the other woman hit her with the whip, including on her genitals. The medical examiner testified that the injuries to the child were consistent with having been made by the whip and strap.

"After trial, *both* the mother and father were found guilty of murder, and both appealed. The case I reviewed was the father's appeal. The court acknowledged that the evidence connecting him to the child's fatal injuries was largely, if not completely, circumstantial. However, expert testimony established that the child's injuries would have been extremely painful and that she would have cried or otherwise expressed extreme discomfort so that he would clearly have known she had been injured. The court ruled that the jury could have concluded that the father either inflicted the child's fatal injuries *or that he permitted another to inflict those injuries,* and thus was guilty by omission."

I said, "Do you have the actual case?"

Mary pulled up the case for me and turned her computer toward me so I could read it myself. I searched for the holding. This case was indeed like ours, and the court of appeals upheld the conviction. The court explained that the purpose of the child abuse homicide statute was to prevent child abuse both by prohibiting the direct infliction of injury on a child and by affirmatively requiring the child's caregiver to take steps to prevent another person from abusing the child, whether by direct intervention, seeking emergency assistance, or notifying authorities.

The law was against us. In my gut, I was absolutely convinced that Kala should not be put in the same category as a killer and was confident we had proved to the jury that Kala was *not* a killer. That she was a victim. The system should be set up to protect and help women like Kala. But Johnson was on a crusade to convict her. With the Guilt by Omission instruction, he could do it.

I asked, "Mary, what do you think? I don't know if we dare leave Kala's fate in the hands of the jury, not if the judge gives the Guilt by Omission instruction. Maybe we should try to make a deal. Or do we roll the dice, all or nothing?"

Mary raised up from the laptop. "Well, it depends on the deal. But I think we should at least try to negotiate something because in my experience, it's extremely rare for a jury to find someone not guilty when there is a dead baby. If Judge Russo gives the omission instruction, I'm afraid the jury will feel like they have no choice but to vote to convict Kala. So... yes, let's see what Johnson will do."

As we entered the courtroom, Johnson closed his file and stood to leave.

"Hey, Johnson," I called out.

"What is it?" he said, not looking at us as he gathered the last of his belongings.

It was killing me, but we needed to try. "It sounded like the judge is on the fence about how to instruct the jury. Maybe we should try to deal the case and make some sort of compromise instead of letting the jury go all or nothing. What do you say?"

"Frankly, after you got in the evidence that Kala's husband may have killed the child, I did consider the possibility that the jury could acquit," Johnson said with uncommon candor. "What are you suggesting?"

Forcing myself to exude confidence, I said, "I'm thinking more along the lines of Child Abuse Homicide as a third-degree felony."

Johnson glared at me. "How do you figure it as only a third degree?"

"Well, the statute says that it can be a third degree if it's negligent conduct instead of intentional or reckless."

"I'm not just going to let her off the hook!" He started to walk away.

"Come on, Johnson," I urged softly, "you're not letting her off the hook. It is a third-degree felony that still carries up to five years in prison."

Johnson asked, "Is Kala willing to accept prison?"

"Commitment to prison isn't mandatory for this charge," I replied. "Considering her lack of criminal history, we'd like to still ask the judge to consider probation. And we would like you to agree to it as well."

"I don't think I can do that," said Johnson. "I have a dead baby. If the judge gives me the Guilt by Omission instruction, I'll get your client for murder even if the jury thinks she didn't kill her child. Under the circumstances, the best I can do is manslaughter with a prison sentence."

"No way," I replied. "That's no deal. We'll take this case all the way to verdict."

Johnson shrugged. Mary gave a head nod toward the door, and I followed her back out into the hallway.

Mary put her arm around my shoulder and walked me to the end of the hallway away from any observers. "Frank, are you sure about this? About not negotiating?"

"No," I admitted, "but one thing I am sure about is that I'm not going to stand by and watch Kala go to prison. If the judge gives the Guilt by Omission instruction, we'll have to come up with a new argument, a new defense."

Behind us the bailiff stuck his head outside of Judge Russo's courtroom. In a loud voice, he announced, "The judge is ready to see you now."

I turned to Mary. "And we had better do it quickly."

Chapter Thirty-Seven

As we feared, after reading the case law, the judge had decided to allow Johnson's Guilt by Omission instruction to be given to the jury. Now he would call the jury into the courtroom, give them each their own copy of the instructions, and read out loud each of some twenty-five instructions on a variety of issues, such as the elements of the offense, how to analyze the testimony of experts and police officers, how the defendant's testimony should be treated the same as other witnesses, and how they should meet together to discuss and decide the case.

Usually, I follow along as the judge reads the instructions to make sure that he or she doesn't make a mistake, or that some rejected instruction does not get into the pile. But not today. Today Mary and I were brainstorming our final argument.

Giving closing arguments in a murder case is challenging enough on any day. But my nervous system was on high alert to the point that on this day, I broke a sweat.

It was only when the judge was at the end of the instructions did Mary turn her computer toward me and showed me the code provision labeled "Compulsion."

As soon as Judge Russo finished reading the instructions, I stood. "Your Honor, if it please the court, we have one more instruction we'd like you to give the jury."

Judge Russo frowned and let out a big sigh. "Please approach the bench, Counsel."

As soon as Johnson and I reached the bench, Johnson said, "This is very unusual, Your Honor. I object."

The judge replied to Johnson, "The fact that something is *unusual* is not a convincing objection, Counsel." The judge turned to me. "But this had better be good, Mr. Bravo, because this *is* very unusual."

Johnson's eyes bore into the side of my head. Trying my best to ignore him, I said, "I realize that. And I apologize for the last-minute request. But it is critical to our defense that the court instruct the jury on the Compulsion defense. That is to say, given the State's new argument that Ms. Tausinga can be found guilty for merely failing to act to protect her child, we want to be able to argue that the only reason that Ms. Tausinga did not do so was because, and let me quote from the code, she was 'coerced by the use or threatened imminent use of unlawful physical force upon her or a third person.' We believe there are facts, as presented by Ms. Tausinga's own testimony, that support this defense."

Johnson's incredulous tone returned. "I object. It's too late now to insert a new instruction. The instructions have already been read, and—"

"Stop right there, Mr. Johnson." The judge raised a hand. "I let *you* add a new theory for your prosecution *after* the trial was already over. I will not hear you complain about timeliness now."

Johnson finally stood mute. Having won the argument and seen the judge dress him down to boot, I gave Johnson a wink to top it off. For a second, he raised his hand like he was going to say something about the wink, which I admit was beyond the call of duty. Instead, he merely pouted and remained silent.

Judge Russo said, "I'll read the Compulsion instruction to the jury and direct the clerk to print and distribute it to them. Then, we'll proceed directly to closing arguments."

After the jurors received the Compulsion argument, Johnson walked past the lectern to stand directly in front of the jury as he began his closing argument.

"Ladies and gentlemen of the jury, as I told you in my opening statement, the evidence has proven that Kala Tausinga is guilty of killing her sixteen-month-old child. First, Ms. Tausinga admitted to the police on the night of the incident and admitted to you when she testified that she told the police she was home alone with her child when he died and that she did not call 911 until six hours later because she was afraid she would go to jail. That evidence is more than enough for you to find her guilty."

Johnson paused. The jury showed no indication as to how they were receiving this information.

"But what about her claim now, at this late date, that it was not her but her husband who killed the child? What of that? Is it merely a desperate attempt by someone facing a murder charge to avoid the legal consequence of her criminal act? Is it a *credible* assertion on her part given that even to make that claim, she had to admit that she's a liar? Obviously, both statements can't be true."

Johnson glanced at me before continuing. He was gloating, as he got ready to fire his next, and maybe most deadly, bullet at Kala.

"And finally, even if for some reason you still had *any* reason to question whether it was Kala Tausinga herself or her husband, Afa Tausinga, who killed the child, as the judge has just instructed you, it does not matter which one of them did it. Under the law, Ms. Tausinga would be guilty by *omission* due to her failure to stop her husband from killing their child or by her failure to seek prompt medical care for him. So, in sum, your two choices when you deliberate on your verdict are guilty or guilty."

Johnson turned and pointed at Kala. "The defendant, Kala Tausinga, is either guilty for killing her son or guilty for failing to protect him." He stood and stared at the jury for a moment longer before slowly returning to his seat.

I stood up and glared at Johnson until he finally sat down. Then I too walked over to stand directly in front of the jury.

"I was glad to see that the prosecutor acknowledged right off the bat the possibility that it was Afa Tausinga, not Kala here, who killed Juna." I glanced over at Johnson just for a second but long enough to see him frown.

"You heard plenty of evidence to show that it was in fact Afa who killed Juna. He tearfully admitted as much to Kala when she came home from the store, and he apologized to her, saying, 'I'm sorry. I'm so sorry.'"

I walked to the wall in front of the jury where the exhibits were placed and picked up two of them. "In addition, you can see from Defense Exhibit number 1 that the handprint on Juna's leg was the size of the medical examiner's hand, and you can clearly see in

Defense Exhibit 2 here that Kala's hand is significantly smaller. These are not merely the arguments of lawyers. They are facts.

"And if there was any remaining doubt in your minds that it was Afa who killed Juna, you heard that Kala Tausinga's four-year-old daughter, in a completely spontaneous statement, said, 'Daddy hit Juna's head on the wall.' So, no, Kala is not guilty of hurting her child. It was, in fact, Afa."

I paused to let the jury sit with the feeling of Kala's innocence. Sometimes, regardless of the law or the facts, a jury makes their final decision on their gut instincts, on how they *feel* about what happened.

After what I believed to be ample time, I broke into their thoughts. "So, what about that last thing? The prosecutor's argument that says you're guilty even though you didn't do anything?"

"Objection," blurted Johnson. "That's not what the instruction says."

Judge Russo did not wait for me to respond. "This is closing argument. I'll allow it."

I turned to the judge and said, "Thank you, Your Honor," as if his ruling supported my argument rather than merely allowing it.

"I see that most of you are taking notes. Good, because sometimes you find the fatal flaw in a prosecution by taking note of what the prosecutor leaves out of his argument. It's not always what he says, but sometimes it's what he doesn't say."

I turned and pointed at Johnson, partly as payback for him pointing at Kala. "In this case, the prosecutor totally avoided mentioning the single most important instruction that the judge gave you today—the

Compulsion instruction."

I sorted through the stack of instructions that Judge Russo had read and pulled out the instruction on compulsion. And then turned again to face the jury.

"Even though it's true that Kala Tausinga did not call 911 after finding her child unresponsive, she is nonetheless not guilty for his death because she was, and I quote directly from the instruction, 'coerced by the use or threatened imminent use of unlawful physical force upon her or a third person.'" I looked up at the jury and waited a moment to let that language sink in.

"You no doubt remember Kala's compelling testimony. When she *begged* Afa to give her the phone so that she could call 911, he shouted at her and told her that if she called 911, he would kill her and her other children. She had all the reason she needed to believe that he would do it. Because he had just killed Juna. Now, *that* is coercion. That is why you *must* find Kala Tausinga, a loving mother, not guilty of killing her dear son Juna."

As I said Kala's name, she clutched the blouse over her heart. Tears flowed freely down her cheeks. I walked back to my seat and put my hand on Kala's shoulder.

Johnson stood up one last time to address the jury. I've never liked it, but prosecutors get to argue twice, because, the argument goes, they have the burden of proof.

"Speaking of leaving things out," started Johnson, glaring at me, "defense counsel left out a part of the Compulsion instruction I want you to look at."

He already had the instruction in his hand. "The second half of the sentence he read to you adds that not only does there have to be some coercion, which I do not admit there was by the way, but also, it must be, and I quote, 'force or threatened force a person of reasonable firmness in his situation would not have resisted.' Ladies and gentlemen, isn't it true that a reasonable person, a reasonable parent, or even each of you in that same situation, would have resisted, would have called 911?"

Johnson paused for effect just as I stood up. I took advantage.

"Objection," I said. "It is impermissible to tell jurors to put themselves in the defendant's shoes."

Judge Russo spoke to the jury without waiting for Johnson to reply. His statement was judicious in that he neither criticized Johnson's argument nor my objection. Instead, he said, "Members of the jury, the statements of the lawyers are merely argument. You should follow the written instructions I've given you in your deliberations."

Although it was unclear whether the judge had sustained my objection or not, what was clear was that I had successfully interrupted Johnson's argument.

He scowled at me before turning back to the jury. "In summary, ladies and gentlemen, when you read all the instructions as a whole, it's clear that the law requires you to find Kala Tausinga guilty."

Johnson sat down, and the judge told the bailiff to take the jury to a conference room to decide the case. After they left the courtroom, the judge told us to stay close by and told the clerk to stop the recording of the proceedings.

Kala said to Mary and me, "Thank you. Thank you both for standing up for me. I will always be grateful."

I put my hand on Kala's shoulder. "Let's see what the jury decides first. Then we'll see how grateful you are."

Kala said, "How long does it take them to decide?"

"You never know. It's about 10:00 a.m. now. They could decide in an hour, or they might not decide today, and we have to come back tomorrow."

Mia came from the back of the courtroom to join us. First, she addressed me. "Frank, good job on your argument."

As I nodded my thanks, Mia turned and gave Kala a hug. They didn't speak but held the hug until the bailiff came to take Kala back to the holding cell. This time, though, he politely waited for them to let go of each other. Perhaps he was willing to allow this violation of court protocol to continue without interfering because he had come to understand that Kala was innocent after all. After Kala left the courtroom, Mia excused herself, saying something about having to make some plans with her new friends.

Mary and I straightened up our files, and Johnson went back to his office, which was right across the parking lot. Mary and I decided to wait at the courthouse. Mary pulled her phone out of her purse and punched in a phone number as she walked out into the hallway. I started thumbing through several dozen emails I had received and ignored during the week.

At 11:30, the bailiff and the judge came back into the courtroom. There was a question from the jury. The clerk called Johnson back to the courtroom. As soon as Johnson strode back into the courtroom, I checked my watch, smiled at Judge Russo, and asked, "Are they asking for a lunch menu?"

Judge Russo read the question. "No, Mr. Bravo, but I'm sure that one is not far behind. This one says, 'We're split over the issue of whether a person can be guilty of murder even if they didn't kill anyone. Can you give us further instructions?'"

Johnson said, "Tell them yes, of course, you can find her guilty. That's the law."

Judge Russo replied, "I'm not telling them to find her guilty or not guilty, Counsel. The only answer I'm inclined to give is to tell them they must rely on the instructions they already have."

I asked, "Is there any indication of which way they're split—guilty or not guilty?"

"No," the judge said.

I turned to Johnson. "If they stay split and there's no verdict, will you dismiss?"

"I hardly think so," Johnson said. "I think she's guilty under either of two theories."

Johnson turned to the judge. "I request that you give them the instruction that they *must* come to a unanimous verdict."

"The dynamite instruction?" I asked without waiting for the judge. "The Supreme Court has disfavored that instruction."

Judge Russo said, "The Supreme Court may disfavor it, but they do allow it, so I'll give it. And I'm going to urge each member of the jury to reconsider their opinion and try to reach a consensus."

"But some members of the jury might feel pressured to change their vote," I complained.

"I've made my ruling," Judge Russo stated with authority.

I took a deep breath and sat down.

The clerk typed up the judge's answer to the jury and took it into the jury room along with a lunch menu.

About fifteen minutes later, another question from the jury came out.

"Can we take our lunch to go? We have a verdict."

After the jury returned to the courtroom and filed into the jury box, the bailiff brought Kala out to stand with us. The judge asked the foreperson if the jury had reached a unanimous verdict.

"Yes, we have."

I wondered if the judge's last instruction had forced whoever was holding out for a not guilty verdict to give up their support for Kala and switch their vote to guilty so that the jury could return a unanimous verdict.

The bailiff took the verdict form from the foreperson and walked it over to the clerk who would read it aloud. The courtroom door opened. Mia made it back just in time to hear the verdict.

I hated this part of the trial. I couldn't help but worry that the verdict might be guilty. The prosecutor gave the jury two different ways to find Kala guilty— because she had killed her baby, or even if she hadn't. I stood there questioning the decisions I had made during the trial, questioning my arguments. Had I done all I could? Did I do enough?

I also loved this part of the trial. The anticipation of the jury's verdict was always intense, but even more so when so much was at stake. I was awake, alive. And hopeful.

The clerk stood like a statue, holding the verdict form, apparently reading it to herself. It was like everything was in slow motion. Eventually she lifted the form, cleared her throat, and read the verdict: "We the members of the jury find the defendant, Kala Tausinga... *not* guilty of murder."

Kala gasped and collapsed into her seat. She must have been holding her breath the whole time. I put my hand on her shoulder to make sure she was okay, to make sure she had heard the verdict correctly.

I leaned over. "Are you okay, Kala? It's *not* guilty."

"Yes. I heard," she replied in between breaths. "Thank you."

Kala scooted her chair forward so she could see all the jurors. She was crying as she said, "Thank you," to them.

Mary leaned in and gave me a hug. "Well done, Counselor."

"Thank you, Mary," I replied. "And the same to you."

I turned toward Randy Johnson and saw that he was avoiding eye contact with the jurors. An acquittal in a murder trial would stain his reputation for years to come. I figured he had it coming, though, for bringing charges against Kala in the first place. And for stubbornly fighting to convict her even after he must have doubted her guilt. Sullen, he slowly started piling the pads of paper and files on his table and put them into his briefcase. Then he quietly turned and walked out the door.

The judge thanked the jury for their service and released them. Turning to Kala, he said, "And you, Ms. Tausinga, are also free to go."

"Thank you, sir."

Kala turned to Mary and I just as Mia joined us.

"The judge said I'm free to go. But I don't have anywhere to go. My aunt and uncle don't want me around my children. I have no money to get an apartment. What am I supposed to do now?"

Mia spoke up. "Don't worry, Kala. You can come with me. I know exactly where you can go. I'll take you there and introduce you to the woman who helped me when I had nowhere else to go."

Chapter Thirty-Eight

"Did you see the paper?" asked Mary as she walked into the restaurant toward Mia and me the day after the verdict. Mary sat down with us, flattened out the paper, and began to read it aloud. "Defense attorney Frank Bravo stated that Kala Tausinga was the victim of domestic violence. He says that she admitted she should have done something sooner when she came home from the store and found her baby having a seizure. But her husband said that if she did, he would kill her and her other children. Bravo also claimed that the prosecutor had put his head in the sand and ignored evidence of the husband's guilt. Bravo added that the husband is wanted for outstanding warrants."

"Sounds like they got it pretty close this time," I said, grinning. "I don't normally talk to the press, but I was pissed at Johnson."

"Johnson had it coming"—Mary waved her hand dismissively— "and you did great. You got a not-guilty verdict for Kala."

"Make that *we,* Mary. I couldn't have done it without you—no way."

"Thanks, Frank."

I turned to Mia. "And, Mia, we could have done none of this without you too. *You* are the one who gave Kala the courage to testify. That's why Mary and I invited you to join us for lunch. We're grateful to you."

Mia smiled broadly. "You are kind to say so. By the way, I'm impressed by the commitment the two of you had to helping Kala. I saw you in action. You never gave up, no matter what. So let me say that I'm grateful to you too."

Looking back and forth between Mia and Mary, I said, "Let's just agree that it took all of us to do it. It didn't seem possible at first. Kala was charged with murder. She told the police that she was home alone with Juna when he died. Kala wouldn't even tell Mary and me the truth. The prosecutor fought us all the way. It was a dead baby case. Everything went against us. But working together, we got a good result for Kala."

"When our drinks get here, let's toast each other for our great work," Mary suggested.

"And toast Kala," added Mia, "for having the courage to come forward and testify even though she was afraid."

"Agreed," I said.

"Mia," Mary said, "it must be fulfilling to be a victim advocate."

Mia nodded. "Yes, it is. Or it was anyway. I didn't tell you, but Johnson fired me from my job."

Mary's jaw dropped. Dishes clanged in the background.

"Oh, my God," Mary exclaimed, "Mia! But why?"

She shrugged and stared at her glass of water. "He found out I was going to see Kala. I told him I believed her to be innocent. I argued with him about not charging Afa. There were lots of reasons I guess."

Mary touched Mia's arm. "I'm so sorry to hear that."

"Don't worry." Mia lifted her eyes. "I plan to find

a similar job with another agency because you're right, the job was fulfilling, most days at least. But it could be frustrating on other days. Sometimes I felt that the system prevented me from helping all the women I wanted to help. At least I used to feel that way."

Mia put her elbows on the table and leaned in closer to us. "Recently, I met a group of women who call themselves The Sisterhood. They help abused women when the system fails."

"The Sisterhood?" Mary said. "I don't think I've heard of them."

"Um, they're not in the book under that name."

Mia squirmed. I assumed she was worried that she had shared too much. After all, Mia had told me that The Sisterhood was a *secret* organization.

"That's just an unofficial name," Mia added. "But you can look up The Refuge if you want. It's a place where abused women can go and be protected."

Mia changed the subject. "So anyway, now that Kala's case is finally over, what are you two going to do?"

"Well, I need to go home and get reacquainted with my husband," Mary said, chuckling. "I've been working so many extra hours that when I finally make it home, he says things like 'Hello, nice to meet you.'

"How about you, Frank?" Mary added. "Last time we chatted, you still didn't have anyone to go home to. Do you think you'll start dating again?"

"No," I replied. "I've been waking up in the night, every night, walking around my apartment making notes for cross-examination and practicing closing argument. That sort of thing is not particularly conducive to dating. I'm totally unattached, and frankly, I'm starting to get used to it. I may never get married again."

Mary said, "Well, that's good for now. You need some time. But never say never."

"But I do have a dinner date with my ex-wife Janelle, though," I said, raising an eyebrow. "Next week."

Mary's eyes opened wide with surprise. "What? With Janelle? *That's* very interesting. Tell us more."

"Well, it's not what you think. It's for my daughter's birthday," I replied, laughing. "Bella said what she wanted for her birthday was to have dinner with me and her mother. I called Janelle and set it up. Where our daughter is concerned, we're both still committed to our relationship as her parents."

Mia said, "Frank, I met your daughter at court. She's so smart and so beautiful. Tell me more about her."

"Okay. She is my favorite subject. She is her junior class vice president. Plays forward on the basketball team. Plus, you were right. She is smart. She has already taken all the A.P. Math classes available. And she still makes time for an occasional martial arts class."

"Come on, Proud Papa," Mary said. "Show her one of those pictures."

I fumbled with my phone until I found an album with pictures of Bella. "Look. Here's a picture of her at age eight doing a flying sidekick."

"Wow," Mia said, grabbing the phone from my hand. "That's great form. How high is she? I can't even see the floor in this picture. And age eight you said? I do martial arts now, but I sure wish I had started younger."

"I started Bella in a self-defense course at age six," I replied, not holding back my pride. "She liked it, so I kept her in it for several years. She got her black belt in karate at age twelve."

"That's awesome," Mia said as she continued to stare at the picture.

Raising an eyebrow, I said, "I'm particularly glad that she knows some martial arts because the prom is coming up soon. She's only sixteen, and even though she's only a junior, she was asked out by a senior kid I don't know. So, I'm worried about her. You know how teenage boys are."

"It's not only the teenagers, Frank," Mary said, laughing.

"Frank, text me the date of the prom," Mia said as the server approached with our lunch orders. "I may be able to get something for her that'll help make her feel safe. Or maybe something that will at least ease your mind."

Chapter Thirty-Nine

Bella grinned and flew into my arms as soon as I came through the front door of the Olive Garden restaurant. "Daddy, I'm so happy to see you."

"Good to see you too, sweetheart," I replied, squeezing her tightly.

"Hey," said Janelle, after a moment, "what about me?"

My ex-wife was smiling, apparently glad to see me as well. "Yes, it's good to see you too."

After Bella released her grip on me, Janelle took a step toward me and started to raise her arms. I quickly met her halfway and gave her a hug. Her warm embrace brought memories of happier times.

"Bravo, party of three?" asked the young blonde hostess in front of a computer at the front of the restaurant.

"Yes," Janelle and I answered together.

I was surprised yet happy. "Still using Bravo?" I asked.

"Yes," Janelle replied. "For Bella. Plus, I don't mind."

"Hey, *Bella*," said the hostess.

"Hi, Amy," Bella said. "How are things since I left? I see you've taken over my job."

"You know, same stuff, different day," Amy said. "Are you coming back? You can have your job back.

I'll go back to serving."

"Thanks. Just kidding about the job," Bella said. "But yes, I think I'll be back. Probably not until summer. I have too much going on at school to work during the school year."

"Well, I'd be happy to see you."

"Me too," replied Bella.

"Follow me."

Amy led us to a booth at the back of the restaurant. I settled in across from Bella and Janelle.

"You like the Olive Garden, right, Daddy?"

"Yes, honey," I replied. "Other than your nonna, nobody makes better minestrone soup anywhere.

"What's new at school?" I asked Bella, as we flipped through our menus.

"Nothing much," she replied. "Just helping plan the prom."

"So, what is the plan?" I asked Bella, raising an eyebrow toward Janelle. I remembered the debauchery engaged in by some of my classmates at my own prom.

"Well, there will be a dance at the gymnasium." Bella glanced sideways at Janelle.

"Go ahead and ask him, honey," Janelle encouraged.

"Daddy," Bella started with the sweetest coy smile, "I need a new dress for the prom."

"I'd be happy to pick something out," I said quickly. "A nice gown, hanging below the knees, maybe with long sleeves and—"

"*Daddy*," interrupted Bella with a pout. "I don't need you to *pick* it."

"Aha, just pay for it," I replied, nodding. "Of course, I will. I'm happy to do it. Happy birthday."

"Thanks, Daddy."

Her smile grew radiant, worth every dollar I'd spend on her dress.

"So, who are you going with? Anyone I know?" I asked, pretending to search the menu.

"Johnny. You don't know him. He plays on the football team."

I peered at Janelle over the top of my menu. "Have you met this Johnny? What do you think?"

She shrugged. "I think that you're never around anymore, which is why you don't know Johnny."

"Come on, baby," I replied. "You don't need to be like that. I am around, whenever Bella needs me."

"And you don't get to call me *baby* anymore."

Bella jumped in. "Stop it! Both of you! This is my birthday dinner. I wanted us all to be together and have a happy time."

The server arrived just in time to force a truce. We each placed our orders. Bella ordered the Tour of Italy dinner. It was a lot, but she had the metabolism to handle it. Janelle, a shrimp scampi, and I ordered my favorite—lasagna classico with minestrone soup.

After the server left with our orders, I said, "Sorry, honey. And I mean that to both of you." Janelle didn't complain about the term of endearment this time.

"Let me try again. Janelle, what do you think of Johnny?"

"What I think is that we can trust our daughter to go with whomever she chooses," said Janelle, sitting back in her seat and folding her arms. She was still leaving it to me to play the bad parent. "You've always been overprotective. You wouldn't even let her cross the street by herself until she was ten."

"I do trust Bella," I replied quickly. "It's Johnny I don't trust." Turning to Bella, I asked, "So tell me the plan. Are you going somewhere before the dance?"

Bella said, "Yes. Everyone goes somewhere to eat before the dance."

"Is that all?" I asked. "I still remember high school. Some people went drinking before the dance, others to the mountains to make out."

Bella glanced at her mother, who I could tell wasn't going to intervene again. "How about this, Daddy? I know that you're a worrier. If anything goes wrong, I'll text you, okay?"

"Okay," I said, understanding that was as much as I was going to be able to get. "It's just that I love you," I said, not feeling any better about it.

"I know you love me, Daddy. And I know that you wouldn't let anything happen to me."

Chapter Forty

"I like your new hairstyle, Kala," said Mary after we got past the reception area of The Refuge. It had been three weeks since Mia had brought Kala to The Refuge, and Mary and I were both eager to see how she was doing now that she was out of jail and the cloud of the murder charge had cleared from her sky.

I added, "Plus, you look strong. And it seems you've got some sun too."

"Thank you. We have access to an exercise room, and I've been walking a lot. And thanks for coming to see me. You just missed Mia. She came to visit me too."

"I'm very glad to hear that Mia is still keeping in touch with you," I said. "She is so sweet. How are things going for you?"

"Great. I love my job now. Xtina is paying me to work in the greenhouse. Because they don't charge me to live here, I've already saved enough to rent my own apartment." She maintained eye contact, and her voice sounded confident. "Xtina said they would either pay for me to continue in school or help me get a new job in town. She says The Refuge has helped lots of women who pay it forward by helping other women from The Refuge." Now, her smile reached her eyes, which danced with hope and optimism.

"That's great, Kala." Mary's voice reflected

excitement and encouragement. "What else are you doing?"

A few women walked through the reception area. One was unkempt and frowning, but the others strolled by with shoulders back and heads held high.

"I'm so busy," Kala announced. "I'm taking classes to get my high school diploma. I go to a support group meeting with other women once a week. They talk a lot about their bad relationships. I don't say very much, but I like to listen. Adya came by and told me that the YWCA's Safe at Home Coalition will help me file for a divorce."

"Have you decided you want a divorce?" Mary asked.

"Yes. I don't want to be with Afa anymore," she announced with strong conviction.

Speaking of Afa, I had a few questions for personal reasons. "Kala, have you heard anything from Afa?"

She nodded. "He called my uncle and said he wanted to get the kids back."

"He can't," I jumped in. "He lost his parental rights."

"I'm not sure he understands," said Kala.

"My uncle Sione said that Afa asked about me and wanted to find me, and that Afa said I was his wife and better do what he said, and that we were going to be together again with the kids. I told Sione *please* don't tell Afa where I am. I don't want to see him. My life is so much better without him."

"Have you been able to see your kids?" Mary asked, staring intently into Kala's eyes.

"Yes! My uncle Sione brought them to visit me. They are so beautiful. He said that I can visit them anytime and that I can take them places too. I thought I had lost them all. I'm so happy I could cry. I owe it to you guys. But Juna, I miss him."

"That's understandable," Mary said supportively.

"I loved Juna so much. I had a dream while I was pregnant with him. In the dream, I saw two graves. One was my father's grave. The other one, right next to it, was a small grave. It was Juna's. That's why somehow, I wasn't surprised when he died at the hospital right after he was born. Or they said he was dead. I thought it was fate. But I prayed to God anyway and asked him to bless my little Juna.

"And then an old man at the hospital did bless him. He blessed him that he would get better so that he could help his mother have a better life. Then Juna came home with me.

"While I was in jail, I kept thinking about the words of the blessing in the hospital, and I know now that Juna's blessing came true. He saved me. Because of him, I am free from Afa. He gave his little life to help me. It was like the blessing said. He was truly a gift from God."

My spine tingled. I was amazed at the spiritual clarity Kala had gained.

"And you two," Kala added after a moment, "you two saved me from the courts and got me out of jail. I am so grateful."

"It was an honor for us to help you, Kala," Mary responded. "But it's a shame it had to come down to us. The system failed you. The police didn't investigate. Your family told you to stay in an abusive marriage. Your bishop didn't help you. And the prosecution made a stupid decision to charge you. Someone should have helped you before."

"Well, no one has ever stood up for me before. Thank you so much. I love you guys."

We hugged. In that moment the work, the danger, and the drama were all worth it. I had helped someone. Justice was served. Or at least a close approximation of justice, which is often the most we can hope for.

In that moment, everything seemed right with the world.

Chapter Forty-One

A week after her last visit with Kala at The Refuge, Mia was driving home from a planning meeting with Zena and Sally. After they found Afa's car and planted the tracker on it, they decided it was time to make a move on Afa.

The sisters engaged in a spirited discussion about what to do. Zena wanted to give him the worst beatdown of his life to make him relive and suffer through every harm he had ever inflicted upon Kala. She wanted to leave him disabled but alive and suffering.

Mia had spoken up to say that Kala was not his only victim, that he had killed a child and had escaped justice. Mia was surprised to hear herself say, "So, shouldn't he have to pay for that?" That is when Sally offered to spirit him away to one of her black sites and to torture him until he begged for death. In the end, Zena and Sally decided to take the case to the board of The Sisterhood for a final vote and decision and had adjourned the meeting.

Mia used her hands-free system to call Kala. "Hi, Kala. I'm calling to see how you're doing in your new apartment."

"Hi, Mia," Kala said, happily. "I'm digging through boxes looking for my favorite nonstick frying pan. My aunt and uncle had boxed up everything I

307

owned when I went to jail and put it in their garage. This morning, some young men from the church brought it all to my apartment, and I'm trying to unpack."

"That sounds great, Kala. But how are *you* doing?"

Kala's voice remained optimistic. "I'm doing well. Truly. The Refuge paid my deposit to move in here and helped me get a job assembling and packaging medical products that pays enough to cover the rent and groceries. The apartment is small, but it is all mine. And it is so peaceful here."

"I'm happy to hear that." Mia couldn't help but smile with the satisfaction of how well Kala has turned her life around.

Kala added, "There is something else I have been wanting to tell you. The YWCA got me a lawyer from Legal Aid who filed my divorce papers for me. They found Afa at his father's house and served him with a copy of it yesterday. Now I am waiting for a court date."

"Good for you."

"And I have more good news. My sister told me that she saw Vai and that he said he wanted to see me. I think that if he calls me, I will see him. Maybe I can make a new future with him."

"That's wonderful," Mia said. "Just know that you don't have to rush into a new relationship. You don't need a new man to take care of you. You should take time to take care of yourself. Then, someday, maybe you'll find the right man."

Bam! Bam! Bam! Kala let out a startled shriek.

Mia shouted, "Kala, what is it?"

Kala replied in an urgent whisper. "It's Afa! He's

at my door!"

"Don't open the door. Hide, but don't hang up."

Mia pictured the roads between where she was and Kala's apartment. Sally and Zena were both too far away. Mia took a hard left. *Only a mile or two.* She pushed her accelerator all the way to the floor and shouted, "I'm coming, Kala!"

Mia swerved around the other traffic as she rushed toward Kala's apartment. She glanced right and left as she flew past a stop sign, grateful there were no cars. Her heart pounded as she approached a red light, and she slowed a bit as she saw two cars entering the intersection from either direction, but she thought there was a sliver of room after they passed, so she stepped on the gas again and zoomed forward as horns blared at her. It was getting dark, and she was going fast, so no one was going to be able to see her license number to report her to police. *The least of my worries.*

"Mia, Mia," Kala whispered.

"Yes. What is it?"

"He's shouting to let him in."

"Where are you?"

"I'm hiding in the bedroom."

"Does it lock? Lock the door."

"No, there's no lock." Kala started whimpering as the knocks resounded louder into her bedroom.

"Be quiet. Try the bathroom. Go in there. Lock it and wait."

Mia's tires squealed around a right-hand turn. "I'm getting closer."

"Okay, I'm in the bathroom now," Kala said after a moment. "But I heard the glass break. I think he broke the window and opened the door. He's shouting something about the divorce papers. He found my address on the divorce papers."

Mia heard loud, muffled shouting, "Open the door! Let me in. I know you are in there. I saw you go in there. Open up!"

Gotta hurry. Mia sped ahead. She had been worried about the police stopping her, but now thought it would be okay if an officer or two followed her to Kala's place. She checked her mirrors. No police. *It's up to me.*

Mia heard Kala shout, "Leave me alone. I'll call the police!"

"Ha! Remember what happened last time you called the police. They arrested *you*."

Kala shouted, "Mia, he is kicking the door. The door is breaking. Mia? Mia?"

"Kala. I'm here. Talk to me."

Kala no longer answered. Mia could hear a struggle, and Kala shouting for help. Afa shouting, "If I can't have you, no one can." But the voices were fading away. Kala must have dropped her phone.

Mia drove as fast as she could. She patted the .38 in the holster under her jacket and checked her pocket. *Dammit.* She wished she had some of Sally's special super-spy lipstick cases.

Seeing Kala's apartment building ahead, Mia screeched into an open parking spot and sprinted for Kala's door. As Mia kicked through the damaged door, she saw Afa holding Kala in the air by her neck. Kala's hands dropped to her sides, and she fell limp.

Mia took three fast steps, leapt into the air, cocked her right leg back, and snapped it forward as hard as she could into the right side of Afa's face. He released Kala as he fell backward and crashed with a thump on the ground, unconscious.

Mia landed on one foot but maintained her balance. Quickly she turned to Kala, who had collapsed to the floor. Mia dropped to one knee to feel her carotid artery. *Are you still there, Kala?*

Yes. A heartbeat. Mia dropped her head to Kala's mouth. Air brushed her ear. She started to reach for her phone to call 911. Afa moved behind her. He was struggling to get up. *No!*

Mia spun toward Afa as he was pushing himself into a seated position, leaning against the wall. She could knock him back down. He was still stunned. She could physically restrain him until police arrived. *But should I?*

Thoughts raced through her mind. Fear and anger collided in her chest. Should she trust in the law like she always had, like she was trained to do, like her job required? Oh wait, no, *they fired me.* When she was in the planning session with Zena and Sally, they had not agreed on what to do to Afa. They were going to ask the board of The Sisterhood for advice. She wasn't sure what she should do now.

Afa's eyes focused now on Mia. Rage blazed in his eyes. Mia's heart jumped into her throat. Memories of Afa flashed through her mind—raping Kala, kicking her belly when she was pregnant, killing Juna, hurting Frank, and now, right now, glaring at her with murderous intent.

Afa was still dazed, and his jaw was broken. She still had a choice. *Was this a choice that Xtina had foreseen, the choice that Xtina had told her she would have to make if she were to join The Sisterhood?*

Pulling the gun from the shoulder holster under her jacket, Mia made her choice.

Mia placed her gun on Kala's kitchen counter, out of Afa's reach, and warily took three steps toward him as he sat stunned on the kitchen floor. There was no need to attract unwanted attention by firing a gun in this apartment building. Plus, the police investigation would continue if no gun were found at the scene of a shooting. Mia didn't intend to be here when the police arrived.

Afa grunted with an effort to stand up as Mia approached. He put a hand on the wall. Just as he got one foot beneath him, Mia unleashed a fierce roundhouse kick that struck him in the face with enough force to bounce his head hard off the wall behind him.

Afa crashed back to the floor. His head wobbled back and forth and fell forward loosely. Mia stopped to consider again what she should do now that Afa was unconscious again. Uncertain, she searched the kitchen for an electrical cord to tie him with. A toaster? The lamp cord?

Mia started to take a step toward the appliances when Afa's hand squeezed her ankle hard and ferociously yanked her foot out from under her, causing her to spin around and crash to the floor on her tailbone, sending a spear of pain down her legs. Still holding her ankle, Afa pulled himself toward her, veins bulging in his hand.

As Afa's grimacing, bloody face approached her, Mia regretted putting her gun down. It was only a few steps away, but it might as well not be there at all. His grip was like a vice on her ankle and prevented her from moving even an inch toward the gun. She cocked her free leg back and fired it forward into Afa's face. His grip loosened, and she tried to shake her leg free. But he still had a hold of her and started again to pull her closer to him.

Fear gripped her heart now too. That last night with Carlos flashed in her memory. *Oh no. Not again.* Afa pulled himself forward and reached out to grab Mia by the hair.

You have the power to fight evil, Mia. Xtina's words steeled her resolve to fight back. She made a fist and with her thumb extended, she jabbed Afa in the eye hard enough to make him jerk backward.

Having some space now, Mia cocked her free leg again and jammed it into Afa's face. Still, he held on. "You fucking bastard," she shouted as she kicked again. "Let go of me!" Mia kicked one more time with all her effort and finally pulled free from Afa. She quickly crab-walked backward and scrambled onto her feet.

Afa growled with effort and dragged himself up to one knee. He lifted his eyes to see Mia. She felt the raw animal intent behind that scowl and steeled herself for action. She knew what she had to do.

Moving quickly before Afa could even start to react, Mia brought her right hand behind her left ear, pushed hard off her left foot, and struck Afa in the middle of his throat with the side of her hand with a force meant to cut right through his neck.

Afa's eyes widened when he couldn't breathe. He put both hands on the floor and leaned forward, trying to choke in a breath.

Mia stood back, waiting to see what happened. In a matter of seconds, Afa's face started to turn blue.

Seeing her opportunity, Mia made up her mind and slipped in behind him. She hooked her right arm around Afa's neck and locked it in place with her left hand.

Afa clamped his jaw down and clawed at Mia's arm, but she held firm. He flailed an arm behind him to try to hit her but couldn't muster the force to hurt her. Still fighting, Afa arched backward and forced Mia backward to the floor with his full weight on her. Mia cried out as she hit the floor but was able to get a better grip around Afa's neck at that angle.

No more, asshole! Mia closed her eyes, grit her teeth, and held on until Afa quit struggling. Then she tightened her grip and squeezed even tighter until she was sure he was dead.

Finally, Mia heaved Afa's heavy corpse off her and rolled to her knees. Breathing hard and crying, she dragged herself to her feet.

She turned and stared at Afa one more time. The mere sight of the brute's face sparked her anger again. Remembering the hours she had spent pummeling the dummy Carlos, Mia wiped the tears from her face, leaned over, and ferociously tried to pound Afa's nose up into his skull until she heard sirens in the distance and worried that they were coming to Kala's house.

Chapter Forty-Two

We had hoped to find Kala awake, but the nurse told us she was sedated and on pain medications. Upon walking into her hospital room and first seeing her, I was shocked by her appearance. She lay on hospital bed, her face almost unrecognizable with massive bruising, cuts, and eyes closed—swollen closed. The backs of her hands and forearms were purple and blue as well from what appeared to be defensive marks. At least the fact that she was here meant she must have been successful.

Mary and I sat in the green chairs near her bed, watching her vital signs on the monitors that were hooked into and onto different parts of her body. Their rhythmic beeps kept interrupting the room's silence but not my thoughts. Not that long ago, I was in this same hospital, lying in a similar bed in a room that was the exact replica of this one. I couldn't help but think Afa was responsible for both hospital admissions. Anger filled me.

The police had found my number in Kala's purse and called to see if I knew anything about what had happened. I called Mary, and we rushed to the hospital.

A young man in his early thirties wearing jeans and a detective badge and gun on the front of his belt strode into the room with a notepad in hand. He glanced at Kala and then at us. "Hello, I'm Detective Mark

Dobbs." Although his guarded eyes didn't move up and down when looking at Mary and me, I got the distinct impression he was sizing us up.

I thought it best if I helped him along and squelched his curiosity about who we were and why we were here. "I'm Frank Bravo, Ms. Tausinga's attorney."

He didn't appear to relax any with my announcement.

His opinion of us didn't matter. Kala had been hurt, hurt badly, and I wanted answers. "Hey, do you know what happened?" My urgent tone even surprised me.

"That's why I'm here," he said, tilting his head toward Kala, "to get more details from the victim."

"Well, she's not talking yet. Can you tell us anything at all?"

He shrugged. "All I know so far is what I heard over dispatch on my way to the hospital. We were dispatched to the victim's apartment because the victim's next-door neighbor—"

"Her name is *Kala*," Mary interjected, with a bit of annoyance.

The officer had flipped open his pad. "Yes, ma'am. Anyway, the next-door neighbor arrived at his apartment after work and stopped for a moment before he went inside when he heard a man shouting angrily at someone, we presume the victim—" He glanced at Mary's set jaw and raised eyebrow. "—uhm, Kala, yelling that he didn't want a divorce, that he wanted her and the kids back. But Kala must have stood her ground because he said he heard a female yelling *no*. The man also shouted something about being blamed publicly for killing someone named Juna. The neighbor ducked away from the window and hurried inside to call 911.

He said he heard a struggle, the woman now screaming for help. Fighting. A door being kicked open. More fighting. A heavy thud. It was already dark, but as the police sirens got close, the neighbor looked out the window and said he thought he saw a young man in a baseball cap sprinting away from the apartment complex."

We all turned to watch Mia burst into the hospital room as if she had come in a hurry. She must have been nearby since it had only been minutes since I called her. Her black hair was damp and hanging loosely around her shoulders. Deep concern etched lines on her face as her eyes focused on the bed where Kala lay unconscious.

"Mia?" said Detective Dobbs. "What are you doing here? I thought—"

"Hi, Mark." Mia nodded toward Kala. "She was a victim from my last case, just before I left the DA's office."

Mia turned away from the detective, and her eyes met mine. She took three quick steps and crashed into my arms, sobbing. We held each other that way for a while.

Detective Dobbs's radio crackled, and he left the room to take a call. Mia sat on the side of Kala's bed and put a hand on her arm and quietly watched her and waited.

I thought it a bit strange that Mia hadn't asked what happened to Kala since she arrived, but I put my arm around her shoulders. "Don't worry. The nurse told us that Kala should wake up soon and would recover completely."

Mia put her free hand on mine. Although her

forehead wrinkled with worry, she managed a little smile. We sat that way, being there for Kala and for each other.

After several minutes of silence, Mia said, "Oh, Frank, I got something for Bella to wear with her prom dress."

Mia pulled a box from the small purse strapped across her body and handed it to me. She nodded at me as an okay to open the box. Inside was a necklace with a shiny black stone trimmed in ornate silver and dangling on a silver chain.

"I like it," I said. "It's beautiful. Thank you so much. She'll love it."

Mia put her finger to her lips and spoke in a quiet voice. "Make sure that she wears it, Frank. And FYI, it has an extremely sensitive long-range GPS transponder in it, and a new high-tech video recorder. It's the latest tech. If you don't trust the guy who's taking Bella to the prom, call me, and I can keep track of exactly where she is."

"I like that idea."

"But Frank, don't tell *anyone* about the transponder. The public is not supposed to have this tech yet. There'll be lots of questions if anyone finds out."

"Well, how did you get it?"

"Remember when I told you about The Sisterhood and how they help abused women when the system fails? If a woman needs help, the organization acts. So, if you ever have a woman who needs help, and the police aren't helping, and the system isn't helping, call me. I'll help."

"Thank you. I will." Cloak and daggerish, but at

this point, I didn't care. "You know I'm glad to have gotten to know you. And I think my daughter, Bella, likes you too. Between meeting you at court and me talking about you all the time. I think she'd like to see you again."

"I'd like that too," Mia said. "But what about you?"

"Me?" Realizing what Mia meant, or maybe just hoping that I understood what she meant, I said, "Yes, me too. I'd like to see you too." Glancing around the room, I added, "But maybe somewhere other than a hospital next time, though."

Mia put her hand on my arm. Maybe it was just the emotion of the situation, but I thought I saw something different in Mia's gaze. The animosity I had felt when we met had evolved to friendly cooperation in Kala's case, and now... what? I know I felt something for her and put my hand firmly on top of hers and squeezed it. She gave me a little smile and then turned her attention back to Kala.

A question filled my mind as we all waited for Kala to wake up. Mary sat in a chair against the wall, staring at nothing. I wasn't expecting her to answer, but I asked the question anyway. "I wonder if they'll charge him *this* time."

"Fuck!" was all Mary said, her normally staid demeanor nowhere to be seen. "*Fuck!*"

"Jesus, I'm sick to my stomach," I told Mary. "They said Afa was mad about being blamed for Juna's death. I'm the one who made a big deal about that, not Kala."

"Well, watch your back," Mary said. "He still might come for you."

Mia turned toward us. She shook her head and looked straight into my eyes. "No, Frank. Afa won't be coming for you. Or for Kala either."

Chapter Forty-Three

Tiny flags lined both sides of every sidewalk on the grassy grounds of the old city government building. Built in the late 1800s, the Romanesque building was a historical landmark. Its granite columns were mined out of the Rocky Mountains that surrounded the city, and the surface of the building was a gray sandstone. On the south side of the tall clock tower, the freemasons who constructed this building had carved a statue of the goddess Justice. It was a perfect location for this event.

A pamphlet on a table at the building's entrance indicated that there were 3,140 flags planted in the grass surrounding the building, which must have been all the flags they had because a large sign stated that the flags represented 5,670 victims of domestic violence in the last year in the city alone.

I stood in front of the Wall of Remembrance. It was covered with photographs and newsclips of the domestic violence victims in Salt Lake City during the past year.

There was a program honoring both the victims and those police and victim advocates who worked to try to help them. A small choir sang. Adya, the director of the Safe at Home Coalition and our expert in Kala's trial, sat up on the stand behind the podium. Other Coalition members were also present as well as leaders from the YWCA.

Several surviving family members of the victims on the Wall of Remembrance came out of the audience and spoke briefly. One man recalled the agony he experienced over having lost a daughter to a violent boyfriend. He lumbered back to his seat in the audience, but before he sat down, he turned back to the stand. With raw emotion interrupting the flow of his words, he asked, "Ms. Singh, how do you manage to do this kind of work every day?"

Adya pointed to the other people on the stand and the participants in the program. "With the love of my brothers and sisters."

Then Kala stood. I was surprised to see her walking toward the microphone. She was such a quiet little mouse when I met her. Unsure of herself as she stood before the crowd, she apologized for not being able to speak in public. But she did speak.

"I am a survivor," she began. "My husband beat me. He choked me. He raped me. He threatened to kill me if I ever left him. He told me I was nothing. I thought I was nothing. I wish I had left him, but I stayed with him. I said it was for our kids. But because I stayed, my son, my precious little Juna, isn't here today."

Kala turned away from the crowd and wiped her eyes before regaining her composure. "After what happened to my son, I thought about killing myself. I didn't care about my life anymore. Sometimes I wanted to go to sleep and never wake up so that I could be with Juna. The pain was too much for me. But I have three other beautiful kids. I am so grateful for my family, and I love them very much.

"The most precious things that I have are my kids.

I know I need to be strong for them. We women need to be stronger. We need to help each other. We need to help our families.

"When I finally told one of my cousins that my husband was beating me, she told me that we Polynesian women get beaten by our men sometimes, but that's the way they are, and we still need to love them. But that isn't right. I'm so sad I didn't take my children and leave. I'm so sad when I think about the past. But we can't stay in the past. We must look to the future. We have to make a new life for ourselves."

As Kala turned and left the microphone, the large crowd clapped firmly for her and continued to clap as the choir director moved to the front of the choir. Then, after the choir sang, everyone was led out to a small courtyard for a candlelight vigil. Young girls wove their way through the crowd, quietly handing out small candles. As we stood in silence in front of the Wall of Remembrance, I marveled at how far Kala had come. She had gone from utter hopelessness at the jail, wishing only to go to sleep and die, to a newfound sense of purpose, and faith, and hope.

After everything I had seen Kala suffer, witnessing her transform into a leader in the struggle against domestic violence and hearing her give hope to others who were suffering abuse renewed my hope as well.

A word about the author…

Ralph Dellapiana is a long-time public defender whose personal experience with the human drama of real cases informs his works of fiction.